"Nice move, Romeo."

Etta's voice was sarcastic. "What did you say to upset Dixie? Did you tell her she was too cute to be a doctor? That she ought to be home having babies instead of delivering them for other women?"

"I didn't do anything, Etta. Don't get on my case."

Etta glared at him as she refilled his coffee mug. "You'd better not treat her bad, Hal. We need her here. You and the other old boys drive her away and you'll have to answer to us women."

Hal watched as Etta turned and left, huffy as the lady doctor had been moments before.

He hadn't meant to drive Dixie away. Just the opposite. He'd finally decided to ask her out for a date. This breakfast was supposed to have been a preliminary. Why couldn't he have talked to her without putting his boot in his mouth?

Dear Reader,

We're wrapping up the holiday season for you with four romantic delights!

Our final Women Who Dare title for 1993 is by **Sharon Brondos**. In *Doc Wyoming*, Dr. Dixie Sheldon is enthusiastic about opening her new medical office in the small community of Seaside, Wyoming... until she meets the taciturn local sheriff, Hal Blane. Blane seems determined to prevent her from doing her job. And he especially doesn't want Dixie treating his mother, for fear she'll unearth family secrets he'd prefer to keep buried.

Longtime favorite author **Margaret Chittenden** has penned a charming tale of a haunted house and a friendly spirit in *When the Spirit is Willing*. Laura Daniels, needing to start over after the death of her husband, moves to picturesque Port Dudley to raise her daughter in peace. But peace eludes her when she discovers that her new home is haunted, and the resident ghost appears to be an aggressive matchmaker!

Two of our December Superromance titles will evoke the sort of emotions the holidays are all about. The moving *Angels in the Light*, by **Margot Dalton**, focuses on Abby Malone, who is decidedly unenthusiastic about her latest story assignment. She absolutely does not believe in near-death experiences. But she has no idea how to explain the new Brad Carmichael. He is no longer the selfish, immature boy who'd simply taken off when she'd needed him most, but a sensitive, gentle man who wants Abby to believe anything is possible.

New author **Maggie Simpson** will charm you with *Baby Bonus*. Susan Montgomery's life is turned upside down from the moment Andrew Bradley knocks on her door to inform her that she has a grandson to care for—courtesy of her runaway daughter and his irresponsible son. Even worse, Andrew is determined to stick around to make sure the baby is raised according to the Andrew Bradley School of Grandparenting!

In January, Lynn Erickson, Peg Sutherland, Judith Arnold and Risa Kirk will take you to the Caribbean, North Carolina, Boston and Rodeo Drive! Be sure to come along for the ride!

Holiday Greetings!

Marsha Zinberg,
Senior Editor

M

Sharon Brondos

Doc WYOMING

Harlequin Books

TORONTO • NEW YORK • LONDON
AMSTERDAM • PARIS • SYDNEY • HAMBURG
STOCKHOLM • ATHENS • TOKYO • MILAN
MADRID • WARSAW • BUDAPEST • AUCKLAND

ISBN 0-373-70574-3

DOC WYOMING

Printed in U.S.A.

ABOUT THE AUTHOR

Wyoming author Sharon Brondos was inspired to write *Doc Wyoming* because of the growing shortage of primary physicians in her home state. Sharon's own interest in herbal medicine is reflected in the character Miss Esther, "who is a combination of many wise old women," writes the author, "and one of my very favorite characters ever." High praise indeed, since *Doc Wyoming* is Sharon's twelfth Superromance novel.

Books by Sharon Brondos

HARLEQUIN SUPERROMANCE

HARLEQUIN CRYSTAL CREEK

PROLOGUE

Wyoming Territory, 1889

THE GEOGRAPHIC STAGE was classic Rocky Mountain.

The drama that was soon to take place there was classic western.

The stage: A wide plain, stretched to the eastern horizon; it was covered with thick buffalo grass, rich grass that had sustained abundant life on the prairie for thousands of years. Gradually, the plain eased upward into a flat, tableland region, the earth rich with minerals that gave the grass even more lushness. Then came the mountains, the spine of the land. High rock cliffs swept upward in ledges and steps into jagged highlands and downward into a V-shaped valley at the edge of the tableland. A creek cut through the valley, and a strip of aspen and pine forest separated the two regions.

Heavy, cold air moved over the peaks to the west, blowing eastward through the area just ahead of an early-winter storm. Wind whistled through the tops of the lodgepole pines. Then, spiced with the sharp-sweet tang of evergreen, it slipped down the mountainside to scour the narrow valley below.

The shallow creek running through the rocks at the base of the steep slopes seemed to shiver and burble along faster, as if it would try outrunning the coming storm. An early-October frost had turned the aspens gold and leached the last of the green from the buffalo grass, but the clear, blue sunny sky lied about the weather.

Snow was due, and the land knew it.

High overhead an eagle rode the wild, unpredictable updrafts, correcting now and then when a tendril of wind from the front hidden beyond the western horizon gusted into the cloudless afternoon above the valley. Two mountain jays skimmed the surface of the water, looking for trout, then flew away into the trees, seeking shelter. A nervous trio of mule deer, a doe and two yearlings, approached the creek and drank deeply before moving back into the pines and a place where they could find protection until the harsh weather passed.

Slowly, the bright sunlight dimmed, but only slightly, as if a thin gauze veiling had been pulled across the sky. Except for the wind and the creek water, the golden valley was silent now. No life to be seen. Even the eagle had abandoned the air above it. Peace, ready to be shattered, settled.

The drama: The thunder began softly, a drumming sound that would have caused the three deer to look up in mild alarm, had they still been out in the open. The noise thrummed up the valley like distant artillery fire, but then it thinned and resolved into the clatter and splash of horses' hooves racing along the shallow creek bed.

Nine horsemen tore into view, their expressions desperate and angry. One rode behind, keeping watch over his shoulder, looking for and fearing pursuit. One rode in front, his gaze steadier than that of the others and raised to the high rock rim above them, to the flat table of land he knew so well.

He was a big man with rough-hewn features and skin leathered by a lifetime in the western sun. His eyes were bluer than the clear sky and his hair a bronzy brown. His wide-brimmed hat shaded his face.

The eight followed the one leader, leaving the water, heading into the aspen trees by the creek and then back up into the huge rocks at the base of the cliff, where they disappeared. For a few minutes, the clacking sound of the horses' hooves echoed in the valley as they rode upward.

Then, nothing. The earth on the tableland was thick and soft enough to quiet shod hooves.

The storm finally blew in, howling, covering the tracks of their passing. It was one of those violent, change-of-season storms, dumping rain, snow and sleet on the land. By the time night fell, the entire valley was covered with an icy, white sheet of winter.

Silence reigned. Time passed. Only once, for a period of about an hour, did human voices break the stillness. Raised in anger and fear, the shouts echoed off the high walls. Then, one sharp, booming sound punctuated the cries. Too short for thunder, too loud to be natural, it rang out. More time passed. Then another unnatural, popping sound. Quieter, but no less alien to the wild land.

And then silence descended again.

Two days later, eight men rode from the valley and cliffs, never looking back. The rider who had led them in remained behind, buried in a shallow grave under rocks and what dirt his companions could manage to pry loose from the freezing land. He died from gunshot wounds, the final result of an argument with his fellow riders. The distrust that had been part of the binding that held the gang together had festered and grown during the enforced period of tense waiting and eventually had ripped the fragile fabric of the alliance.

Death had been the outcome, not the intention of the enterprise. And a good man had lost his life, needlessly.

He'd died under an assumed identity.

Later, when spring came to the land, by chance he was found and reburied deep in the earth by another than one of the eight. An innocent who nevertheless knew fear and had assumed guilt. The burial was done secretly and in fear and still no one knew who the dead man really was or why he had ridden with the desperate eight.

No one, that is, who would or could tell.

Yet.

CHAPTER ONE

Seaside, Wyoming, 1993

"COME ON. YOU CAN DO this," she told herself. "Just stay awake for another hour or so."

She rested her forehead against the cold, hard steering wheel of her Suburban and closed her eyes for a moment. *Just a moment to rest...*

The pale gold rays of Wyoming's rising summer sun lit the darkness behind her tightly shut eyelids, but she settled for seeing nothing but gray for a short time. Dr. Dixie Sheldon was bone-tired—even more tired than during the grueling days of medical internship and residency. Could she handle three long years of this? She'd been at it for less than three weeks, and this morning, it seemed like a lifetime.

Maybe, Dixie reflected, it was because she was no longer a young intern, full of pride, energy and enthusiasm—and just plain older. She *did* still have the enthusiasm, though, most of the time. She smiled, then opened her eyes.

She was here, in Wyoming, and it was neither a dream, nor a nightmare. Reality lay before her—but with a touch of fantasy. She looked around, and for a second, felt as if she'd been sent back a hundred years to a time when the West was young. In some ways, it was fantasy and illusion. In other ways, it was not...as she'd learned the hard way.

Dawn turned the main street of Seaside, Wyoming, into a pearly rose dreamscape that looked like a western movie set. If she squinted, the pavement on Main Street became hard dirt, marked by horses' hooves and wagon wheels. The concrete sidewalks became wooden planks. The buildings fit in perfectly, many of them being nearly a hundred years old. Behind the nineteenth-century street-front facades of wood and stone, modern businesses waited for full morning, but right now, the place was authentic Wild West.

Especially evocative was the jail-courthouse building where she had parked a few minutes ago. The soft pink sandstone did nothing to offset the ugly implications of the bars on the small windows and the heavy wooden door. If there had been a sign saying, Abandon Hope All Ye Who Enter, the grim effect would have been complete.

Dixie shook her head, throwing off the fantasy. Fatigue made her muscles feel loose and weak, and she wondered at this unusual state of enervation. It had to be caused by more than one all-nighter with a woman in labor. She'd sat through plenty of lengthy births, and this one had been relatively easy—a breeze, in fact. So why the fatigue?

She looked at the jail.

Maybe it was because, in a few moments, she would be dealing with Hal Blane.

Sheriff Hal Blane.

He was a bad guys' nightmare in cowboy boots. A big, rugged, tough lawman with dark blond hair and piercing blue eyes. A western sheriff right out of central casting. A man who seemed part of the wild-and-woolly legendary West, but with effective influence and power here in the present.

Almost enough influence and power to have prevented her from getting this job. From what she had heard, he had a negative attitude toward her probable ability and potential as a general-practice doctor. He'd been against her before he'd even set eyes on her, she'd been told.

Dixie sighed, gathered up herself and her medical bag, then got out of the big vehicle. It was high enough, and she was short enough that she had to jump to the ground. She shut the door, took a deep breath, squared her shoulders and turned toward the jailhouse.

When she came through the front door, Dixie noticed that the morning light barely illuminated the office, adding once more to her sense of being in the past. The small room was grim and gray and typical of Old West jail offices. The sense of theater here was strong, and the place seemed naturally to wait for a movie director to order it floodlighted and to yell "action" as the actors assembled. She saw Hal Blane seated in the shadows, at his desk. A large shadow in the shadows. Lurking.

Dixie waited a beat, but no one yelled or spoke or moved. She couldn't see Blane's face, so she wasn't even sure he was awake. She cleared her throat, loudly, and he stirred.

"Good morning, Sheriff," she said, managing somehow to sound alert and professionally cheerful. "Sorry to take so long getting to you."

Blane rose like a large and dangerous mountain lion, too quickly and smoothly for a man who might have been napping. He'd been awake, she realized, but he'd made her speak first.

He ran a hand through his thick hair. Stretched his arms, then moved toward the rear of the office. Not a word of greeting. She could see he had on his regular tan uniform, but the material looked creased and rumpled. He must have been sitting in that chair all night, she thought, waiting for her. Finally, he spoke, the sound of his voice a grudging rumble.

"The prisoner's back this way, Doc. He's George Preston, a local yahoo who sometimes works as a ranch hand and usually gets drunk on Saturday night. This week, he decided to extend the drunk into Sunday. He isn't hurt bad, but he's bleeding some. We did what we could while we were waiting on you. Glad you could find the time to work us into your schedule." Sheriff Hal Blane turned his back to Dr. Dixie Sheldon and opened the barred door that led to the jail cells.

Dixie glared at his broad shoulders, thinking how best to respond. "I was out delivering a baby," she said. "Since Deputy Travers told me on the phone that your prisoner's case wasn't life-threatening, I thought getting the baby a good start in this life was more important."

Hal Blane turned around. A patch of morning sunlight hit his face, spotlighting him, giving a healthy, appealing glow to his tanned skin. His hair was bronze in the light. "Did Betsy Dumont finally have that kid?" he asked, and smiled for the first time. It changed him completely. "Boy or girl?"

"Boy."

"Well, I'll be..." The smile got wider. The man seemed bigger. Bigger, but...friendlier. "That's great," he added, moving one step toward her.

Dixie took a step back, remembering. Though she had seen him around town since she'd arrived for good, her original encounter with the sheriff had been months ago, in March, when she'd been interviewed for the position of primary-care physician for SeaLake County. On that occasion, she'd faced the entire, almost all-male contingent of county commissioners and their chief employees, Blane among them.

It had not been a comfortable or pleasant interview, but she had gained enough of their respect during it to get the job. Admittedly, they were also resigned to the fact that not many young doctors, male *or* female, were willing to spend three years of their professional lives literally stuck in the middle of nowhere. Seaside was in the middle of an ancient seabed where fossils outnumbered living humans by a large percentage.

She wasn't quite sure whether to place Hal Blane in the fossil or living human category. Oh, he was an attractive enough man with his solid, utterly male, features and his blue eyes and his muscles, but he was antediluvian, mentally and socially, she was sure.

He was also one of the few eligible bachelors in town, a fact of little interest to her, but not to others. It hadn't taken the gossips long to let her know he was available, that his divorce had been an ugly event years ago, that his ex-wife had left the state for good, abandoning both him and a male child, and that he didn't date locally. And to inform her that he was one of the two people who'd voted against her taking the job, because she was a woman. As that was apparently his only objection, she had assumed he disliked women on principle, probably as a result of his unhappy marriage. At least, he'd seemed concerned enough about Mrs. Dumont to indicate he wasn't a complete misogynist.

"Is she all right?" he asked, resting one big fist on his hip and the other hand against the jailhouse wall. From that position he seemed to loom over her. "I mean, did the delivery go all right. Were you able to handle...?"

"Betsy's had five kids, Sheriff. She hardly needed me there," Dixie responded. "But I did my bit, thanks. Now, where's my next patient, your prisoner?" She crossed her arms, waiting, feeling the pressure of his stare, but willing herself to face it directly. This was the closest, physically, they had been in the three weeks since she'd set up practice in Seaside. She realized that he disturbed her.

It was more than his size relative to hers. It was...almost a negative force. A force that would continue to oppose her. One she was going to have to encounter on a regular basis. One she wasn't going to be able to overcome.

"He's right down here, Doc." He jerked his thumb toward the cells.

Dixie nodded and moved past. Not an easy task, given the narrow space and the size of the man. She was used to feeling small, being just five feet tall in her socks; something about Hal Blane made her feel insignificant, as well. It wasn't a sensation she liked. But, here it was, uncomfortable and undeniable. She could sense the spicy-sweaty male scent of him, not unpleasant, but strong, almost challenging, and she wasn't sure she'd be able to keep from flinching as she went by him.

But she managed, and then she moved forward down the hallway. Though the jail area looked dingy and dirty, there wasn't a musty smell. Whatever else she thought of the sheriff, she had to admit he kept a clean and sanitary lockup. The prisoner-patient was in the last cell. George Preston, she reminded herself.

She could see the man's huddled form, face to the wall. She reached for the door, grabbed a cold metal bar, pulled on it. It was locked. She heard the clink of keys. The sheriff reached around her and inserted one in the door. His arm brushed against hers . . . warm . . . The key turned and the lock clicked. The door swung open with a dull clanging noise.

The injured prisoner didn't move.

"What happened to him?" Dixie asked, keeping her tone low. She stepped into the cell. Blane followed her.

"He's a troublemaker. He seems to enjoy it, even when it hurts him. He got into a knife fight with the wrong man. An Indian who didn't take kindly to George's attitude about Custer and the Battle of the Little Big Horn." He paused. "Don't have the other man here, but I know where to find him when I have to. Unless George wants to press charges, I'm leaving Toby alone. George asked for it. Started breaking up the bar before he turned on the Indian. Like I said, he isn't hurt bad, but he's cut up in a real creative kind of pattern. Bet you never saw anything like it before, Doc."

She glanced up at his face, saw nothing there to indicate humor or mockery. He was studying her, however, and she knew she was being tested in some way. "I worked emergency room detail every Saturday night for a year," she said, still speaking softly. "I don't expect I'll be surprised."

Blane's eyebrows went up, but he said nothing.

Dixie moved to the prisoner. She could smell stale, sour sweat and booze and blood—Saturday-night drinking and fighting. It was the same in downtown Chicago or Denver or Seaside, Wyoming. It didn't matter where she was. Men drank and fought and bled. So, what else was new?

She touched the man's shoulder and spoke to him gently. After turning him over, she looked at the damage and was not impressed. Certainly not horrified. She opened her medical bag. He was cut from the edge of his eyebrow down across his cheek and chest, but the gash wasn't deep. Just a shallow furrow which would, nevertheless, require some careful stitching. She started to take out instruments and set them on a clean towel. The patient opened his eyes and stared up at her. Fear and pain twisted his coarse features. And, not unexpectedly, surprise.

"Hello there, George," she said, softly, soothingly. The man's eyes fluttered. "I'm going to fix you up so you feel better," she added, slipping on clean, sterile gloves. She saw the prisoner give the sheriff a look filled with alarm.

"Don't you worry," she added. "I'm not police. I'm a doctor."

Hal Blane stepped back a bit so he could see the lady in action. He'd heard from others that she was all right when it came to treating sniffles and kids' fevers and even setting a broken bone over to the Edwards' place when one of the cowhands had busted an arm, but how, he wondered, was she going to take the kind of mess Toby Daniels had made of George Preston? Preston's homely face looked like a jigsaw puzzle with a couple of pieces gone, anyway, but now it was bad enough to curdle milk, even with most of the blood mopped up and the scar crusting dry. George's face looked real damned ugly.

She didn't flinch, and Hal decided he had to give her credit for that. Even he had felt a little queasy when he'd tried to wash away some of the blood earlier. The cut wasn't deep, but went from eye to belly button.

"I've got to clean him up better, and then I'm going to have to put in stitches," she said, her attention on the patient, but her words clearly addressed to Hal. George was still too drunk to speak, anyway. "He'll need an antibiotic shot, too, as well as a tetanus booster. This isn't going to be very comfortable for him," she added. "Could you help me, Sheriff?"

"He won't like it, but too bad. That's what I'm here for, I guess," Hal replied. He unfolded his arms and pushed away from the bars. "Just tell me what to do, Doc."

She stared up at him, her big blue eyes seeming to bore holes in him. "Okay, I will. Roll up your sleeves, put on these gloves and don't call me 'Doc,'" she said, her voice tightening and hardening on the last phrase.

After that, however, she didn't make a single nonprofessional comment. With a gentle, but sure touch, she mended George's hide. Hal kept pace with her work, acting, he realized, like a nurse to her doctor, but not really minding. She was doing a good job, her small hands moving skillfully. Nice to watch, in fact, if you didn't mind she was sewing flesh not cloth. George grunted once or twice, indicating mild pain, but he didn't complain aloud. Doc Sheldon knew her stuff.

And it started a change in Hal's determinedly negative attitude. For the first time since he'd set eyes on her last spring, knowing she was going to get the job in Seaside, Hal decided having this woman as the only physician within hundreds of miles might not be so bad. Of all the men who'd voted on whether to hire her, he knew he was the most likely of all to have need of her professional services, since his job held the highest risk of physical injury. It concerned him that she might not be competent to handle an emergency, in spite of her training. It was one thing to deal with blood and trauma in a hospital environment, and quite another to deal with it on-site, without proper equipment or other physicians right at hand to help out if things went wrong.

Now, watching and working with her, he decided maybe she'd do, after all. A jail cell was a far cry from even the most primitive of emergency rooms, but she was coping well. In fact, she seemed downright at ease in the place. George still looked like Frankenstein's monster when she was done with him a good hour later, but he was stitched up neat as a quilt and hadn't squalled at all about her hurting him. He had regained full consciousness for a while, sobered by time and pain, but apparently her kind, reassuring words and the pleasing sight of Doc Dixie had kept him quiet and meek as a lamb.

Hal understood George's almost reverent silence. One of the reasons he'd voted against her was her feminine good looks. She was tiny, barely reaching the five-foot mark, he was sure. Tiny, but built fully enough to silence any man for an appreciative moment of appraisal. Her short hair was dark, almost black and looked like silk. Her features were just shy of perfect, with a pair of blue eyes that seemed almost too big and wide for a grown woman, and high cheekbones that made her look elfish. A cat's face, definitely pretty and appealing.

Maybe, too appealing. Such an attractive women wasn't made for rough and ugly work like this, he figured, sewing up drunks in a one-horse town jail. She needed a city or at least a big hospital to shine in, a place where she'd get the attention she had to be used to and maybe even needed, looking like that. Must have had men praising her and courting her most all her life. She was just too darn pretty to be a country doctor. He wiped some blood off his gloved palm and wondered exactly how soft and silky her hair would feel.

Hell of a thing to be thinking of!

"You almost finished?" he asked, standing up and stripping off the gloves.

She hesitated, regarding her patient. "Maybe. Have you got someone to watch him?" she asked. "He's not likely to need any further attention, but I do want to be called immediately if he's in any real distress."

"Travers is out front," he said. "Heard him come in while you were finishing stitching George together." He put his hand on her elbow, steering her out of the cell. "Just tell him what you want."

"Okay." Dixie let him guide her outside, and when he stopped to close and lock the cell door, she gently disengaged herself from his grasp. He made a sound deep in his broad chest, but otherwise ignored her move away from him.

They returned to the office without saying anything more, and she stood quietly, waiting and watching, while he spoke to his deputy. Ted Travers was a young man with a nice face marred by a scraggly attempt at a rust-colored mustache. She decided that Hal Blane looked old enough this morning to be the youthful deputy's father. The long night had etched his face, and she wondered if hers looked as haggard. Probably, it did.

Even haggard, he looked good, if you liked the rough-hewn, western type. And she did. She'd grown to young womanhood in Laramie, where cowboy-stud types abounded, along with the academic/university males. It was a good place for men-watching—women were outnumbered by a considerable margin—and she had devoted her teen years to careful study. Dixie had nourished a weakness for those cowboys when she was young, but she was sure she'd outgrown it by now. Too many times she'd fallen for a man with all the qualifications to turn her on, except one: he kept any brains he had to himself. She knew herself well enough to know that any permanent relationship she had in the future would depend first and foremost on being able to share equally in the thinking department.

Ted Travers turned to her and asked for instructions, so Dixie took a piece of paper from the desk and scribbled out a list of warning signs he should watch for in the patient. "If he starts to complain of a fever, let me know right away," she added. "But I think he'll be fine. Most of his discomfort's liable to be from a hangover."

"Yes, ma'am." The deputy grinned and took the paper. "Ole George did tie one on last night. He sure put on a show for us once we got him locked up. What kept you so busy, you couldn't come right away, ma'am?"

"Betsy Dumont had her baby," the sheriff said. "Doc here delivered her a boy."

"No kidding?" Another grin. "Bet Tag's happy. He's been complaining he wanted another boy after those three little girls. What's he gonna call him?"

"I suspect he'll name him after his daddy. He loved that man, he really did. I was there when he died, and Tag cried like a baby, himself. You know his old man ran sheep up to..." The sheriff's voice droned on, dispensing information about the Dumont ancestor.

Left out of the conversation, Dixie turned away. She should leave while she was unnoticed, she decided. The two men were leaving her, the newcomer, out. She headed for the door, feeling every minute of the long night on her neck and shoulders, longing for the oblivion of sleep.

"Hey, Doc."

She turned around, ready to correct him again about calling her that, then decided it wasn't worth making it an issue. He'd call her what he wanted when he wanted, regardless of her objections.

He was that kind of guy.

"Breakfast?" Hal asked, the shadow of a friendly expression on his face. "I'd like the company." He rubbed his hand over his chin, and she could hear the scratch of whiskers on his palm.

"Sure," she said. "Why not?" The man was actually making a hospitable gesture. Doing something nice. "I'm hungry," she added, her spirits rising into a state almost resembling her normal cheerfulness.

The town of Seaside was not large, so they set off on foot. Most of the main establishments were within a fair shouting distance of all the others. Even her clinic was just off the main street, not so far from the jail that she wasn't able to hear the comings and goings of the law while she dealt with her patients and their families.

The café was almost empty. The morning sunlight gleamed on the scrubbed linoleum floor and Formica countertops. Fresh coffee, frying bacon, yeasty cinnamon rolls—the smells lingered in the air. From the rear, in the kitchen, came the soft sound of a country-western radio station and the louder clatter of pans and utensils. By now, nearly seven a.m., Dixie knew that most of the folks who ate breakfast there were already filled up and gone to work. Life began early in Seaside.

She and the sheriff took a booth in the back, away from the heat of the sunny front windows. They greeted the waitress, wife of the cook and co-owner, Etta Jennings, and then they both ordered while she poured coffee for them into thick white mugs.

"Want some sweet rolls?" Etta gestured toward the kitchen with a twitch of her head. "Sal made 'em fresh this morning." She balanced her thin frame first on one foot, then the other, as if standing there and waiting for them to decide what they wanted was putting a strain on her arches and back.

"Sal makes them fresh every morning, Etta," Hal replied, his tone weary.

"I'll have one," Dixie said. The smell of the cinnamon and yeast was making her mouth water. "And grapefruit, please."

"You, Hal?" Etta regarded the sheriff.

He shook his head negatively. "Just get me my usual," he said.

Etta slapped her hand on her lean hip. "Never gonna get fat with an attitude like that, Hal Blane," she said.

"Good." He buried his face in his coffee mug. Hiding a smile, Dixie realized. Etta departed, muttering about stubborn customers who'd never try anything different, and Hal commented loudly that too much sugar and fat weren't good for anybody. Dixie sensed the byplay was a regular morning occurrence, a kind of friendly joshing between old neighbors.

Feeling left out of the local scene once more, she sipped her own coffee. It was fresh, strong and rich, which brought her emotions back into line. "Ahhh," she sighed. "Elixir of wakefulness. I may even manage to get in my clinic hours today before I pass out."

He watched her over the rim of his coffee mug. "Think that's such a good idea?"

She smiled at him. "When I was in medical school, I remember going four days and nights without sleep once. Just making it on caffeine and nerves."

"How many patients knew you were wired like that?"

She quit smiling. "None, of course."

"Sounds like a bad idea to me."

"It is." She sipped more coffee, feeling the cells in her brain come back to life. "And it isn't. While it's an experience I'd never willingly repeat, at least for the rest of my life I'll know I *can* do it, if I have to."

He frowned. Questioning.

"I mean I can stay up way past my normal limits and fight for human life. Suppose just as I was done with George a disaster of terrible proportions had happened around here. One that demanded I be able to perform, no matter how tired I was. I'd been up with Mrs. Dumont all night, I'd patched up poor old George and ..."

He grinned, looking down at his coffee. "I get the point, Doc," he said. "Yeah, it is nice to know you can operate on the afterburners, but..."

"But what?"

He looked up. "Why should you?"

"You mean, why am I a doctor?" She leaned forward, resting her elbows on the tabletop. "Why did I choose a profession that makes such demands?"

He nodded, a smile still turning up the corners of his mouth.

"Why are you a cop?"

The smile faded. Fled, really. His face resumed the hard, stern planes she was used to. "It's a job I can do," he said.

"Nothing more than that?"

He cupped his hands around the mug. "Sometimes. Yeah. Sometimes it is more than just a job."

"Okay." She tried to look encouraging, hoping he would see that she really was interested. "Tell me about one specific 'sometimes.' Give me an example of an experience you had that made the job worthwhile."

He shook his head. "Doc, I'm too tired to talk." He leaned back in the booth as Etta set their plates down. "Let's just eat, okay?" He stuck a spoon into his bowl of steaming hot oatmeal and began shoveling.

And that was that.

Surprised at his bluntness and rudeness in response to what she'd meant as genuine interest in him as a person, Dixie settled back into herself and ate her breakfast in silence. He wasn't worth getting upset over, she told herself. She tried to ignore his presence and enjoy the cinnamon roll. He remained, however, at the edge of her awareness, sitting across from her, silently, sullenly devouring his meal.

Etta wandered over. "The roll okay?" she asked. "Sal wants to know what you think, Doctor."

Dixie smiled, glad for the distraction. "You tell Sal that I've had cinnamon rolls in New York and Chicago that couldn't hold a candle to this." She took a healthy bite. "These are the best!"

"I'll tell him." Etta smiled crookedly. "He'll like that. Thanks." She glanced at the sheriff. "Oatmeal okay?"

"Uh-huh." Hal looked up at her. "You tell Sal the lumps are good, as usual. Best I've ever eaten. New York lumps couldn't compete."

Etta looked back at Dixie, and the two women exchanged wry grimaces before Etta shrugged and left.

"You were making fun of me," Dixie said. "That wasn't necessary. I was only trying to be pleasant to Etta."

"I wasn't making fun of you. Don't be so sensitive. I was only trying to joke. I made a mistake thinking you could take it." He put down his spoon. "Lady, maybe you're just a bit too touchy."

Dixie glared back. "Maybe I am touchy, but I hope I'll always think about other people's feelings as well as my own. And as for being sensitive, in my profession I think it's an asset to be sensitive, not a liability."

He said nothing for a moment. "It's a liability to care too much. It'll break you. If you let it."

She sat back, considering what he had said and the kind, gentle, warning way he'd said it. Was he speaking out of personal experience? Was this an opening into his real self? If so, should she take the opportunity to probe?

"I think I know what you meant by that," she said, speaking slowly, choosing her words with care. "And I think you meant it to be a friendly statement. But I want you to know, Hal Blane, that I resent it. I resent the way you and some others have treated me since I got here. And

I reject the notion and your assumption that I would be too weak to bear up under the double burden of being both responsive and responsible.''

"That's not what I meant! I . . ."

"Oh, I think it was exactly what you meant." She wiped her sticky fingers clean and set down the napkin beside her plate. "Thanks for breakfast. I enjoyed it, though the company left something to be desired." She took out several dollars and put them by her plate. "Here's my share." She stood up. "See you, Sheriff. I have a clinic to open. I have a job to do. One I do well, thanks very much."

And she left.

Hal sat still. He put both palms on the table. He took a deep breath. He picked up his coffee mug. The coffee was cold.

Etta came over and poured him a fresh cup. "Nice move, Romeo," she said. "What'd you do? Tell her she was too cute and pretty to be a doctor? Tell her she ought to be home having babies herself instead of delivering 'em for other women?" Her expression was neutral, but her tone was serious and chiding. "Don't treat her bad, Hal. You know we all need her here. You and some of them other old boys drive her away, you'll all have to answer to us women, you know. We all like her a lot."

"I didn't do anything, Etta. The lady's been up all night, and she's tired enough to be prickly as a porcupine. Wasn't my fault. Now, don't get on my case." Hal took a big swallow of the coffee, scalding his tongue. He glared up at Etta. "Tell Sal the lumps in the oatmeal were cold, too," he said, using gruffness to hide the hurt feelings that stung him. Etta left, huffy as the doctor had been. Hal hung his head and studied his coffee, wondering at himself. At women. At life in general.

He hadn't intended to drive the doctor away. Just the opposite. Because of the way she'd handled herself this morning, he had finally decided he liked her well enough to ask her out for a date when the opportunity arose. This breakfast was supposed to have been a preliminary. Damn. Why couldn't he have talked to her without putting his boot in his mouth?

CHAPTER TWO

DIXIE MADE IT through the morning on caffeine and adrenaline before exhaustion hit her again. When it did, she gave a silent prayer of thanks that she had only one more patient to see before noon. After that, she'd ask Fran to tell people to come back later in the afternoon, after she'd slept. Or let Fran see the cases that she was capable of handling.

Fran Coble could do plenty. She was a registered nurse who'd come out of retirement to provide the only medical care people had had for months, until Dixie came. She smiled as the older woman came in to the office with a chart.

Fran was tall, slender and gray-haired, and a stickler for traditional office protocol. Though she called Dixie by her first name outside the clinic, here, she always referred to Dixie as "Doctor." She didn't joke about people and she didn't gossip, making her unique here in Seaside. She was a person whose professional judgment and personal advice Dixie had come to trust and depend upon in the space of a very short time.

"Who's next?" Dixie asked, stretching her arms over her head and groaning. "Hope it's nothing serious. I'm about to fall asleep right here at this desk."

"Don't know if it's serious," Fran said, setting the chart down. "But Hattie's been complaining about chest pains for months, now. I think..."

Dixie picked up the chart. "Chest pains? Hattie? A woman?"

"Yes, Doctor." Fran stepped back and folded her hands in front of the starched white skirt of her uniform. "She's fifty-eight, postmenopausal, thin..."

Dixie stood up. "Have you run an EKG?"

"Several." Fran looked pleased with herself. "Read the reports. I sent them down to Casper for..."

"Oh, I see." Dixie ran a finger down the chart. She studied the attached EKG tapes and the reports from the cardiologist in Casper. "Normal. Normal, and normal. So, why...?"

Fran raised her eyebrows. "She's in the examination room, Doctor. And I think you'll understand why, once you talk to her."

Dixie smiled again, wearily. "You're not much help, Fran. For once, I wish you would gossip. I gather there's a family situation that I ought to know about."

Fran nodded. "There is. But you need to hear it from Hattie, I believe."

That got Dixie's attention, and she felt the gears of her brain engage, overriding the weariness. "What's her last name?" Dixie flipped the chart over.

"Blane." Fran paused. "She's the sheriff's momma."

"Oh."

"Uh-huh."

"I'd have chest pains, too." Dixie laughed. "Lead on, Fran."

AFTER DIXIE FINISHED the examination, she had Hattie Blane dress and come into her office. The woman was upset, with tears glimmering in her eyes, when she took a seat. She was thin and gray, a pale, shadow of a woman. The bones of her face indicated a structure that might once have been beautiful, but was now stark and gaunt. "I know all the other doctors say it's just in my mind, Dr. Sheldon," she said. "But I feel terrible and my chest *hurts.*"

"I believe you," Dixie said. "And I don't think you're imagining the pain. But organically, you're healthy. I've given you a complete workup, and I can't find anything wrong. The other reports indicate you've been fine all along. What I'd like to look at is your everyday situation. Maybe there we'll find an answer."

"You mean, I need to see a psychiatrist?" Hattie's thin lips pulled tight. "That it's all in my head? That I'm crazy?"

Dixie sat in her office chair, relaxing as best she could under the tense conditions. "You're not crazy, Mrs. Blane. Neither am I. But we both react to things around us in ways that show up in physical symptoms from time to time."

"Do you have chest pains?"

"No. I have severe headaches, though. Real wall-climbers, I have to confess."

Hattie sighed. "So does Artie. He gets those things you call migraines. He gets so sick . . ."

"Migraines? Who's Artie?"

"My grandson. Arthur. He lives with me."

"I see. Any other people living with you besides Artie?"

Hattie shifted her position on the chair. "Well, actually, I live with my son. It's his house, you see."

"Oh."

"But I take care of them both." She raised her hands, displaying long, graceful fingers beginning to show the signs of labor and advancing age in the large veins and chapped knuckles. "I work hard, Doctor. I don't just lie around, taking up space. Not even when I feel terrible. I never let the boys know what's going on."

"I'm sure you don't, Hattie." Dixie set the woman's chart on the desk. "How do you feel about that?"

Hattie Blane shrugged. "I don't mind. We all have to work, don't we? I mean, that's what we're here on earth to do." She sighed and looked up at the ceiling. "Of course, I did enjoy work more when I was younger. When my husband was alive, and we lived out on my family ranch. Then, every task seemed to have more...purpose to it." Another deep sigh. "But nothing lasts forever, does it?"

"No," Dixie agreed. "The good things don't, but more importantly, the bad things don't, either." She watched Hattie's face for a response. None came. She was as deadpan as her laconic lawman son. "Hattie," she said, "I want you to plan to come in every day this week for a visit. We'll just sit and talk."

Hattie Blane looked horrified. "Why, I can't do that, Doctor Sheldon!" She wrapped her arms tightly around herself. "We can't afford it, and I don't have time." She put her hand to her chest. "Besides, I don't see how just talking will help me with the pain."

Dixie tapped a fingernail on the chart and thought a moment. "Hattie, do you do much baking? I mean, feeding two men must..."

"Of course I bake." Hattie sat up straighter. "Every Monday for forty years, I've baked, had bread in the oven. Even when Hal was a baby, I—"

"Okay," Dixie said, interrupting so she wouldn't think about the sheriff as a baby. The concept was so bizarre, she was afraid she might start to laugh. "Why don't we do this, Mrs. Blane? Forget about coming in every day. You bake as you normally do on Monday, then on Tuesday morning, you come in for an hour, sit and talk to me, and bring me some baked goods instead of worrying about payment."

Hattie Blane's face seemed to light up and grow younger. "Oh, why that's what my momma did when she was living and had to take us children to the doctor. She and my poppa never did have two extra dimes to rub together, you know. Everything went to keep the ranch running. But she'd pack up some things and..."

"Goods for services. It is a tradition of long-standing." Dixie stood up. "In this day of insurance and government health systems, most people don't want to work it out that way, but I'm happy to do it, if it's all right with you."

"It's just fine." Hattie took a deep breath and patted her chest. "I don't know, Dr. Sheldon. But I think I feel much better already."

"Good." Dixie smiled. Of course she felt better. Relief of anxiety did that. "Go see Fran about setting up a regular appointment on Tuesday mornings." She stopped when she saw that her patient's face had taken on a somber expression. "What's the matter?" she asked.

"Um." Hattie's eyes glazed slightly. "I'll have to check on that time each Tuesday, I'm afraid. It depends on when Hal needs me to be home." She put her hand back on her chest. "His schedule is rather unpredictable, you know."

"Have you told him anything at all about your physical problem? Mentioned the pain even once?"

Hattie brushed back a stray strand of gray hair. "Why, no, of course not. He has enough on his mind with Artie and his job and all. I just wouldn't bother him with my troubles."

"Bother him now." Dixie took out a prescription pad and scratched a note on it. She tore off the sheet and handed it to Hattie Blane. "Give this to him. And to your grandson, and anyone else who tries to interfere with your coming here on a regular basis.''

Hattie took the paper and read:

To Whom It Concerns,
On Tuesday mornings, Mrs. Hattie Blane is to spend one hour with Dr. Dixie Sheldon. This is a medical prescription for her chronic pain condition.

She looked at Dixie. "Doctor's orders?''

"That's right.''

"You...you won't tell anyone else? I wouldn't want anyone around town to know I was having...some sort of weaknesses.''

"I don't tell anyone anything about my patients.''

Hattie nodded. "That's true enough,'' she said. "The only complaint I've heard about you, dear, is that you never gossip like old Doc Whitcomb used to do. Why, when he'd spend Saturday night down to the Starlight Bar, by Sunday morning everyone in town'd know everything there was to know about the aches and pains and sins of their friends and neighbors.''

Dixie managed a wry smile. "Not my style.''

Hattie smiled back. "You are an improvement, believe me.''

"Thanks.'' The words warmed Dixie's heart. Especially since this woman's son had been such a jerk earlier in the day.

Later on, however, Dixie pondered what she had gotten herself into with her new patient. If, as she suspected, Hattie Blane was suffering from deep-rooted psychosomatic pain, she was liable to need special care and help for a good while. She needed to be led by the hand, at first. Then she needed to view her problem as part of a whole-life situation and start managing the healing process herself. Hers would likely have to be a long-term commitment to therapy—months, maybe years.

Dixie wondered if she was right to start something that she might not be around to finish. There was no way to answer that question yet, but it bothered her, nonetheless.

So tired, she was having trouble thinking straight, Dixie took the rest of the afternoon off and lay down on the couch in her living room, determined to nap. But sleep wouldn't come. Drowsy but awake, she watched her thoughts chase one another around in her head.

The small house that the town and county had given her as part of the deal was cozy, freshly painted and cleaned to sterile conditions by the volunteers who had welcomed her. Nevertheless, it wasn't home, and she didn't quite feel at ease, yet. The furniture obviously had been collected from attics and basements and donations from all over town; it was clean and comfortable, but not much could be said for the decor. She was grateful, but looked forward to the day when she could set up her own furniture in her own home.

Her own home... That was going to be a dream that would have to wait. And waiting on dreams was not a good way to fall asleep. She considered taking to her bed, but that was against the rules—sofas for napping, beds for sleeping.

She also considered writing some letters—a task she'd been promising herself she'd do for weeks now. She had friends who'd like to know where she was and what she was up to these days. M.J., down in Casper. Reily over in Salt Lake. She smiled. Even Charlotte, the woman who'd lured away her last boyfriend. The guy wasn't worth a fight, so Dixie had given up gracefully, and she and Charlotte still remained friends.

But talking with any of them, even by letter, wasn't appealing right now.

Finally, she got up and went over to the rough wood bookshelf that held her collection of volumes on herbs and other natural healing methods. Drawing her finger down the spines, she considered which would best relax her.

Dixie had a lot of books. It wasn't long before she was yawning, and even less time before she was finally back on the couch asleep without even opening a page.

HAL BLANE WATCHED his mother as she bustled around the kitchen, getting dinner on the table for the three of them. Artie was still upstairs, doing whatever it was he did in the depths of his room, but he'd been called. "You feeling all right, Ma?" Hal asked.

"I'm fine." She stirred the contents of a steaming pot. "Just fine."

"I saw you coming out of Doc Sheldon's office this noon."

"Oh?" She drained vegetables over the sink.

"Seeing the doc?"

"Now, why would I do that?" Hattie turned back to the stove. "Would you put the butter on the table, please, dear?"

"Ma." Hal opened the refrigerator. "Is something wrong with you?" He took out the butter plate and set it by the homemade bread.

"Not a thing. Would you call Artie again, please? We're about ready to eat." She wiped her hands on her apron.

"Ma, I saw you. Leaving Dixie Sheldon's office. I'm your son. Tell me what's going on."

Hattie faced him. "Hal, I'm having some indigestion, or something. I just went in to get checked. Dr. Sheldon said I was fine."

"Indigestion?"

Hattie touched her chest. "It's just . . ."

"Ma, are you having chest pain?" Hal moved closer, studying his mother's face. She did look drawn and tired, now that he paid closer attention. Was her skin just a little bit gray, too? He felt a chill of fear deep inside. His father had had that color not long before his fatal heart attack.

"She says it's not my heart." Hattie looked sideways, not meeting his gaze directly. "Nothing to worry about."

Hal put his hands on her shoulders, shocked at how thin and frail she felt. "Ma, how can I not worry? I don't want you getting sick or hurting."

She put a small, slender hand on his arm. "Well, I went to see the doctor, didn't I? And I'm going again. She'll take care of me."

"Sure." He frowned. "I'm calling that specialist in Salt Lake tomorrow, Ma. Remember he said if Dad had come to him earlier, he could have . . ."

"I will not be driven all the way to Salt Lake," Hattie stated. "There's just no need for it, even if we could afford it. I'm content with Dr. Sheldon's diagnosis. Besides, how would you manage? You have your job to do twenty-four hours a day, and—"

"I have a good deputy. And what do you mean, we can't afford it? We can, too. Somehow. I've got insurance for my family, and you certainly qualify as family. You know that. Whatever it takes to keep you feeling all right . . ."

"Dinner ready yet?" Artie Blane came into the kitchen. "Hurry it up, Grandma. I got things to do tonight."

Hal turned around and snapped at his fifteen-year-old son. "We'll eat when it's ready, and not a minute before, you hear me?" He took a step forward. "Don't go ordering your grandmother around like that."

Artie Blane was not impressed or intimidated. "Yeah, Dad." He slumped down on a chair. "Sorry, Grandma." He stared at the table, at his fingernails, at the ceiling. At the clock on the wall.

"We're ready to eat now," Hattie said, giving her son a warning look. "Let's try to have a pleasant dinner together, shall we?"

"Okay." Hal pulled out a chair. "But we're not finished talking about this doctor thing, Ma. Later on . . ."

"We are finished," Hattie said. "Now, Artie, do you want gravy on your meat or beside it?"

After dinner, Hal broke family tradition by insisting that his mother take the evening off and go watch TV while he and Artie cleaned up in the kitchen. Hattie protested and Artie whined, but Hal prevailed. He and his son washed and dried the pans and dishes in silence while Hattie's television show sounded in the background. Finally, Hal spoke.

"Your grandma's been to the doctor. That's why I wanted to give her a break tonight."

"She sick, again?" Artie glanced over at his father. For the first time that evening, his young face showed emotion. He was a past master at the teenage deadpan, Hal thought. Now, however, he did look concerned.

"I don't know," Hal answered honestly. "She says, no. But she's going back to see the doc next week."

Artie smiled, relief showing. "Well, if I had reason, I'd sure go see the doc."

"Yeah?" Hal put away the big frying pan. "Why's that?"

"She's pretty, Dad. You know that. I've seen you watching her." Artie's grin widened. "She's *real* pretty, isn't she?"

Hal stared. When had his little boy become this...this almost-man? Looking at Artie now was somewhat like looking into a mirror of his own past. The boy had lost that slender, delicate blondness he'd inherited from his mother and was slowly shaping into a replica of...

Of himself! Hal looked away. "She may be pretty, sure," he said. "But I wonder how good a doctor she really is. I'm worried enough about your grandma that I don't want to take any chances." He started to slip into a gloomy mood. Words flew around in his mind, but he didn't speak any of them. Spoken words, wrong words, he reflected somberly, were what usually got him in trouble with people he cared about. He started to brood on his failure to communicate successfully with the pretty doctor that morning. Perfect example.

"Hey." Artie's sharp tone brought his father's attention around. "Who are you kidding? You're worried? You?"

"What's that supposed to mean?"

"I mean, how come you're all of a sudden worried?" The boy's expression was angry and defiant. "I've known she gets spells and feels bad. You're never around here to see how she gets."

"What do you mean? I—"

"I caught her one day crying and holding her chest, Dad. But you were off chasing down the guys who took one of Fred Benson's cows. When you came home, I tried to tell you, but you didn't want to listen to me. You just ignored me and went upstairs to your books and stuff. You never listen. I think you just flat-out don't care."

"That's not true. I—"

"It is, too! You care more about those damn books and old papers than you do—"

"Hal? Artie?" Hattie came into the kitchen. "What's the matter? Why are the two of you yelling?"

"It's nothing, Ma." Hal gave Artie a warning look. "You go on back and relax."

"Yeah, Grandma." Artie put his hand on her shoulder and steered her around toward the living room. "Dad and I were just talking, that's all."

"You were yelling."

Artie shrugged and smiled. "Grandma. You know how us boys are."

She smiled and kissed him. "Yes, I do," she said. Then she let him guide her out of the kitchen.

Hal was deeply touched for a moment by his son's concern and ability to charm and soothe his grandmother. It wasn't until he heard the front door close that he realized Artie had also used the occasion to escape finishing his chores and the house, as well. He clenched his fists and hit the edge of the kitchen sink. If he weren't so tired and if Hattie wouldn't know right off that something was wrong, he'd take off after that kid and show him once and for all who was the boss around this house!

Or would he? Maybe he'd just drive Artie away as he had driven his mother away fifteen years ago. She had wanted him to be kind and understanding all the time and Hal Blane was not cut of that particular cloth. So she'd left with the first man who'd come along and given her the tenderness she'd craved. Hal knew he was too gruff, too grumpy, too unemotional, but he couldn't help it. He was not a man who ever cried, but at that moment, he yearned for the release of tears. What a goddamn relief it would be to just bawl! What a blessed relief!

After a few minutes, he controlled himself enough to go into the living room and tell his mother that he'd be upstairs reading. He asked if there were anything she needed before he went.

There wasn't. Hal knew in his heart that wasn't true, but he couldn't think of a thing to do about it.

THE NEXT MORNING, Dixie opened the mail Fran had stacked on her desk. Most of it was from various government offices and insurance companies who needed her to fill out forms so that she could collect Medicare and the like, but one envelope was marked the California Whole Medicine Research Hospital. As Dixie held the envelope, she noted without surprise that her hand was trembling slightly. No wonder. A great part of her dreams for the future depended on the contents. She took a deep breath and ripped at the paper.

Fran came running at the sound of Dixie's delighted cry. "What's the matter? I heard you yell and..."

Dixie waved the letter. "Read this, Fran. I'm in! Once I've done my three years here, I have a place in research at the medical center. And, there's more!"

Fran read, then spoke. "They want you to collect data here?" She frowned and took off her glasses. "Data on what?"

"Natural medicine. Folk medicine." Dixie got up and moved around the office. Her energy level was back to its normal high. "This place is perfect, you know. Off the beaten track. Distant from big modern medical centers. People have had to depend on themselves for healing for over a century." She whirled around. "This may actually be the best of all possible places for me right now, Fran. I can start here, and who knows how far I can go someday!"

Maybe, she thought, *even the Nobel Prize awaited down the line.* Someday...

CHAPTER THREE

THE SUMMER SUN beat down on her head as Dixie ruefully eyed the broken-down Suburban. She was going to need some serious help to get towed back into town. In the meantime, she was stranded, stuck out in the middle of nowhere. And Nowhere, Wyoming, was serious nowhere.

It was Friday. Four days since she had seen Hattie Blane and three since she had received the wonderful letter from California. After that high moment, reality had returned to rest heavily on her shoulders. Until a few minutes ago, she had been returning from a house call to an outlying ranch where three kids were down with chicken pox.

Three kids. Chicken pox. She was thinking more like a country doctor than a Nobel Prize-winning researcher when she'd responded to that one, she thought wryly. Rather than have the harried mother and father pack up all three and drag them into town, she'd elected to drive out and pay a house call.

The children had been cranky and uncomfortable, but were surviving the itchiness and enforced isolation from the rest of the children in the area. Dixie had examined them and recommended long baths in cool water with lots of baking soda or cornstarch thrown in, then she'd started back on the dirt road toward home. She'd heard the ominous knock in the engine right away, but had chosen to ignore it.

Until even the knock had ceased. The engine had died, groaning and coughing like a tubercular patient in the final stages of the disease, and once it stopped, it would not turn over, no matter how much she fussed and cussed at it. Thankful she had a cellular phone, a gift from her parents, she'd called Fran, and help was on the way. All she had to do now was wait for some knight in a shining tow truck.

Waiting, however, was hot work. The Suburban was in a deep, wide canyon. High rock walls loomed skyward on either side, making an earthy furnace of the place. Dust from the dirt road rose in the air. Sun blazed like a spotlight overhead. The temperature was well into the nineties. And she had no water with her.

She knew better. Knew much better than to go out without water and survival equipment, even in the summer. She'd grown up in this essentially rural state where the human settlements were sometimes hundreds of miles apart and a stranded motorist risked death as well as serious discomfort in the days before the cellular phone. Even now, it could happen. Phones didn't always work. Everyone with any sense carried the essentials in car or truck, no matter what the season or how long the journey. One never knew.

Well, she knew now. Angry at herself, Dixie sat sideways on the driver's seat, crossed her arms and sweated in the heat. She'd left both doors open in case a breeze took mercy on her.

None did. Minutes ticked by. Fifteen. Thirty. Forty-five... She got hotter and more annoyed at herself. And at whoever was supposed to be on the way to her rescue. They were certainly taking their own sweet time!

She turned on the radio, which pulled in nothing but the country-western station out of Cody down here in the canyon.

She turned it off. There was no point in wasting the batteries.

She shifted to the passenger side, hoping it would be cooler. It wasn't.

She got out and stood in the shade of the canyon wall. Heat radiated off the rock, making the shady area an open oven, baking her already heated skin. She moved back to the car. A plume of dust appeared on the far side of the draw. Her lips were dry and starting to hurt. She rummaged in her medical bag, found a small jar of Vaseline and smeared some of it on her mouth. That brought temporary relief. The plume of dust now had a sound to it. Dixie shaded her eyes with her hand and squinted into the harsh sunlight. Someone was coming.

But it wasn't a tow truck.

Hal downshifted his modified Jeep as he approached the doctor's stalled vehicle. The air in the canyon was hot as hell, and he could see from here that she was looking pretty wilted. He cursed the fact that Al Pringle had been too busy working on Dan Foster's tractor to take the time to do this chore. Of course, Hal understood that in this land that depended on agriculture for life, tractors came before females, even if they were doctors who'd probably just run out of gas. He wasn't relishing the idea of dealing with Dixie Sheldon under these conditions.

When Fran had called him, though, pleading with him to rescue her boss, he really couldn't beg out of the job in good conscience. He was, after all, the sheriff. Protect and Serve. He pulled to a stop, let the dust settle a little and got out.

"Hello, Sheriff," she said, sitting there, her chin on her hand, watching him. "Hot enough for you?"

"Yeah, I guess." He watched a trickle of sweat run down her face. Her usually pale skin was flushed with the heat, and he could see a fair amount of it, since she was wearing a loose, sleeveless dress. Blue color, soft-looking material. Appropriate for the weather, but not very doctorlike. More...feminine than he would have expected. He tried out a smile. "It's for sure hot today," he agreed, tilting his hat back on his head. "Want a lift?"

She didn't move. Didn't smile. "I'm waiting for a tow." Another trickle of sweat ran down her throat to disappear into the top of her dress. The material under her arms and breasts was already stained darker blue. Hal tried not to stare at the way the damp material outlined her shape.

"Well." He took off the hat and wiped his face with a handkerchief. "I don't know how long that might be. Al Pringle owns the only tow truck in town, and he's fixing a tractor right now."

"I'm not leaving my car."

"You can't stay here. Not in this heat. Come on, Dixie. It's safe enough out here. Nobody's going to bother it."

"Maybe not. But I don't care to leave it. If nothing else, the temperature may harm the engine."

Hal jammed the hat back on his head. "Let me take a look at it." He moved around to the front of the Suburban. "Crack the hood, will you?"

She got out and came over to him. "Do you know anything about auto mechanics?"

"Some."

She put her hands on her hips. "Gee, Sheriff. How would you feel if I was going to operate on you and you asked if I knew anything about surgery and I said, 'Some'?"

"It's not the same thing, and you—"

"I know that this car has to last me for at least the next three years, and I don't want anyone touching it who doesn't know exactly what he's doing."

"How about spitting in my eye, Doc. I did come all the way out here just to help you, you know."

She looked even angrier, then suddenly apologetic. "I'm sorry, Hal. I do know that. It's not your fault, and I'm wrong to snap at you. I just..."

"It's hot. You're worried." He tilted the hat back again. "I understand." She had, he realized, called him by his first name. She looked small and helpless. Her vulnerability caught at him, and he *wanted* to help. "No need to apologize," he added. "I sure sympathize."

"Thanks."

"Why don't you let me look, anyway. What harm can I do, just looking?"

"All right. I suppose you can't hurt it much more than it already is." She didn't smile back. She looked downright grim and certainly unhappy at the prospect of letting him root around in the guts of her precious car.

"Good to be appreciated." He went around to the front of the Suburban again. "Crack the hood."

Dixie did. Five minutes later, the engine was humming like a new machine. Hal slammed down the hood and took out a handkerchief. He wiped his hands. He did not look at her.

"I'll follow you into town," he said, walking back toward his Jeep. "Just in case."

"Hal."

"Yeah?" He half turned.

In time to see her smile as wide as the morning sky—at him. "Thanks," she said. "You're terrific! A real lifesaver. If I weren't so sweaty and stinky, I'd kiss you, I swear!" Then, she surprised him once more by pursing her lips and blowing a kiss at him. She looked terrific doing it—young and vital and deliciously female.

A real about-face for the usually solemn Dr. Dixie Sheldon. Was it really just because he'd fixed her car? Or was there more to it? He liked what he saw when he looked at her and wondered if she felt the same about him. He entertained himself all the way into Seaside, thinking about that.

WHEN THEY PULLED UP in front of the clinic, Dixie got out and went over to the Jeep. "It's still making a funny noise," she said, worry crinkling the soft skin between her dark eyebrows. "I think I'd better let Al have it in for a checkup."

Hal stayed in his seat, but he nodded. "Might be a good idea," he agreed, watching her without staring, using his side vision to study her face. Enjoying himself for the moment. "I just reconnected a hose, but you might have other parts loose. One of the belts is frayed, I know."

She smiled. A small smile, but genuine. "You're a good sport. Thanks again. Tell me, how did George Preston make out? Did my stitching hold him together until he got into court?"

"George is fine. He's back riding fence up to Dalton's north pasture. Bragging about his pretty doctor and the fine scar he got."

"He's not still in jail?" She frowned again. "But I thought..."

Hal shrugged. "Nobody brought charges. It was enough he got cut, had a hangover and spent the weekend in the clink. He's not really any problem to society, Doc. Don't you worry."

"Odd justice around here, I have to say," she murmured. Then, her thoughts seemed to change. Her frown lines deepened. "A while ago, you called me by my first name. I like that better than 'Doc.' Think you can manage?"

"Sure. Dixie." He leaned forward to shift gears, then sat back. "Say, could I ask you something?"

Dixie sensed a change in his attitude. "You can ask. Is this a medical matter?"

"Kind of."

"Then come on inside. My office is air-conditioned."

She turned and entered the clinic. He followed her inside, his big boots making clumping sounds on the old hardwood floor. She moved almost silently on her thin sandals, which summed up the difference between them, he realized. He made noise; she didn't.

Dixie waved at Fran, who was in the back section of the front office, rummaging through the file cabinets. Fran gave the sheriff a double take, grinned and waved back, then went on with her business. Dixie opened her office door and motioned him to enter. "I'll get us some pop," she said. "I know I'm dying of thirst, and you must be, too. What would you like?"

"Nothing. Thanks." He went in, sat down, took off his hat and closed his eyes, breathing in the cool air. "Nice in here," he commented. "Jail's not air-conditioned."

Dixie regarded him for a moment. "I'll bring you a soda, anyway. I hate to drink alone."

"If you want."

She left him and went down the hall, thinking dark thoughts about Old West machismo and Hal Blane's apparent need to stick to the Code. He had to be thirsty, no matter what he said. When she returned with the cold soft drinks, he seemed to be dozing in the chair.

His eyes opened instantly when she snapped the tab on the can. She handed him a soda and went behind her desk to her own chair. "Now," she said, after taking a long, thirst-quenching swig and having the satisfaction of seeing him do likewise. "What can I do for you, Hal?"

"It's about my momma."

"Hattie?" Dixie sat back and took another drink. "What about her?"

"You think...um...do you think she's sick?" He sat forward on his chair, his big hands embracing the pop can. "She says she isn't, but..."

"But?"

"Well, my boy, Artie, he sees her more than I do, and he thinks she might be..."

"Hal." She set the can down on her desk. "I don't want to alarm you, so I'll say this. I don't think your mother is physically ill. She's not in any immediate danger, if that's what's worrying you. But she is exhibiting signs of anxiety."

"Chest pains?"

"She did say..."

He shifted position on the chair. "My daddy died of heart disease," he said, his voice low and soft. "If Ma has any trouble like that, I want to know. Straight up. No lies."

"She has trouble. But not..."

"I want to take her to Salt Lake. See a specialist."

"That's certainly your privilege. I'm a general practitioner, that's all. A specialist would be great for her. I wouldn't expect any other kind of response from a person who was worried about someone they love."

"You're not...upset I want her to see someone else?"

"I made a diagnosis, Hal. Based on some tests and my own examination." She clasped her hands and placed them on the desk. "But I admit I'm not perfect. I don't ever expect to be perfect, in fact. So if you want a second opinion, I can give you the name of an excellent psychiatrist in Salt Lake who..."

"I'm not talking about a shrink, Dixie. She's not crazy. I want her to see a heart specialist."

"I just told you, she does not have a problem with her heart..." She sat back, looking at the man in front of her. "Okay. I'll set it up for you. When do you want to go?" If he was determined to find out for himself, it was certainly his right to do so. And maybe Hattie herself needed one more outsider to confirm what Dixie had told her. Maybe then the counseling would be more effective.

Maybe.

He sat forward. "Next week, I suppose. But I don't know when I can take off, so I can't say definitely right now."

"Hal." Dixie tapped her pen on the desktop. "You need to arrange your priorities. I've tried to tell you that your mother has no heart problem, but you don't seem willing to accept that right up front. When I offer to set up an appointment with a cardiologist, you can't waffle around about the time. She's very busy. You have to take what she'll give you."

"She?"

"Dr. Lauren Becker is the best cardiologist in—"

"I want to take my mother to Tim Reed. He was the doctor who told us what killed Pa. He's—"

"He's retired, Hal. How long ago did your father die, anyhow?"

"I was about Artie's age." He shifted in the chair. Rubbed the back of his neck, didn't meet her gaze. "Fifteen. I was just fifteen. That was around twenty years ago."

She felt a shadow of the pain that fifteen-year-old Hal Blane had suffered. She spoke softly. "Lot of changes in medicine since then."

He shifted again. "Yeah. Well. If Reed's retired, I guess I don't have a choice. When can we see this Lauren woman?"

Choosing to ignore his tone of voice, Dixie put her hand by the phone. "I'll call right now and see what her schedule will permit."

He set his jaw. "Do that. Whenever it is, I'll make arrangements."

Dixie reached for the phone, but it rang before she could pick it up. "I'll let Fran get that," she said, sitting back. "She knows I'm in conference with you, so unless it's an emergency, she'll—"

"Doctor." Fran appeared at the door, rapping on it once and opening it as she called for Dixie. "It's an emergency. There's been an accident way out at the dinosaur dig. They say it's bad. They need you right away."

HE DROVE her there. It made no sense to do anything else. She had to get to the site as soon as possible, and certainly her own vehicle wasn't reliable, so she strapped herself in to the passenger seat of the Jeep without comment. He turned on the siren to get them out of town, and then used the bar lights to justify speeds of nearly ninety miles an hour. Dixie said nothing. Speed was necessary, and he drove with skill, his entire attention on the road.

She used the time to study him and to think.

Something about the man definitely appealed to her and that was crazy. Since their first encounter, he'd succeeded in regularly annoying her. Oh, there had certainly been moments now and then when he'd been pleasant. But overall, her impression of Hal Blane wasn't positive. Not at all.

So, why did she find herself enjoying this wild ride by his side?

Maybe, she thought, it was because he seemed so competent to do the job. She didn't know many people she'd trust to hurtle her along at speeds this high.

Or maybe it was the way his hard profile looked beneath the edge of his cowboy hat. It made him look stern, manly, secure in his identity.

Maybe that was part of the appeal. A throwback he might be, to times when men were men and women worked hard and had kids until they dropped dead of it all, but at least he seemed sure of himself—a hard, certain, dominant male. . . .

Oh, brother. Was that it? She looked out the window at the dusty summer land that flashed past. It had been a long time since she'd been in a romantic relationship. Was she acting like a wild female animal in heat responding to the lure of the alpha male?

Ridiculous! She folded her arms and stared out at the Wyoming hills. If she needed a man at all, which she was sure she did not, she needed one who would be a partner, a fair match for her in the brains department. Not someone who could only dominate her physically. Make her feel womanly and delicate like Blane did . . . She was too intelligent, too sophisticated to fall into that sort of trap!

Wasn't she?

They drove for another few minutes along the paved highway, then he jerked the steering wheel to the right and turned on to a dirt path leading toward plateau land and the mountains. "They're going to be right up in that cut," he said, indicating a low notch in the higher land. "Hang on, Doc."

She did. Forgetting her senseless musing about her feelings regarding him, she concentrated on keeping her seat. Her teeth rattled, and her kidneys screamed, but she didn't say anything. Not about the ride. Not about being reduced to "Doc" once more. Neither her comfort nor her dignity seemed to matter. An injured person waited, and she was a healer, not a fighter.

They drove along the flat prairie, kicking up a high plume of dust, then eased onto the slope of the tableland. The track twisted and turned, rising upward in a steep grade toward the top of the plateau through land that was gray and purple and beige with spots of pale green sagebrush bunched into sheltered areas. Hal shifted gears and the engine groaned before responding. Dixie glanced at him, wondering if anything was wrong with *his* vehicle, but she saw no sign of alarm on his face. No sign of any emotion.

They slowed, and there was the camp. Farther over to the right, beyond the edge of the plateau, she could see pine trees, then aspens and the bottom of the valley, cut by a small stream.

"Digging for dinosaurs," Hal commented, his tone dry. "They swarm up here every damn year and throw dirt like crazy as long as the weather and their grant money holds." He pushed the Jeep over the top and down into the hollow.

Dixie held on tight. "You don't like it?"

"Didn't say that. But it seems strange to have eastern university folks backed by big bucks out here looking for creatures that lived when this was all ocean, when what we need now is to direct some of that energy and money to the local people who are needful today."

She thought of the clinic with no hospital nearby, the decrepit jail, the generally run-down appearance of the town that Hal Blane called home. She sensed a depth of feeling there that she hadn't imagined in him before. "I see your point, I suppose, but isn't the knowledge they gain here by digging up the past worth something?"

"Didn't say it wasn't. Just said it was strange." He pulled to a stop a few yards from a cluster of tents. "Different needs. Different values. Different attitudes about what really matters... Well, here we are at Harvard Square West," he added.

People in tan work clothes came running toward them. They did not look as though they were from Harvard or any other Ivy League school. They looked rough and dirty and upset.

"Watch out," he said softly.

Dixie glanced at him, alarmed, her fingers hesitating on the door handle. "Why? They need me. I'm not afraid."

"No, you aren't, are you?" He was smiling at her in that wry, sideways manner he had. "No, I don't mean you should be scared. It's just the boss man. The director's a cranky cuss from Harvard," he said, explaining. "Been running this show for years. Big shot back there, I understand. Name's Oscar Hayden. *Professor-Doctor* Hayden. And don't forget that. He won't. Thinks he's king of the universe. You watch yourself."

"I can do that. But thanks for the warning." She got out.

"Dr. Sheldon?" A tall worried-looking woman with sun-bleached blond hair, a lanky frame with zero body fat and skin that had been weathered by heat and sunshine greeted her. Worry lines cut into her face and forehead. "Dr. Sheldon? You're the local physician?"

Dixie nodded.

The other woman smiled, relief in her blue eyes. "I'm Winnie Nash, temporary director of this dig," she said.

"This is my first year out here and I didn't know what to do for emergency medical help. Dr. Hayden's not here, so I called the nearest town for help. You're a godsend! Thanks for coming so quickly. We've got a student down in a ravine. A boulder fell on him, and I think he's got a crushed leg. I didn't want to move him until a doctor was on the scene."

The words tumbled out of her, making Dixie aware that she was extremely agitated. She could tell Winnie was terribly concerned about the situation and the well-being of the student, and Dixie immediately liked this woman.

She held out her hand and they shook. The paleontologist's hand, long and broad, almost swallowing Dixie's. "I'm Dixie Sheldon," she said. "And you did the right thing by not moving him, yet. Take me to him." She looked back at Hal again. "Sheriff Blane here can help us move him when I'm ready."

Sheriff Blane did more than that. Once Dixie started to work on the patient, Hal was right there by her side, helping just as he had when she'd worked on George in the jail. Almost without thinking about it, she issued him gloves and orders, as if he were a paramedic or a nurse who had trained and worked with her for a long time. He did his job efficiently and without asking questions, obeying her to the letter.

Not much later, the injured student was on his way by Life Flight helicopter to the regional medical center in Casper. The damage to his leg was severe, though not immediately life-threatening. The worst danger had already been attended to by Winnie Nash's quick first-aid techniques. Dixie called for the helicopter in the confident hope that the leg could be saved by speedy surgery. Winnie, grateful that her youthful charge was in good hands and clearly relieved that she had done the right thing by calling in the local physician, invited Dixie to stay for dinner.

"You, too, Sheriff," she told Hal. "But if you need to get back to town, I can drive the doctor home later after we eat."

Dixie expected him to take that opportunity to depart, but to her surprise, he did not. Instead, he favored both of them with a slow smile that stirred her more than she cared to admit. "I reckon town can take care of itself for a while longer," he drawled. "I've always liked it out here at night. Especially in summer when it's warm like this. Don't get much chance to enjoy it, these days. So, I'll stay."

And he did, and it was pleasant to have him there, Dixie discovered. There were layers to Hal Blane that surprised her. Layers she would never have suspected and might never have seen if they'd been relating the way they did in town. Here, though, his defenses seemed down.

And, possibly, so were hers.

CHAPTER FOUR

Dixie relaxed completely for the first time in months. The atmosphere of the camp was warm and homey, in spite of its being outdoors. She found that her first impression had been right: she did like Winnie Nash.

She was pleasant to be with, humorous, easygoing and gentle in her ways. Her charming nature emerged once she was no longer so anxious about her injured worker.

The rest of the crew seemed likable, too. The scholarly paleontologists proved to be just like any other group of folks camping out in the West. As twilight darkened into night, a bunch of them gathered around a large fire in the center of the camp, to sing songs and tell stories. Winnie joined them after supper, inviting her guests to do the same, but Hal and Dixie chose to remain apart for a while. At Winnie's tent, they had their own fire and their own form of singing and storytelling. They began to share themselves with each other.

Wrapped against the evening chill in a large jacket loaned by Winnie, Dixie sat on a log next to the usually taciturn sheriff. Both of them were poking at the small fire with sticks and opening up about themselves as if they were trusted friends.

"When I was a little guy, my daddy used to tell me the stars up in the summer sky were all flashes of sunlight on the shiny horns of heaven's cattle herd," Hal said. "Then, he'd kind of look at me just to see if I was buying that stuff.''

Dixie hugged her knees to her chest. "And did you?" she asked, really wanting to know. Suddenly, the concept of Hal Blane as a child fascinated her. He was so somberly, solidly *adult,* it was difficult to imagine.

"No." He grinned, making her wonder if he was telling the truth or just spinning her a pleasant yarn. "But I pretended I did, just to make him happy."

"My folks are a little more on the pragmatic side," she confided. "No tall tales or fairy stories for me. I was the first kid in my class to know Santa and the Easter Bunny were Mom and Dad."

He seemed to think about that for a time. "What about religion? Did they deny you that, too?" He didn't sound impressed with her parents.

Dixie shrugged. If he didn't like her history, that was his problem, not hers. She was in no mood to quarrel. She just wanted to talk. "No. They didn't *deny* me anything like that. But I was left to make up my own mind about God."

He didn't ask what conclusion she had come to.

"I think anyone who works in medicine, with its life-and-death decisions, sooner or later has to come to grips with matters of religion," she went on. "I know I have."

"Law enforcement's like that," he said. "Life and death come often enough, a man better make his peace early on." He stared at the fire.

In profile by the firelight, he seemed older, more careworn, even more ruggedly western....

More dangerous. And, oddly, more interesting. Actually, exciting. The glow of the flames made his skin look like hard bronze and even his hair seemed metallic, the way it shone. The cragginess of his features reminded her of an unfinished sculpture—too rough for real male beauty, but with an underlying pattern of pleasing shape and symmetry. He looked . . .

For a moment, she slid back into that fantasy of the nineteenth century that had gripped her before, when she'd sat in her car outside his jail. "Have you ever shot anyone?" she asked, the question slipping out before she could stop herself. Embarrassment filled her the moment she realized what she had asked.

He turned his head slowly and looked at her. "You mean, have I ever *killed* anyone? That's what you want to know, isn't it?"

Dixie swallowed, her mouth suddenly dry. "Sorry. I don't know what I was thinking. That was a terrible question. I shouldn't have asked it. That was unforgivably rude. Forgive me, please."

"Yeah. Don't worry about it. But I do get asked that now and then. Surprises me, your doing it, though."

"Let me explain, please." Dixie made a wide gesture with her arms. "It's . . . it's this place," she said. "It excites something strange in my imagination. It makes me feel like I've gone back in time to the Old West. Gunfighting and stuff like that. It's weird. For a second, I could even see you as an old-time marshal or sheriff. I can't explain it. It happened to me the other day, too."

He looked at her, questioning without speaking.

"It happened at dawn last Sunday. When I came to patch up George," she said. "I was tired, I know. But I was sitting in my car and, for a minute, the whole town seemed to shift back in time. The sidewalks seemed made of wooden planks. The street seemed hard-packed dirt. And you . . . When I saw you in the darkness . . . Well, you looked like someone out of a John Wayne or Clint Eastwood movie."

Hal laughed. "Tell me more, lil' lady," he mimicked. "Make my day."

She laughed, too. "Okay. Have fun. But it's happened twice now. And, believe me, I am not a very imaginative person. Quite the opposite, in fact."

"I don't believe that." He smiled, taking the sting out of his words and any tension out of the awkward situation. "I think you're a pretty remarkable woman, Doc Dixie."

"Thanks. I'll try my best to live up to that." She shivered and drew the jacket closer.

Hal moved over and put his arm around her shoulders, sharing his considerable warmth with her. The gesture was a friendly one. Romantic, but not sexy.

"Gets real cold out here at night," he commented, looking back up at the sky. "No matter how hot it is during the day."

"I know. I remember. On summer nights when I was a kid my friends and I would string up a sheet between two trees and pretend we were camping out, until it got so cold we had to go inside."

"Where was this? I figured you for a city child."

"I grew up down in Laramie. I guess that's a city compared to Seaside, but it's not New York, by any stretch of the imagination."

"Laramie. Your folks . . . ?"

"Teach at the university."

"Oh."

Dixie looked sideways at her companion again. His voice had an odd tone. "My father is a historian," she said. "Mom teaches English. They're both Ph.D.'s. It got funny sometimes, hearing them both called 'doctor.' Now, me, too."

"Doctor, doctor, doctor. Who's the real doctor?"

"Something wrong with that, Hal?"

"No." His arm left her shoulder, and he moved away slightly. "I'm just jealous, to be perfectly honest with you."

She regretted the loss of his warmth. "Why's that?"

His mouth twisted. "I wanted to go to college. Really wanted it. Couldn't manage it, though, mostly because of money, but also time and circumstances. Because my mother was a widow, I felt I was responsible for her. And then I went and got married." He paused. "We had Artie right away. So I took some courses over at the community college and then went down to the law enforcement academy at Douglas. No college degree for me."

Dixie felt uncomfortable and unsure of what his confession entailed. "Why would you need college, if you were going to be sheriff here?"

He smiled at her again, the expression open and not wry at all. "I didn't need it, but I wanted it."

"Then, I'm sorry you didn't get the chance."

"Me, too." He looked at the fire. "But my boy will."

"That's Artie?"

"Yup." He picked up his stick and poked at the coals again. "I guess my mother told you about him."

"She mentioned him."

"He's . . . he's a good kid. Just kind of difficult to handle right now."

"How old, Hal?"

"Fifteen."

Dixie laughed. "I've never met a teenager yet who wasn't a trial. Myself included." She laughed again. "I was fifteen when I first ran away from home."

Hal turned quickly to stare at her. "You? I can't see you as a runaway."

"Oh, there's a lot about me most folks wouldn't guess at these days. I was one wild kid." She tucked her hands into Winnie's jacket pockets. "But that's all in the past." She nodded in the direction of the main camp fire. "Say, do you want to join them for a while before we go back to town?"

Hal stood up and held out his hand to her. "I think we should. Haven't been very sociable, sitting over here by ourselves, have we?"

She took his hand and rose. "No, I guess not."

They continued to hold hands as they walked over to the others. Only when they reached the group did Hal release her. Dixie missed his touch when he let go. Compared to hers, his hand was huge and rough-skinned, yet he had held her so gently. So... securely.

A few minutes later, they were sitting with the others. Apparently, the sheriff of SeaLake County was known to more than one of the diggers.

"Why, hello, Sheriff," said the young man strumming a guitar when they entered the light of the fire. He had long dark hair pulled back in a ponytail and the shadow of several days' beard growth on his tanned face. "I heard you were the one who ferried the doctor out here. How are you doing?"

"I'm doing fine, Hastings," Hal said. "And you?"

"Just fine." He strummed a minor chord. The man regarded Dixie curiously. "Are you the doctor?"

"Yes."

"Well, you take good care of this cantankerous lawman, please. He saved my life last year." He punctuated the sentence with a major chord.

Dixie looked at Hal.

"Rattlesnake," he said. "Bit him. Hastings, everybody, from now on, any of you have any medical problems, you won't have to put up with my ham hands."

There was a spatter of applause and murmurs of welcome. About fifteen people sat around the fire. Dixie noted that most of them were younger than her. Tanned and fit-looking with long or extremely short hair. No one had on jewelry, makeup or anything resembling fancy clothing. They looked like hard workers who liked what they did. "Hope you don't need me, but if you do, I'll be here for the next three years," she said.

"Why?" asked a woman with sun-streaked brown hair. "I mean, you can't be making much of a living practicing medicine way out here. There just aren't that many people."

"True enough, and that's the problem." Dixie sat down. "Rural medicine here is based on paybacks," she said. "I got my medical education on the state's dime, so now I owe three years or lots of money." She smiled. "The years are a little easier to come by, right now."

"What do you plan after your tour of duty's up?" Winnie asked. "Stay here, or move on?"

Dixie remembered the letter. "I have an offer I can't refuse," she said. "I applied to a medical center in California that specializes in investigating and utilizing natural and folk medicine under modern scientific techniques and methods. It's a dream job."

"Sounds like a great idea," Hastings said. "Using old wisdom to enhance modern science."

Dixie smiled, the remembered excitement of getting the letter returning to her. "There's more. I'm under contract to them while I work here."

"How's that?" Hal asked. He'd put his hat back on, and his eyes were shadowed.

"I'm to collect data locally," she explained, "record it and send it to the center. They'll start setting up a computer program based on my material, so that when I go there permanently, I can get right to work."

"Sounds convenient," Hal drawled.

"For them," Winnie added, her forehead creased in a frown. "Dixie, are you sure they aren't taking advantage of you? Are you getting any compensation?"

She shook her head, unwilling to admit the point both of her new friends were making. "It doesn't matter. I have a job offer."

"You have a job here," Hal said. "Folks need you. How much do they need another doctor in California?"

She was pensive for a moment. "Maybe they don't, Hal. But I need them. I've dreamed of this project ever since I started medical school."

"Well, then." Hastings strummed his guitar. "Sounds like you ought to go for it. Let's see, your name's Dixie? What a coincidence. That's the title of my next song."

Everyone joined in on the chorus, including Hal, Dixie noted. She couldn't be certain because so many people were singing, but his voice sounded unusually good.

Then Hastings held out the guitar. "Go on, Sheriff," he said. "Show us how it's supposed to be done."

Hal shook his head, refusing the guitar. "No. We have to be getting back to town."

"Oh, come on, Hal," Dixie said. "Please. I'm in no rush. I'd like to hear you play."

He hesitated, but took the guitar. His hat cocked back on his head, he settled against a log and placed the instrument on his lap. Dixie watched and waited.

What happened next amazed, delighted and mystified her.

Hal Blane not only sang well, he played like a professional country-western star. She didn't know much about the technique of playing stringed instruments, but she did know talent when she saw and heard it. Yes, she mused again, Hal Blane had many more layers than were apparent at first glance.

They stayed for another hour while Hal gave a mini-concert of western ballads and cowboy songs. The others, including Dixie, joined in when they knew the words, but the sheriff carried most of the music alone. He had a pleasing baritone that was too rough to be professionally perfect, but sounded just right that night under the open sky and stars.

Dixie was enchanted.

Finally, he called it quits. "I really do have to get on back to town now," he said. "And I know the doc's tired, too."

"I am," Dixie admitted, rising to her feet reluctantly. "But I am having such a good time, I hate to leave."

"Come back during the day sometime," Winnie said. "Dig with us for a while. Do you some good to work on the past instead of the present."

"I might do that. Thanks. What kind of past does this area have, anyway?" She glanced at Hal, thinking he might have the most interesting answer.

Hal settled his hat down on his head. He surveyed the night scene, taking in the mountains above the camp and the cliff and creek area below. "You're on part of what used to be the old Kedrick ranch," he said. "Rich tableland here. Good pasturage." He left the circle of the firelight and walked out into the darkness beyond. No one else spoke, and Dixie heard what he said next clearly.

"This land belonged to my people at a time long past."

"Native Americans?" Winnie asked.

"No. Buccaneer English. The Kedricks. On my mother's side. A bad lot. Sailed the seven seas, then ended up here on a dry one. SeaLake County." He continued to gaze out into the night. "We took it from the Indians. About a hundred years ago." He made a sound like a laugh, but it was too thin to be real mirth. "And then the U.S. government took it from us." He took off his hat and slapped it gently against his leg as if to dislodge dust. "Only fair, I guess." He turned around and looked at Dixie. "Coming, Doc?"

Dixie murmured an assent and said her goodbyes. Hal's declaration had been mysterious and dramatic, and now she was itching to know the details.

Details might help her understand her patient, his mother. Details might help her understand this man who was becoming more and more interesting the more she stayed around him.

However, he contributed little to her store of knowledge. On the way home, he turned on his tape deck and discouraged conversation by playing loud country music. Hank Williams and Jim Reeves commanded the stage.

Dixie didn't try to compete. She sensed that by playing the music, he was saying he wanted to ride in peace, if not quiet.

When they returned to town and drove up to her house, he shut off the tape. "I know doctors and sheriffs don't have weekends like most folks," he said, not looking directly at her. "But if you aren't busy tomorrow night, would you like to go out with me? For dinner?"

"Sure," she replied, a little surprised, but pleased. "I'd like that a lot, as a matter of fact."

He turned toward her and smiled. "I promise to be in a better mood than when we had breakfast last week. I wasn't real pleasant, then, I know."

"Is that an apology?"

"Guess so."

"Then, I really am looking forward to tomorrow." She slid across the seat and kissed him, briefly, but square on the mouth. His eyes widened in surprise and appreciation, and she grinned. "Night, Hal. Thanks for rescuing me this afternoon."

"My pleasure." His voice was low and soft, almost a deep purr. Like the noise a contented lion might make.

She got out, shut the door and asked through the open window, "What time should I be ready tomorrow?"

"Um . . ." He touched his lips, thoughtfully. "Five. It's a long drive to the place I have in mind. It's beyond Cody, over in the national forest." He smiled again, the expression oddly shy. "Kind of a gourmet spot, if you want to know the truth. Can't say it's health food like the stuff you probably enjoy, but it's good. Real good. Bring your appetite. Dinner takes three hours, minimum."

"No kidding? I'm intrigued. Should I dress up?"

"Wear what you want. This is still Wyoming."

"Right." She slapped the side of the vehicle. "Anything from jeans to black tie is all right."

"You got it." He sounded happy, and in the light from the dashboard, Dixie saw a much younger, more relaxed Hal Blane smiling at her.

She took that image to bed with her, and though she dreamed of old-time western sheriffs and macho gunfighters, when she woke up at dawn, she was thinking of the real man she was beginning to know.

To know and, surprisingly, given her first impressions of him, to like.

SHE SPENT the next morning over at the clinic, even though it was Saturday, and the place was theoretically closed. In practice, she had plenty to do, catching up on the inevitable pile of government paperwork and seeing two patients with minor emergencies, a cracked wrist on a child and a horse bite on a careless cowboy. Then she went home for lunch. While she was eating, the phone rang.

Dixie tensed, thinking it might be another medical situation that required her presence, but it was her parents, calling from Laramie. She had already shared with them the happy news about Cal Med earlier in the week, so she had no special information to report.

She spent a pleasant twenty minutes listening to them recount their activities and give her the campus gossip. But when her mother started to inquire about her private life and learned about her date that night with Hal, Dixie found herself getting defensive.

"He's not a hick sheriff, Mom," she said, when her mother, Dr. Philomena Sheldon, decried her daughter's interest in the lawman. "I mean, he's local, all right. Very local. But I think he has some real depth and breadth to him. Not limited by his environment to—"

"Oh, Dixie," her mother said, interrupting. "You know what they're like. Those macho, cowboy types just never manage to grow up. I thought you got them all out of your system while you were in high school. Goodness knows, you dated enough of them to find out what they really wanted, which you and I both know wasn't an exchange of intellectual opinions. And if they don't want uncomplicated sex, they want a wife who'll tend the hearth and home, attend their every male whim with a smile and silence. That is not for you, darling girl!"

"Mom, I—"

"Your mother's right, dear," her father added. "Listen to her. The last thing you need is involvement with a man who'll hold you back."

"I am only having dinner with him! I'm certainly not marrying him!"

Her comment was met with silence followed by indulgent sighs and softening comments.

"Of course. I suppose that's all right," her father said.

"It is. Now, darling. We love you and we tend to overreact where your future is concerned."

"I know. I know. It's okay. Say, I forgot to ask. How's Aunt Vi?" Dixie managed to redirect the topic of conversation to Raymond Sheldon's ailing sister. While her parents filled her in on Violet's latest batch of medical problems, Dixie reflected that they did, indeed, overreact where she was concerned. They always had.

She was their only child, and all their parental hopes were pinned on her. They'd done a fair job, she had to admit; satisfied with their own career goals and professional gains, they had infused her with ambition. She'd been taught to let nothing stand in the way of achieving her dreams.

Well, as far as she was concerned, nothing and no one was. End of discussion.

Before she was through with the phone call, however, she did have one more question to ask. "Dad, have you ever heard of a Kedrick that owned land up this way? Took it from the Arapaho, I think. And then lost it."

Her father was silent for a moment. Wyoming history was his specialty. If anyone would know, he would. "I don't suppose you're talking about Robert Kedrick, are you?" her father asked.

"I don't know. Maybe. Who was he? What about him?"

"Well, I ran across some material on him when I was researching an essay for that history text the department's putting together. The man was supposed to have led or at least been a part of a crew of outlaws in the year Wyoming got statehood. A little over a hundred years ago. Robbed some big gold shipment from the army, and the rest, as they say, is history. The Treasury Department under William Windom had a full-scale war declared on the good old boys responsible. Windom didn't last out the hunt, and I believe Charlie Foster picked up the reins of control, so there was some spillover of administrative leadership. Eventually all of them were caught, except Kedrick, of course."

"Robert Kedrick?"

"Yes. He never was found. Some say he was killed by his own men after he hid the gold. They got mad when he wouldn't tell them where it was and shot him. The treasure was never found, in any event. Some say he got away to South America and spent the loot. Deserted his family, if that's the case. Wife and a couple kids, as I recall. His descendants still live up where you—"

"Dixie, why do you want to know about that man?" The question, hard-edged and probing, came from her mother. "That sheriff doesn't have you out looking for outlaw fool's gold, now, does he?"

"No." Dixie made some quick mental connections that shook her. Hal had said the land belonged to his ancestors. He'd used the term *buccaneer,* one that certainly had outlaw overtones. He was probably related to the infamous Robert Kedrick, then. Fascinating!

"No, Mom," she said. "Don't worry. The only digging I'm likely to do this summer is with a group of Harvard paleontologists. Their crew boss is a woman named Winnie Nash. A professor. I think we're going to be friends." She decided there was no need to reveal the possibility that her date tonight had renegade blood in his veins!

She'd made the right decision. Her response made her folks happier. The talk then centered around her possible friendship with Winnie Nash. When she finally hung up, Dixie knew she had left her parents with a good feeling about her current situation. It was odd to be their "darling child" when she was over thirty, but she supposed she'd always be that to them, no matter how long they all lived.

There wasn't anything wrong with that, really, as long as it didn't influence her.

She spent the rest of the afternoon napping and preparing for her date with Hal. Some of that preparation included a warning to herself that she shouldn't allow her curiosity about the Robert Kedrick/Hal Blane connection to get in the way of having a pleasant time with a man who was obviously making an effort to be friendly.

But Dixie had never been short on curiosity. Curiosity had motivated her career choice, and so the best-laid plans...

CHAPTER FIVE

HAL PAUSED in front of the hall mirror to check his reflection on the way out the door. He needed a haircut, but otherwise he looked passable. When Artie walked into view behind him, they stared for a moment, reflection regarding reflection. Then, Artie spoke.

"You seeing Cyn tonight?" he asked, his youthful face blank of expression, but the light of amusement in his blue eyes. He made the name sound like "sin."

"No. I'm not taking out Cynthia," Hal replied.

"The doctor!" Artie's face broke into a wide smile. "You're going after her?"

Hal controlled his temper with no problem. Artie couldn't rile him. He intended to stay calm tonight. "Dr. Sheldon and I are going to dinner, son. I'm not 'going after' her or any other woman."

"Yeah. Right." Artie resumed his blank look and stuck his hands into his jeans pockets. "And with that shirt on, you ain't likely to get one, either. At least not one with the class of Doc Dixie."

"What's that mean?" Hal looked in the mirror again, momentarily shaken into self-consciousness. "What's wrong with this shirt?"

"It's old and it's checked, for one thing."

"So?"

"Dad. If you're taking out a lady who's used to the big city, you ought to wear a nice Sunday shirt, at least." Artie walked around his father. "And a tie."

Hal smiled. Artie sounded just like his grandmother. "Thanks, son. I just wasn't thinking."

"S'okay. I do that myself a lot." Artie walked out the front door. "See you," he said just before letting the screen door slam shut.

Hal went back into his bedroom and changed, thinking that Artie's criticism of his shirt was a good sign. The boy was finally taking an interest in something outside of his own dark, broody thoughts.

He put on a white shirt and a string tie with a big turquoise stone and silver tips. Then he combed his hair again. He was ready.

As he drove over to the doctor's house, he whistled a cheerful tune. He was pleased that he'd made the move to ask her out. She'd disturbed him from the beginning for a variety of reasons, and getting to know her better could relieve a lot of the tension, personal and public, between them. After all, they were destined to work more or less together for the next three years, and it would be better if they were friends. Maybe, pretty good friends, if he was lucky and didn't put his foot in his mouth again.

That *was* his motivation, he thought. *Wasn't it?*

Usually, when he was after female companionship, he took out one of the single women in the area. Widows and divorced ladies as well as spinsters like Cynthia Hydeck over in Powell. They enjoyed the outing, the good times, and they made no attempt to attach strings to the relationship if it turned from warm to hot during the evening.

He assured himself that this date with Dixie Sheldon was no different.

Asking her out had been an impulse, pure and simple. The last thing he'd planned to do on Friday was ask Dixie Sheldon for a date.

He *had* asked, though, and he wasn't sorry. He parked, walked up to her door and rang the bell.

She came out of her house, greeting him with a smile that nearly melted the silver tips on his tie, and he was glad he'd listened to Artie about his clothes. If he'd stayed in his old shirt, he would have felt outclassed to an embarrassing degree. She was wearing a dress—a nice one. First time he'd seen a woman living in Seaside wear a dress two times in a row, he thought. Usually, if a skirt ever did appear, it was on Sunday or some special social occasion. Wyoming was not skirt country. Seaside was downright opposed to the garment. Most women wore jeans or some other kind of pants.

Hal liked to see women in skirts. When Dixie sashayed down the walkway, chatting away about her morning at the clinic, and how nice the weather was now that it wasn't so darn hot, he found himself enchanted beyond expectation. Listening to her talk was fun and entertaining. Being with her was...

Whoa. He shouldn't be letting her get to him so quickly, shouldn't really let her get to him at all. They'd just have a good time, nothing serious.

They drove out of town toward the west, and the need for conversation trailed away as the scenery took center stage. The road ran along a flat plain surrounded by hills that soared up to become high mountains. It was like driving at the bottom of a flat bowl with a jagged, cracked rim. The summer sun was still high, drawing short shadows on the ground from the few buildings and fewer trees. Dixie sat back, relaxing and reveling in the open spaces.

After a while, though, she got restless. "So," she said. "Tell me all about this place you're taking me. Fran was impressed, but couldn't say much about it, since she hasn't been there. Says it's almost impossible to get a reservation unless you book months in advance. My curiosity is up."

Hal glanced over at her. The sight of her gave him a thrill. She looked extremely attractive, sitting there in her nice dress, with a pleasant smile on her face. He was glad—darn glad!—he'd had that impulse to ask her out.

"It's kind of hard to describe," he said. "It's owned and run by a couple who dropped out of the New York rat race to open up a restaurant. It may be in the middle of nowhere, but everyone who likes fine food has heard about it. They get patrons making reservations months ahead from around the world. Literally."

Patrons? Dixie examined the word. It was not a Sheriff Hal Blane word, not the sheriff she knew, anyway. "How did you get us a reservation on such short notice, then?"

He shrugged. "I did them a favor once. They're grateful. And they like me, I guess."

She laughed. "Was it a sometimes-it's-more-than-a-job sort of thing? The sort of thing you wouldn't tell me about at breakfast the other day?"

Hal slowed the Jeep. "Damn. You hold a long grudge." He scowled, and for a moment, Dixie thought she'd lost him. When he began to talk, she realized he'd only been thinking, considering the best way to tell his story.

"It was a few summers ago," he said. "Ray and Sandy Fawcett had just moved out here and set up shop. No one had lived back in that area for almost a decade, and the forest critters figured it was still their territory, pure and simple."

"Forest critters? As in deer and bunnies and squirrels?"

"Sure. And as in moose and grizzlies, as well. Bambi and Thumper were no real problem, but the other ones were too big and too comfortable to willingly be invaded by humans." He paused, chuckling. "I was over at the Park County fish and game office when the Fawcetts came in, howling bloody murder about a big grizzly bear staking out their back door. Two New York City dudes. You'd have thought Godzilla was on their trail."

"Oh, my! What did you do to help?"

"Mostly common-sense advice. Fish and game added its two cents, too. Don't leave garbage around. Use bearproof trash containers. Make lots of noise. Keep pets on leads or in kennels. Eventually, the animals get the idea and keep their distance. Grizzlies don't like people any more than people like them. All you have to do is use a little care and common sense."

"Sounds good, but not good enough to entitle you to a table whenever you want one. There must have been something else."

"No. That's it."

"Come on, Hal. You're lying to me."

"I swear."

"Hal . . ."

"Okay." He looked over at her. "I just don't want to do or say anything to spoil this evening. That's all."

"And you're afraid that if you tell me the whole truth, it'll put me off, somehow? Come on, Hal. I've undoubtedly seen worse than you can even dream of. I worked ER, remember?"

He was silent.

"How're we supposed to get to be friends, if you don't trust me with your less-than-pleasant past?" She laughed, keeping the mood light. "I'll tell you mine, if you tell me yours."

Hal reached down, picked up a tape and shoved it into the player. Ronnie Milsap sang about Carolina love. The sheriff cleared his throat. "Well," he said, "I-was checking by the Fawcetts' restaurant one afternoon. Just to see if the grizzlies were under control. There was no trouble with the bears, but there *was* a summer infestation of motorcycle gangs. They'd driven the bears and most of the other animals clean out of the woods, and were harassing customers trying to leave the restaurant."

"I've heard about those gangs," she said soberly. "Sometimes they traveled through Laramie on the way to Sturgis for the summer rally."

"Uh-huh. Anyway, I took some action that put an end to any trespassing in the woods near the Fawcetts' place."

"You strung wire?"

He slowed and stared at her. "How did you...?"

"It's a classic ploy. I'd have been disappointed if you hadn't thought of it."

He grinned again. "Actually, I never had to do it. Just had to kind of say I was going to."

Dixie tried to envision the scene. "Tell me."

Hal shrugged again.

"Not much to tell. When I drove up to the place, I could hear 'em. Yelling. Engines snarling. I took out my shotgun and strolled up the hill where I saw a bunch of 'em doing doughnuts and wheelies in the garden."

"Lord!"

"Tore it all up. And the Fawcetts had been trying to grow herbs and stuff for cooking."

"Where were they? Were they hurt?"

"No. They were holed up back in the house, trying to call for help." He turned off the main highway on to a county road that led back into the forest. "Did I tell you the original site was a guest ranch?"

"No. And don't change the subject. What happened with the bad guys?"

"Oh, I just suggested that they take their fun on back to California or wherever it was they came from."

"And they listened? Respectfully? And obeyed you, immediately?"

"Not exactly." His teeth showed. "I had to convince the leader. And fire a few rounds of buckshot into his Harley. After that, it was pretty smooth sailing. Especially when I suggested what barbwire strung at neck height along a dark road at night might do to a biker."

She clapped appreciatively. "You know, if you let yourself go a little, you'd be an excellent storyteller. You really keep a person on the edge."

"Thanks. Anyway, the upshot is that Ray and Sandy don't have any trouble now with human or animal varmints."

"You're hard-nosed about the human ones, aren't you?"

"It's my job."

"But it's more than that, isn't it? I mean, you seem to take it personally. Just like I—" She suddenly realized what she was about to say.

"Like you what?"

"Nothing. I just see you as being pretty intense about your work. That's all."

"Um." Hal didn't believe her, but he let it go.

Dixie settled back into her seat, thinking how close she'd come to getting on the topic of Robert Kedrick. She was so curious, questions almost came slipping right out. Sometime, she knew she'd ask, and Hal would answer, and she would know what she wanted to know.

But not now. This was not the time or the place for that.

Now, other matters were on the agenda. Friendship, fun, good food. Perhaps a little romance, and none had much to do with the past.

They drove on down the county road for a while, then turned on to graveled dirt. Hal cleared his throat. "Thanks for what you said about my storytelling," he said. "I do like spinning yarns, but I prefer true stories to made-up."

"I expect you have lots of them," she replied, encouraging him. "Being sheriff here can't be dull."

"It is and it isn't."

"Give me some more examples, please."

He didn't speak right away. Instead, he pulled over to the side of the dirt road and stopped his Jeep. Silence.

"Why'd you stop?" Dixie unfastened her seat belt. "Is something wrong?"

"Yes." He unhooked his belt and faced her. "What the hell do you want to know about me, Dixie?"

"I..."

"Come on. You've been picking at me like an old scab. Wanting to know this. Wanting to know that. What's really on your mind? And don't lie about it. I'm an expert when it comes to lies. I'll know."

"How?"

"I just will. Now, out with it!"

Dixie regarded him. He wasn't being angry or menacing, or using any other macho technique to get her to talk. He was asking with a sincere desire to know, which worked on her where anything else would have failed.

"I want to know about your relationship to Robert Kedrick, the outlaw," she said.

"How in blazes did you find out about...?"

"I asked my father who Kedrick was and what he'd done. I think I told you my dad is a historian, so when I was talking to my parents this afternoon, I mentioned the name of Kedrick, because I was curious after what you said about the land last night. Dad remembered some details about the stolen U.S. Army gold and Robert Kedrick. Now, I'm asking you. Who or what is or was he to you?"

Hal's face turned brick red, then, the hot color subsided. "You constantly surprise me, Doc," he said, his tone soft and thoughtful. "Constantly." He refastened his seat belt and started the engine again. "Haven't had anyone do that to me in a long, long time." He pulled back out on to the road.

"Wait! Aren't you going to answer me?"

He didn't look at her. He just continued to drive slowly down the road. "Robert Kedrick," he said, his tone reflective, musing, almost musical. "Robert Kedrick was my great-granddaddy."

"He was?"

"He was. And he's not the first of the line to go bad, either. Doc, I come from a long string of rogues, rounders, roughriders and general bad guys. Even my daddy's honesty was suspect for a while before he died. I'm the first of my kind to take the side of the law."

"Sounds like a ballad."

"Could be." He glanced at her. "Satisfied?"

"Not really. But I appreciate being told. Sorry if I stepped on your toes."

"No problem." He sped up a little and soon they pulled into a clearing that held several large log buildings. "Here we are," he said. "Hope you're hungry."

Dixie looked around. Four other vehicles were already parked in the dirt lot. "Here?"

"Yep."

"You're kidding."

"Nope." He flashed a smile. "Trust me, Doc."

"Didn't you just confess that all your ancestors were rogues and rough characters? And I ought to trust you?"

"I said I was on the side of the angels, didn't I?"

Dixie regarded him for a moment. "You know, Hal Blane, if I didn't have a fair amount of good sense, I might just find myself liking you."

His smile widened. "Good. Let's feast."

And feast they did. The Fawcetts were gourmet chefs who clearly loved what they were doing. In the pleasant company of four other couples, Hal and Dixie enjoyed a meal not just fit for kings, but emperors. From the opening drinks and hors d'oeuvres to the ending coffee, desserts and cognacs, the dinner was an astonishing experience. Seven courses long, it took over three hours, as Hal had warned.

The best part for Dixie was being able to get up and walk outside between courses. It was during those pauses that she and Hal made the most progress in deepening their knowledge of each other.

Hal had been warmly greeted by Ray and Sandy Fawcett, a couple who looked a little like the nursery rhyme characters, thin Jack Sprat and his heavy wife. They didn't introduce him to the other guests as the sheriff, nor did they mention why he was such a favorite. When Hal introduced Dixie, it was as his friend, not as Doctor Sheldon. The others seemed to assume they were a couple who lived nearby, and didn't ask outright about their professions. She wondered why there had to be so much secrecy about their jobs.

During the first eating break, Hal had suggested they take a stroll outside in the moonlight. They walked over the dirt-and-grass yard in the direction of the unoccupied corral.

"Why did you keep quiet about what we do?" she asked. "Who we are?"

Hal had put his arm around her shoulders when they left the group. Most of the other diners had remained up on the front porch of the restaurant, a few had slipped out by the back to indulge in cigarettes. So, they were essentially alone and unobserved. Now, he gave her a gentle hug. "Can you imagine a bigger wet blanket on an evening like this than knowing you're sitting down to eat with a cop and a doc?"

"Speak for yourself, Wyatt Earp! I'm no wet blanket."

"I haven't noticed any designated drivers," he said, continuing as if she hadn't spoken. "And I know they're not all planning on spending the night here. However, I also know the pace of the meal tends to allow for sobering up before everyone heads out onto the highway."

"You could say that."

"Yes. I could. But I don't want to make anyone self-conscious. They're paying a lot of money to enjoy this, and I don't intend to interfere."

"I wouldn't, either. Being a doctor hardly makes me the public watchdog you seem to be."

"Maybe not. But, this isn't exactly health food we're chowing down on."

"No, it's not. But as long as you don't eat this way all the time, you're entitled to indulge."

He gave her another hug. "Come on. Confess. You're bothered. I can see you biting your tongue when that fat guy dives into his plate."

"He's not my patient. He hasn't asked my opinion. If he wants to live that way, that's his right."

They reached the corral. Hal took his arm off her shoulders and rested his forearms on the fence. "Know what my opinion is?'' he asked. "I think you're a terrific person.''

His tone and manner were different now. Softer. More...seductive. Dixie glanced at him, sideways. "Is that a prelude to a kiss?'' She looked up at him, gazing into his eyes.

Suddenly, all the sensual feeling she had almost forgotten, certainly neglected in her life for so long, came rushing in on her, and Dixie was swept up by the sensation of falling right into Hal Blane's blue eyes. It was a feeling of erotic surrender that almost overwhelmed her. She could not tear herself away.

She *wanted* him! And she knew he wanted her, too. It was so sudden, the desire took her breath away, and for a moment, she was on emotional and physical overload. She swayed a little, catching at his arm to steady herself.

It was like catching hold of an oak tree, an iron bar, a solid anchor.

Safety.

"Hey,'' he said, pulling her closer. "What's the matter? Too much *vino?* Or...?''

She kissed him then, and it wasn't just good, it was so erotic it set her whole body on fire. She lost almost all sense of who she was, aside from being the woman who wanted this man. She clung to his neck and pressed herself against him. He felt so strong, so solid, so securely male. And he kissed her with a carefully checked passion that reflected her own feelings.

Finally, she broke loose and stepped back, her heart racing and her breath coming fast. He was staring at her, astonishment only one of the expressions crossing his face.

"S-sorry,'' she stammered. "I don't usually do that sort of thing on the first date.'' She turned away, feeling the heat of embarrassment in her face. "Sorry,'' she repeated.

He covered her shoulder with his hand, fingers digging into her gently, caressingly. His breath was warm on her cheek and ear. "Don't apologize, Dixie. You just did what I was wanting to do and was afraid to try."

She turned. "Hal, we can't..."

"Why not?" He looked down at her, his eyes hooding slightly. "Because I'm just a small-town cop? Uneducated? Or..."

"Damn you!" She stepped back, her voice low but intense. "That has absolutely nothing to do with how I feel about you. So get off that right now, mister!"

He smiled, but there was a touch of regret in the way his mouth lifted at the corners. "You're sure?"

"Yes."

"Then...?"

She shook her head. "I don't know. It's too soon, I suppose."

He touched her face again. "I don't know, either. But I have learned over the years that sexual attraction is something that has its own timing. I'd have thought that as a physician, dealing with people's private lives on a regular basis, you'd know that, too."

Dixie relaxed. "Hal, I may know how to set a broken bone and sew up a cut, and I can do an adequate job of counseling, but I am not an expert on my own emotional matters. Particularly where sex is involved. I—"

The rest of her sentence was cut off by the soft ringing of the dinner bell. The next course awaited.

"We'll continue this," Hal said, his hand still cupping her cheek.

"I know," she replied, leaning into his palm and kissing it. She felt him shiver, and shivered, herself.

They walked, hand in hand, back to the dining room.

Halfway through the course, Dixie realized that part of what bothered her about the intensity of her sudden attraction to Hal Blane was the doctor-patient relationship she had with his mother. Hattie was coming in to her office on Tuesday to begin talk-therapy sessions, and Hal was sure to be included in his mother's conversation. Getting involved with him might mean she couldn't treat his mother objectively.

Dixie pondered the matter, thinking she still had plenty of room to maneuver, if she wanted to end things here and now. The evening could end as soon as dinner was over, or it could go on. He'd made it clear that she was setting the pace. It was up to her, not him.

But fate wasn't ready to let the evening end so easily. After dessert, a sinful little number mildly named a "chocolate bonnet," just swimming in fat and carbohydrates, Ray came over and said, "I understand from Hal that you're interested in herbal cures and folk medicine, Dixie. How would you like to pay a call on one of the strangest and wisest practitioners of that kind of stuff you'll ever have the opportunity to meet? Her name, as far as any of us know, is just Miss Esther. She's kind of a local legend, as well as a self-proclaimed witch. A good witch, of course. I wouldn't be putting you on to a bad one. Not with Hal as your escort. No, ma'am."

"Sounds like a chance I would regret turning down. Does she live near here?"

"Ray, I don't think that's such a good idea," Hal said, an expression hovering between concern and amusement on his face. "Dixie, Esther is . . . I mean, you wouldn't be interested in her. No science at all where her stuff is concerned."

"Dixie is interested," Dixie said. "Science is wherever you find it."

"You'll be sorry," Hal said. But he looked amused.

And that sent her curiosity level right through the stratosphere. "Can I meet her tonight?" she asked. "Or is it too late?"

CHAPTER SIX

IT WASN'T TOO LATE. Ray explained that Miss Esther kept night hours and lived just a few more miles into the forest. He began to describe a weird but good-natured medicine woman who performed minor miracles out of her kitchen with herbs and incantations. Sandy joined them and added a tale or two to the legend. The other guests were only mildly interested in the topic and wandered off to the lounge in search of more jovial discussions, leaving the four of them alone in the dining-room area. Dixie was beginning to think she was the target of a jest, when Hal surprised her by growing serious about the matter.

"Old Miss Esther is no joke," he said. "You'll see," he added darkly.

Ray explained that Miss Esther didn't approve of motorized vehicles near her digs and that any who dared come too close found only trouble. When Dixie asked what Esther had thought about the motorcyclists, Ray just pointed at Hal and said, "He came along and took care of it, didn't he?"

"Sure, but..."

"We didn't call him or expect him," Ray added. "He just showed up."

Dixie looked at Hal. He shrugged. "I had no particular reason, like I told you. Happened to be in the area, and I just dropped by."

"Miss Esther takes the credit for conjuring him up," Sandy Fawcett said, her tone soft and serious. "And I almost believe her. She is a wonder, let me tell you. When you meet her, you'll see what I mean."

As they set off on foot in the moonlight, the pine forest around them was singing with summer-night noises, and she became aware that something more than curiosity was drawing her to the "medicine woman." She felt oddly magical, as if the world she had known were changing with each second that passed.

She knew part of that magical feeling was because of Hal. After their kiss, when the earth had seemed to move beneath her feet, his presence had become an intoxicant to her. She hadn't had much to drink during dinner, only sipping at the superb wines. Nevertheless, she felt as giddy and reckless as if she'd slugged down every drop set in front of her.

"I got the impression you know this old woman," she said, moving closer to him and taking his arm. "What's the deal?"

"No deal." He kicked at a stone in the path. "I just know her from when I was a kid."

"And?"

"And I run across her now and then. She's been living out here since the beginning of time, I think."

"You're teasing me."

Hal stopped. "No, Dixie. I'm trying to keep from kissing you."

She moved closer. "Why?"

He touched her face. "Because, if I kiss you, it's likely we won't make it up to Esther's place any time soon. She'll be real upset, then, and I don't care to risk offending—"

"How does she know we're coming?"

His smile was wide and white in the moonlight. "Easy. Big old black crow tells her when anyone's coming. 'Caw, caw,' he says. Saw him fly away out of that tree over there just a moment ago."

Fairly sure now that she was being teased, Dixie shut him up with a kiss, but just as she was beginning to get serious about it, a raucous, squawking sound startled her. She screamed and pulled away.

Hal laughed and held her shoulders. "See? I told you." He pulled her back against him and embraced her tightly. "Let's go visit Esther," he said. "Then we can see what else is in store for us. She'll tell us."

"No. Don't tell me you're willing to ask your fortune from a...a..."

"A witch?" Eyebrows raised, he looked down at her. "Was that what you were trying to say?"

Dixie shook her head. "This is getting too strange for me."

"Just wait," he said.

They kept on walking for a while until they were far enough from the restaurant so that only the natural sounds and smells of the woods surrounded them. The trees were thick enough to block out much of the moonlight, as well.

"Are there bears around here?" she asked, holding on to his arm.

"Probably."

She tightened her grip.

"But don't worry. They won't bother us now."

"Because we're off to see the witch?"

"Don't joke about it. I told you she takes things like that seriously. And it's not a good idea to make fun of her."

"Sorry." Dixie subsided into silence. She was absolutely certain she was being led into some sort of practical joke. She didn't know Hal well enough to tell if he had a good laugh at her expense up his sleeve, but surely no one could believe in fortune-telling, magic and witchcraft, white or black, in this day and age.

Finally, they came to a clearing in the center of which was a small log cabin. The front door was wide open and light streamed out onto the swept dirt yard. Firelight flickered eerily on the ground and surrounding trees. Off to one side was a small corral. Two dark shapes moved about inside the enclosure. One whinnied softly. Horses.

"Oh, my," Dixie said, her voice catching in her throat.

Hal put his hand on her back and guided her to the door. "Don't say anything you or I might regret, please."

"Hal, I—"

"Is that you, young'n?" A thin, querulous voice called out. "Harold Kedrick Blane? Is that you and your woman?"

"What?" Dixie whispered. "*What* did she say?"

"Shh." He pushed her forward. "Evening, Miss Esther," he said, his tone friendly and respectful. "Yes, it's us."

Dixie found herself propelled gently but firmly through the door and into the one small room that made up the cabin's interior. She wasn't sure what she had expected, but this wasn't it.

A tiny, ancient person was sitting in a rough-hewn wooden chair by the fireplace. She wore layers of clothing and was huddled in a huge quilt. In a different setting, Dixie would have assumed she was looking at a bag lady.

Now, she thought she might be looking at a real-life, female Yoda, instead. The wrinkled, brown face held eyes that sparkled with life and intelligence. "Hello," Dixie managed to croak. "I... That is, we..."

"Hush, child." The old woman stood up, shedding the quilt and moving closer. She reached a twisted claw of a hand to touch Hal. "You've changed, boy," she stated, her voice deeper now. "You look older. Sadder."

"It's nothing, Miss Esther," Hal said. He didn't look at Dixie. "I've just been working too hard. That's all."

"No." The old woman stared. "It ain't. Don't lie, boy. It's the curse of your people, lying. Gets 'em into boiling water, whether they be good folk or not."

"Sorry, Miss Esther." Hal put his hand on Dixie's shoulder. "This is the doctor."

"I know." Esther didn't look at Dixie. Her dark eyes seemed to be boring holes through Hal. "She ain't your problem."

Hal fidgeted and his palm on Dixie's shoulder got warm. "I didn't think so...," he began, obviously struggling for words.

"Miss Esther," Dixie interjected. "I hear you have a great knowledge of herbs and healing. Would you talk to me about it sometime?"

The old woman turned slowly toward Dixie. "Surely, child, you can see this man needs healing. You're a doctor. You must know."

Dixie held out her hands, palms up. "But, I don't."

Esther stared at both of them for a long, uncomfortable moment. Then, she turned away. "Let's have some tea," she said. "I picked some sweet leaves yesterday."

She waved a hand at the hearth, and they both moved quickly, sitting together by the fire while the old one stepped into the dimmer regions of the room and began to putter with objects that rustled and rattled. Sweet, pungent smells swirled around her in the dark air. Dixie reached for Hal's hand and held it tightly.

She wasn't scared—far from it. Her heart beat rapidly with excitement. Although things here were a bit spooky and definitely weird, she was thrilled. Miss Esther seemed to be the genuine article—a wise woman who lived in harmony with the wild, raw land and its healthful bounty. How old was she, really?

"You okay?" Hal whispered.

"Sure." She squeezed his hand. "I wouldn't trade this experience for anything. Thank you for bringing me here! She's...wonderful!"

"Don't get all worked up about me, young'n," Miss Esther declared, her voice disembodied in the dark. "I ain't nothing special. I just lived a long, long time. Woman learns things, living this long." She appeared in the light again, bearing a small black pot, which she hung on a hook and swung into the heat of the fire. "Water'll be a few minutes boiling," she said. She settled back into her wooden chair. "Now, tell me what you want, girl."

Dixie leaned forward, releasing Hal's hand. "Everything," she said. "I want to know, what you know."

Esther stared at her for a long time, then, started to laugh. "You hear her, boy?" she asked Hal. "She wants to know what I know."

Hal wasn't amused. "That's why I brought her here to meet you."

Esther sobered. "You understand what it means if she learns my ways?"

"No, I..."

"She won't ever leave. Are you ready to have that happen to you, boy?"

Dixie glanced at Hal. He had a totally unreadable expression on his face. "Is that water about ready?" he asked.

Esther sighed, the sound a combination of weariness and exasperation. She put her hands on the arms of the chair and rose. "I see," she said, heading back into the darkness. "You ain't willing, Hal Blane. Leastwise, you ain't yet."

Dixie looked at Hal. Nothing.

Esther returned, carrying a tray with cups. She set the tray down on the hearth. Dixie moved nearer Hal. "May I help?" she asked.

Esther looked sharply at her. "Maybe," she said. "Maybe you can, child," she added, her tone now musing instead of curt.

She offered no suggestions or orders; she simply ignored Dixie and pulled the pot out of the fire. Wrapping one hand in part of the old quilt, she poured steaming water into the cups. A sweet, musty fragrance filled the room.

Dixie sniffed at her cup appreciatively. "Oh," she said. "This is wonderful!" She sniffed again. "Chamomile. I can smell that. And a touch of mint. But what else?"

Esther didn't reply.

"That's all legal herb stuff, isn't it, Miss Esther?" Hal asked as she solemnly handed him his cup. "Nothing chemically creative in here, is there?"

The old woman grinned, revealing fine teeth.

But she didn't answer.

She took her own cup and settled back in her chair. "Drink your tea, Harold Kedrick Blane," she said. "And see."

Dixie smiled into her cup. The woman was teasing him, but not unkindly. Since she hadn't received a direct answer to a direct question, she was going about it sideways. Not an uncommon diagnostic technique for any physician faced with a recalcitrant patient. But...

But what was going on with Hal that Miss Esther thought he needed treatment? Dixie's amusement and curiosity passed into anxiety. What was wrong with Hal might have something to do with what was wrong with

Hattie. Dixie stopped thinking of this as a game and set-tled in to observe as closely and objectively as possible.

Esther started to hum. The sound was so soft at first, that Dixie thought it was the wind in the pine trees. But after a few more minutes, the tune became recognizable, if not remembered. It was soothing. She felt her eyelids droop.

She's hypnotizing us, Dixie suddenly realized. The herbs in the tea were relaxants. The warmth of the fire, the slug-gishness from the wine and the meal, the late hour... All combined to make hypnotism of willing subjects easy as a cakewalk.

Dixie was not willing; she struggled to stay alert. Hal's head was resting against the warm stones of the hearth, his eyes were closed and the cup tilted in his hands. Dixie caught it before it spilled and fell. Hal's body relaxed, his features softened and he began to snore softly.

"Good." Esther stood up, showing none of the slow-ness she had exhibited before. "Don't worry. He'll just sleep a little bit and be fine," she said. "Come into the night with me, girl." She held out her hand.

Dixie took Esther's hand, unable to stop herself. She knew no fear, only excitement and intense curiosity. This was a right thing! A good thing.

The two women walked outside, hand in hand. Though it was after midnight, the air was still warm and soft against Dixie's face. The old hand in hers was small and delicate, mostly bones and wrinkled skin. "Did you really know we were coming?" she asked.

Miss Esther sighed. "You know, it would be nice if I could do all those things folks think I can do." She pointed to the edge of the woods where two large tree stumps had been shaped into smooth stools. "Let's sit and talk."

The positions of the seats made the cabin and the clearing look like a small stage. One of the ponies in the corral whickered, a gentle, soothing sound. The firelight seemed softer, and the moon stronger. Esther sighed again.

"Do you love that man?" she asked.

"I... No. This is our first date. I just recently decided I even liked him. Love's a long way from that."

Esther smiled. "You want each other. You share desire. That's not so far from love, girl. You ought to know that by now."

Dixie squirmed. She didn't want to talk about Hal. Or desire. She wanted to talk about Esther. "What else was in the tea?" she asked. "It sure took him down in a hurry."

Esther shrugged, the movement a mere lift of bony shoulders. "Boy was tired. He drank what you and I drank. Nothing more."

"Nothing less?"

"Ha!" Esther's hand grabbed Dixie's arm. "You are a sharp one. You might make a healer in time."

Questions whirled in Dixie's mind. "May I come and learn from you?" she asked.

The old woman looked at her. A look so direct and clear that Dixie almost quailed beneath the power of it. "Why?" she asked.

"Because... Because I want to know."

"You have ambitions." The old eyebrows rose.

"Sure. I admit I do, but..."

Esther laughed again, the sound simple and reassuring. "Okay, child," she said. "You can come up here anytime. But I warn you. No magic here. Just years. Years and years..."

"It's not magic I'm after," Dixie explained. "I have a contract with a medical center in California to collect data on folk medicine while I'm here. If you'd be willing to be a part of my research, I'd be very happy.''

"Why's that?" The sparse white eyebrows went up again.

"Because I think you have a lot to teach me. And if I share it with others, we might help people who need it.''

Esther fingered the material of her skirt. "I'm part Shoshone. Did Hal Blane tell you that?''

"No.''

"Well, my ma was full-blood. And she taught me most of what I know and do. I have both white and Indian blood. So, I use both worlds in my healing.''

"I'm interested. Please, go on.''

Miss Esther stood. "Not tonight. Tonight, I have something to say to the man, not to you. But you come on back anytime, Doctor Woman. You must. Because we were meant to share.''

"All right." Dixie stood, too.

But the old woman motioned her to sit again. "I need to talk to him alone. You wait. He'll be out, directly.''

Dixie watched Esther's bent figure as she moved slowly across the yard to the front door of the cabin, then went inside. In the darkness behind her, Dixie heard small noises. Rustlings and chirpings. Birds, insects, mice... Definitely not bears. A gentle breeze began, sighing through the high tops of the lodgepole pines. She slipped into a meditative state.

How peaceful this place was. How... holy. Restful and rejuvenating. Though she should have been completely exhausted after the events of last week and two late nights in a row, she felt energy flowing through her veins. Not flooding, just flowing. Nice. Pleasant. Relaxing.

She shut her eyes. She heard the forest sounds, the soft voices from the cabin, smelled the horses and the pine trees and the wood smoke. And once again, she had that feeling of being in the Old West. It enveloped and embraced her. Comfortably. Like Esther's quilt. Her eyelids were too heavy to lift for a while.

When she opened her eyes, Hal was standing in front of her, a smile on his face. "Hey, sleepyhead," he said. "Time to hit the trail."

Dixie stood up in a hurry. "I wasn't asleep," she said.

"Right." He leaned forward and kissed her gently. "Just like I didn't doze for a few minutes in front of Esther's fire. Come on," he said, putting his arm around her shoulders. "Let's go home."

"Shouldn't we say goodbye, or something?"

He shook his head. "She said for us to go on home. She's headed for bed, herself."

As if on cue, the front door to the cabin swung slowly shut. The firelight dimmed. Night settled over the clearing.

They started walking toward the path that led back to the restaurant. "What did she say to you?" Dixie asked.

He walked more slowly. "To be perfectly honest, I'm not sure. When I woke up, she was there, muttering stuff at me. I didn't hear it all clearly, and I didn't think it would be polite to tell her to speak up. She's such an old lady."

"She seemed to think what she had to say was important enough to say while you were alone."

"Well, I didn't hear anything important."

He sounded a little tense about it, so Dixie dropped the topic. She moved closer to him as they entered the trees, and he took her hand in his. The atmosphere between them calmed and returned to a semiromantic state.

"So, what did you think of her?" he asked after a few minutes.

"I like her. I respect her. I'm really interested in her."

"Good."

Dixie stopped and pulled on his hand to make him halt. "Hal, why did you bring me here? What reasons did you have?"

"Reasons?" He shrugged. "I had none. I didn't even intend to go calling on her. That was Ray's idea, remember?"

"Oh, yes." *But you could have primed him,* she thought. *Asked him to set it up.*

But why would he? Even with what she knew to be the rural tendency to test "newcomers" by telling them tall tales, Hal just didn't fit the bill of a practical joker. No. She was making too much out of the mystical feelings she'd experienced for that timeless moment.

Hal just did not strike her as a conspirator-type. For all of his apparent depth, he still seemed a pretty straightforward guy.

He surely kissed like one, anyway.

"Come on," he said. "It's late."

They walked on, both thinking so loudly they might as well have been shouting. Finally, they reached the restaurant parking lot and Hal's vehicle. All the lights were out in the buildings, and a sense of sleeping peace lay over the scene.

"Hard to imagine motorcycles here right now," Dixie commented as he opened the passenger door for her. "It's so quiet."

"Usually is," he said. "Way it was meant to be," he added, getting in beside her. He started the engine. "Sometimes I almost wish they'd cordon off the borders of this whole state and not allow any motorized vehicles inside. Just horses, oxen and wagons, like it used to be."

Dixie laughed. "Now I know you're a man from the past, recommending that kind of life."

Hal drove out onto the dirt road. "There were drawbacks," he said. "But by and large, I think it was probably a more fulfilling kind of life."

"Short, though. Think about it. If it hadn't been for the helicopter, that man at the dig site would have died yesterday."

Hal was silent.

"And I would certainly never have gotten into medical school in a past century."

"No," he said, slowing to drive past a group of three deer browsing at the side of the lane. "You'd have been married long ago, and have a house full of kids."

"Grim thought,"

"Is it?"

"Well, not if that was the only kind of life I could have. But..."

"But not for you. Not now." Hal speeded up, the Jeep's headlights cutting through the night, revealing the highway just ahead.

"That's right. I don't think I'd have liked to be around a hundred years ago."

They drove onto the blacktop and rode along in silence for a while.

"Me, neither, I guess," he said finally. "Nostalgia is great, but when you really look at it, the past was a pretty rough time to be alive. When I think about it, all of my family would be dead. Me included."

"Your son?"

"Was a problem birth." He leaned back, one hand on the wheel. "I'd have lost them both even ten years before." He shifted forward. "At least, that's what the doctor told me."

"Your wife didn't want other kids after that?"

"No. What she didn't want was me."

"Then..."

"Let's talk about something else. Okay?"

"All right. Would you have died in the old days?"

"Probably. But you know, you might have made it to medical school."

"Huh?"

"Yeah. Let's see. Well, there was..."

Dixie listened, amazed, as he listed names, dates and places. Historical facts adding up to the unavoidable conclusion that, yes, women had managed to get medical degrees before the turn of the century. Though small in number, they did do the same jobs the male doctors did. Even surgery.

"How do you know all this?" she asked.

He shrugged again, lifting his big shoulders in that gesture she was growing to recognize as an indication of shy pride. "I like history," he said. "Read all the time."

"I see." She lapsed into thoughtful silence.

Hal drove on, reacting now and then to deer alongside the road. He was so used to doing that, he hardly needed to slow...

And then, he found he was slowing. Driving at a lower speed. Almost stopping...

"What's wrong?" Dixie asked, sitting up. She'd been dozing and thinking. Mulling over what she'd learned about the man beside her. "Why are you stopping?"

"I..." Hal felt sweat breaking out on his face, even though the late-night air was cool. "I don't know. I just..." He let the Jeep cruise to a halt.

Right in the middle of the road. A wave of dizziness hit him, and he bent over the steering wheel, willing his brain to stop spinning around.

"Hal!" Dixie had her seat belt off in a moment and moved toward him. "Hal, talk to me!"

He sat back up straight. "It's okay," he said, staring ahead, not looking at her. "I'm all right."

"Sure you are." She reached around him and unbuckled his seat belt. "You've stopped in the middle of a highway in the dead of night, and you're just fine. Let me have a look at—"

"No!" He pushed her away. Hard enough that her head cracked against the passenger-side window.

Dixie yelped in pain.

Hal moved even more quickly and gathered her to him. "Dixie, I'm sorry!" He cradled her head in his hands. "Are you hurt?"

"Yes," she yelled, her voice muffled by the position of her face pressed against his shoulder. "You pushed me!"

"I'm sorry." He moved back, releasing her. "I wasn't thinking. I just...reacted."

"I'll say." She rubbed the back of her head. "I'm going to have a goose egg there."

He put his hands on the wheel. "Let me get us out of the middle of road." He drove to the shoulder and pulled off. Two deer bolted out of the shadows and ran in front of the headlights.

Dixie watched them dash across the road. Then she watched Hal turn off the Jeep engine. He didn't look at her or speak, he just stared out of the window into the darkness. Her head hurt, but the fear of him that suddenly filled her hurt worse.

No.

Not fear. Something else . . . Something . . .

Awe.

Awe? She cleared her throat. "Hal, what's going on?"

"I don't know." His voice was deep, but thinly pitched. "I wish I did. I can't believe I let myself hurt you like that." He did not turn to look at her. "I kind of . . . lost myself there for a second."

"It was accidental." She risked moving closer. "You didn't mean it."

"I didn't want you to touch me," he said, his tone flat and emotionless. "I . . ."

"Hal, what was in that tea?" She put her hand on his shoulder. "Could it have—"

"No. She wouldn't do anything to hurt us."

Dixie pulled back. "Well, you seem to have been affected by something. Either the tea or something you ate, I'd say. I'd like to run a few tests on you when—"

The police radio interrupted her. The dispatcher was calling for Hal. He picked up the mike and keyed it. "Seaside One. Go ahead." Nothing in his voice indicated that anything out of the ordinary had just happened.

"Sheriff." The voice of the dispatcher was tight and tense. "Better head on up to the dig camp. They've got a DB for you."

"Say again?" Hal's hand shook. "Details?"

"None. I repeat, a DB. And Dr. Nash says she wants Dr. Sheldon to come along, too. I knew you were out together, boss, so I . . ."

"Thanks. I'll get on it. Over and out." He keyed off and hung up the mike.

"What's happened?" Dixie strained to read anything in

his face. Anything at all. The features were carved bronze. "Is a DB a..."

"A dead body." Hal turned on the engine. "Let's go, Doc. We have some work to do, you and I."

CHAPTER SEVEN

NEITHER OF THEM said a word as Hal drove at top speed to the dig site. Dixie was constrained both by her concern for their safety as he flew along the dark road, and by her thoughts about his behavior of a few moments ago.

They finally reached the site after an hour of silence. Coming over the rise once more, this time in the dark, Dixie saw that the area was lit up by floodlights. People moved around, casting long shadows in the bright artificial light.

Hal made no comment. He just drove into the camp and stopped. He opened his door and got out.

Dixie reached for the handle of her door, ready to join him, but the rapid approach of a large, bearded man made her hesitate. The man wore the standard site outfit of desert khaki. He was bushy-faced and burly and should have looked like a friendly bear.

But he didn't. Dixie glanced at Hal. His body had taken on a posture and attitude she didn't recognize for a moment.

Then, she did. It was the posture of a man ready for a fight. Quickly, she opened her door.

"Took your time getting here, Sheriff," the bearded man bellowed. "And just what the hell do you think you're doing, bringing one of your local bimbos along?" The floodlighting was behind him, putting his face in shadow, so Dixie couldn't read his features clearly, but there was no mistaking the hostility in his tone and stance.

Hal nodded curtly. "Hayden," he said, acknowledging the man. "This is Dr. Sheldon, the county physician." He gestured toward Dixie. "She's going to do the ME work for me." He did not introduce the man.

Dixie stepped forward. So *this* was the director of the dig. She looked around for Winnie. "Where is Professor Nash?"

"She's here. Or there, staring at the find just like everybody else." Hayden laughed, an unpleasant, rasping sound. "So, this is the new doctor? I heard what she did for the young Layton kid the other week." He frowned, then held out his big hand to Dixie. "Sorry, Doctor," he added. "I'm upset about all this. You understand? I'm Professor Oscar Hayden. Director of this...project."

Feeling a crawling sensation in her palm, Dixie went ahead and took the professor's hand. "I think I do understand," she said, noting that the man's skin was warm, almost hot. "Can we see—"

"Where's the body?" Hal interrupted. "Who found it?"

Oscar Hayden turned toward the sheriff. "Nash better tell you," he said, his tone much less aggressive. "I got here just *after* they found the thing." He gestured for them to follow and started walking back toward the floodlight.

Glancing at Hal, Dixie hesitated. He had that stone-face look again. He needed . . . She didn't know what, but she knew he needed something from her. Then, she heard Winnie calling her name.

"Dixie! Thank goodness you came, too!" The tall woman ran up to them, ignoring Hayden. She spoke to Hal. "You're going to need her help identifying the dead," she said.

Hal regarded Winnie. "What do you mean, 'the dead'? Is there more than one body?" His voice seemed to have an echo out in the darkness beyond the floods. His tone was cold and emotionless.

"Well, no, but..."

"Nash!" Hayden had stopped and listened to the conversation. "Cut out the chatter. Just show them, will you?"

"All right." Winnie gave Dixie a pained look. "Come on. It's over there in the side of the cliff." She started off, Hal right by her side, his pace as fast as hers.

Dixie trotted to keep up. "The cliff?" she asked. "You found a body in the cliff?"

Winnie nodded. "We were starting an exploration trench late this afternoon. Just setting out to see what might be in the area, and one of the kids located... Well, let me show you, first. It's easier to explain if you can see."

"All right," Hal said.

They strode through the camp, following Winnie to the edge of the cliff above the creek. Dixie remembered what Hal had said about the area; that it used to be his family's land. She wondered what he was thinking about right now.

"Why didn't you call it in before?" Hal asked. "Why wait until so late?"

"We didn't know what we had until about two hours ago," Winnie explained. "And then we called."

"It took that long to establish you had a body?"

"We're professionals," Winnie replied. "We don't just fling dirt around. We knew we had a body. We didn't know what kind until we worked on the site."

"You excavated it?" Dixie asked.

"Millimeter by millimeter," Winnie answered. "We treated the exhumation as we would an ordinary dig."

"Then, it wasn't... recent?" Hal asked.

"See for yourself." Winnie stepped off the edge of the cliff and down a few feet along the side until she reached a ledge. Some footholds had been cut into the hard dirt, and the going seemed relatively easy. The ledge ran along the face of the cliff and around a bend. Bright light shone from a point beyond.

But it was very dark where the light failed to cover. Dixie shuddered before she took that first step behind Winnie and Hal. She did not allow herself to glance to her right, down into the darkness of the valley below, but she could hear the soft voice of the creek as it cut through the night and the sighing of the slight night wind in the tall trees standing just out of sight.

"Nearly as we can figure," Winnie was saying, "this area was all part of the tableland decades ago, and only recently did the edge of the cliff erode enough to expose it. I expect that the extreme winter you had in the mid-fifties might have started the process, but..."

Hal stopped. Dixie nearly ran into his back. "Are you saying that this body has been buried here for decades?" he asked. "Since the fifties?"

"Since long before that," Winnie said. "I can't tell yet, but it looks to me like it's over a hundred years since this person took a living breath of air."

"A hundred years?" Dixie repeated. "My gosh! Are you sure?"

"I think it's likely. But..."

Hal said nothing. He shoved past Winnie. At the next turn around the face of the cliff, the ledge became wider and the slope from the top less acute. More floodlights were set up on the ledge, shining onto a cavity in the ground. It was as if some giant scoop had attacked the earth, taking out a monster-size lump. There, at the base

of the scooped section, still cradled in its grave, the body
lay.

It was only a skeleton. Totally bare of any flesh. Hal
stopped beside the trench and drew in a breath. He didn't
know what he'd been expecting, but it certainly wasn't this.
He felt confused and oddly spooked, almost scared. "How
long did it take to uncover all this?" he asked, staring
down at the thing.

Dark, empty eye sockets stared back at him. The skull
was clean, but mottled from where the soil had lain on the
bone for many years.

"Six, seven hours," Winnie said. "It didn't take long to
establish the bones as human and not of great age. But we
still didn't move fast. We didn't want to disturb anything."

Hal squatted on his heels by the grave. "You sure
didn't," he said, admiringly. "Good, careful work, I'd say.
Look here." He pointed at the line of arm bone and wrist.
"It's bent, just like the body was tossed down and then
covered up..." His tone changed. He fell silent, studying
the scene. Why the hell was this bothering him so much?
There was no logical reason for the feelings he had. He'd
seen plenty of worse graves uncovered in his professional
career.

Dixie came up behind him. She'd been to crime sites and
scenes of violence in the past, part of her training in emergency medicine. But this, an ancient death, a long-ago vi-
olation of a human being, disturbed her deeply. The body
and most of its clothing had decomposed in the earth,
leaving only grayish-brown bones and a few scraps of
cloth, leather and small pieces of metal. One of them
caught her eye.

She moved up, next to Hal and knelt down beside him,
tucking her skirt up under her legs. Without touching

anything, she pointed into the grave at a small, round, shiny object lying beside the skeletal hip. "Isn't that a coin?" she asked.

Hal nodded.

"It looks . . . wrong," she said, sitting back and placing her hands on her thighs. "Too clean."

Hal looked at her. "You've got a good eye," he said, softly, his voice so low that she barely heard him. "It *is* wrong." He inched closer to the grave. "Very wrong." He stared down.

She waited.

"Who found the body?" he asked, turning his head and directing the question to Winnie. "Who found it *first,*" he added, emphasizing the last word.

"Um." Winnie frowned. "I can't say. There were five or six kids at work here under Oscar's supervision, and..."

"Get Oscar down here."

"I'm here," a deep voice responded. Oscar Hayden stepped out of the shadows into the light. "What do you want, Sheriff?"

Hal stood up. "I want a step-by-step account of the exhumation," he said. "I want to know who did what and where and for how long."

Oscar nodded. "I'll do the best I can. We did keep a log, just as if this was a legitimate paleontological find. But you'd better ask the others, too. Check on me. My memory's not as exact as it was a few years ago." He smiled wryly. "That's why Dr. Nash is here to help me."

"All right," Hal replied. "Winnie, can you also set us up in a spare tent for interviewing?"

"What?"

"I need to talk to the crew," Hal said. "I need to interview them. Understand? Just to get the story straight for my own satisfaction."

"Well, I guess—"

"Of course she can," Oscar interrupted. "We really do want to cooperate."

Dixie found the man's agreeable manner surprising. She'd expected outright hostility. Maybe even defensiveness. But, after all, they were dealing with an unexplained death, no matter how far back in the past it had happened.

The men spoke to Winnie, making arrangements. Not listening, Dixie leaned forward again, studying the skeleton. That was where she could help. Although forensic pathology had never been her favorite subject, she had learned her lessons well. She'd known she would be responsible for medical examiner's work in the county, because she was the only scientifically trained professional immediately available. She bent down, putting her face close to the ground, examining the bones. She even sniffed, smelling, trying to sense the manner of death using all of her faculties, as she'd been taught.

No go. The bones were far too old. They smelled musty, but not unclean. All the flesh had long gone and no sense of corruption remained. Still on her knees, she moved around until she was at the foot of the grave.

She studied the bones. From the position of the limbs, the body had definitely been dumped carelessly in the ground before being covered with dirt. She looked up at the side of the cliff. Judging by the depth at which the grave was found, the final resting place had been shallow. Probably hastily dug...

She looked back at the bones, focusing on the rib cage...

Murder! "He was shot," she announced. "In the back." She straightened up and pointed at the rib cage. "See that section of rib that's shattered? A bullet entering the upper back, just around the heart area, would have made exit damage like that. I . . ." She saw something and hunkered down again.

"What?" Hal stood over her.

She scooted around to the skull. "I think there's another . . . Yes!" She put her head down right next to the bones. "See?" She put her finger near the small hole in the side of the skull. "It's tiny. I can't place that size of entry hole. It seems almost . . ."

"Let me see." Hal gently moved her aside and took her position. "Damn," he said softly. So softly, the curse was almost a prayer. "Hell and damnation."

"What is it? What have you found?"

This time, the question came from Hastings Clark. The young scientist stood out of the light, at the turn of the ledge. Dixie couldn't see his face, but she heard the eager curiosity in his voice. "We don't know, Hastings," she said. "It looks like—"

Hal straightened. "It doesn't look like anything right now," he said loudly, interrupting her. "Could be an insect bored into the skull." He looked at Dixie, his eyes speaking to her. "We can't tell yet, can we?" he said emphatically.

"No. We can't. That's what the postmortem's for."

"Well, I wondered." Hastings came into the light. "Looked like you two had made some kind of discovery about our friend here," he said. "I helped uncover him. Makes me feel a kind of . . . connection with him. Have to admit, I'm just about burning up to know what took him out. And why."

"Are you?" Hal reached down into the grave and carefully picked up the shiny coin. "This your dime?" he asked, holding it so that it gleamed silver in the light. "Maybe fell out of your pocket while you were dusting off the bones?"

Hastings laughed. "Maybe. Have I spoiled the grave?"

Winnie came over and knelt down again. She examined the spot where the coin had been. "Hastings, don't joke," she said sternly. "If you dropped the coin, tell us. Something's been here a long time, and it sure wasn't a common, modern-day dime." She took a small brush from her shirt pocket and flicked twice at the earth by the skeleton's hip. "There's a definite depression that's too deep to be caused by a coin like that."

"It says 1987." Hal read off the date. "I'd say this guy has been here a bit longer than that."

"It is a male," Dixie confirmed. "Pelvic structure shows me that. A big man, from what I can tell by the bones in this awkward position. I'll have to lay him out straight to be more accurate." She leaned over again, looking at the teeth. "And as Winnie has already determined, not too old, either."

Hal stood up. "I'm going to get my camera," he said, placing his hand on her shoulder. "Don't let *anyone* near this," he added.

"All right," she said.

"We took pictures," Oscar said. "Lots of them."

"Good. I'll need to see them." Hal stepped toward the darkness. "Now, I'll take some of my own." He disappeared. Winnie followed him, telling him where they were going to set up a place for him to question the other diggers.

Oscar Hayden moved closer to Dixie. "Sheriff's a bit on edge tonight, isn't he, Dr. Sheldon?"

Dixie stood and brushed dirt off her skirt. "I suppose he is. It's late. We were out for dinner. I don't think he expected to get a call like this." She placed herself in a position whereby the professor couldn't get closer to the grave without bumping into her.

"That's not what I mean."

She regarded the bearded man. "What do you mean, then, Professor?"

Hayden's eyes narrowed for a moment. He smiled thinly and shrugged. "I thought you two were well enough acquainted for you to understand." He turned. "I guess I was mistaken." He walked away into the darkness the way Hal and Winnie had gone.

"What's that supposed to mean?" Dixie rested her hands on her hips and stared after him.

"He's just a first-class jerk, Doctor," Hastings said. "Can't hack the full summer at a dig site anymore. His heart, or something. He's over the hill and hates it. Takes it out on everyone. Don't let him get to you."

"I won't." She smiled at the younger man. "How long have you known the professor?"

Hastings rolled his eyes. "Long enough. He's my degree advisor. I *have* to be nice to him."

"Lucky you."

"Yeah." Hastings took a step toward the grave. "Hey, seriously, now, Doctor. What do you think about this?" He gestured toward the bones. "'Murder most foul'? Or just an unlucky cowboy?"

"Why do you say cowboy?"

"Well, he could have been a rancher, I guess. Look here." Hastings squatted and pointed. "He wore boots. There are rivets from his jeans. A belt buckle. No telling what we'll find once you get the bones out and we start sifting the soil."

"What about that dime?"

"I have no idea. One of us must have dropped it." Hastings stood. "Or maybe the grave was found before and covered back up. Think about that. What if..." The younger man's expression darkened.

"What if what?"

"Nothing." He waved a hand. "I just have too much of an imagination, I guess."

Dixie intended to push a little. She was curious about that imagination and what it might be devising, but just then Hal reappeared, carrying equipment, a big camera setup and a large bag similar to a medical case.

"You know how this is done?" he asked.

"Sort of. I've had a little ME work. Plenty of theoretical training, anyway."

"Okay." Hal set his things down and rolled up his sleeves. "Everybody else out," he said. "I called Ted, my deputy. He'll be here soon to conduct interviews and take statements. Professor, I want prints of the pictures you people took. Hastings, I want you to rack your memory and tell me the name of every person who stood near the grave. I want the owner of that dime."

"But..."

"No buts. Do it!"

Hastings nodded and looked hurt.

Dixie spoke up. "I think you might consider Hastings's idea, Hal," she said. "About that dime."

"What idea?"

"Just that...," Hastings began.

"Suppose someone had found the grave a few years ago, Sheriff," Professor Hayden said, interrupting his student. "Couldn't the dime have been dropped in then?"

Hal frowned, considering. "Why cover it back up? And you people said it looked undisturbed."

Just then, Winnie appeared. "It *was* undisturbed," she said. "I'll stake my professional reputation on that. The soil was hard-packed. No one has looked in on our friend there since the day he died."

"Or the night he was murdered," Hal muttered.

Dixie looked at him, but saw nothing in his face. Stone. Solid rock.

"Maybe," Winnie admitted. "But determining cause of death is your job, not ours. We just compile data."

"And, my dear colleague's professional reputation notwithstanding," Oscar Hayden said, "the grave site could have been disturbed. The landslide that took off that part of the tableland and cliff edge created loose dirt. It's not likely, but it is not impossible that someone else found the bones a few years ago."

Winnie said nothing. Clearly, however, she was annoyed at having her judgment challenged.

"Well, be that as it may," Hal said, "Dr. Sheldon and I have some work to do."

"If someone else did leave that dime," Hastings said, "maybe it was to confuse anyone else who might find the body. About the age of the bones, that is."

Hal regarded the student. "Why would anyone want to do that?"

"I don't know." Hastings shrugged. "Just a thought."

"Umph," Hal said. His impatience with the "thought" and the thinker was clear.

Conversation faded after that. The three paleontologists left the scene. Without any more comment, Hal set to work, studying, recording and photographing the grave site. Dixie followed his lead.

They worked together with remarkable harmony. She had just about finished before she realized that they had performed their tasks as a team. As if they'd been partners for years instead of hours. As she carefully laid the last bone in the body bag, she looked over at Hal and saw he was smiling at her.

She brushed some dirt from her hands. "Are you having fun?" she asked.

"In a strange way, I am," he admitted. "We're good together, Dixie."

She smiled, but felt her face get a little red. "That sounds romantic, and this is hardly a romantic setting."

"True enough." His expression sobered. "I'll tell you now I don't usually end my dates squatting by old graves." He gestured out past the edge of the cliff. "Look. Dawn's starting to break."

Dixie smiled and blushed a little more. "So, on our first date, we spent the entire night together."

He didn't smile, but the expression in his eyes warmed considerably. Dixie held his gaze for a long, delicious moment. Then she looked down at the body bag.

"Doesn't seem right, somehow. Feeling good while we're working on this poor man."

"Maybe not. But somehow, I don't think he'd mind."

She looked back at Hal. He had a faraway expression now. Almost a dreamy appearance. "Hal?" she asked. "What are you thinking about?"

He shook his head. "Nothing. I... The past, I suppose. His time... Nothing." He got up. "Come on. We've done what we can here. Let's go."

Dixie was reluctant to let him drop the subject so easily, but they were both tired and she still had no business probing his psyche. The time for that would come, she reminded herself. And felt another twinge of professional conscience at the possible conflict. She would have to be very careful to keep her focus on Hattie's needs, and not her son's.

Once they were back up in the camp, Hal went off to see what his deputy had come up with during interviews. Dixie had the responsibility of seeing that the body was brought to the specimen tent where a thorough examination could take place.

Winnie assisted her. "Have some coffee first," Winnie said, handing her a large, steaming mug. "It's morning."

"I know!" Dixie sipped caffeine gratefully. "Do I ever know." She laughed. "Seems like every time Hal Blane and I work together, we end up seeing the sun rise together."

Winnie lifted an eyebrow.

"Oh, come on," Dixie said. "I don't mean it like *that* ."

"Well, too bad. He seems to be a heck of a man."

"In his way, I suppose he is." Dixie turned, set her coffee mug down on a bench and said, "Now, let's see who and what we've got here."

Winnie, wisely, dropped the topic of Hal and moved in to help take notes and measurements. A tape recorder hung on a wire over the table, and Dixie spoke toward it as she did the postmortem.

By the time they finished, the sun was blazing down outside and in spite of the big meal she'd eaten the night before, Dixie was faint with hunger. Winnie snagged a student worker and sent her for rolls, doughnuts and more coffee. When the goodies arrived, the two women settled in to eat.

"So," Winnie said, munching on a roll. "What do you think?"

"About Hal?"

"No!" Winnie laughed. "I'd forgotten all about the living. The dead are much more interesting. It's my business, after all. What do you think about our friend, here?"

Dixie regarded the bones. After taking samples for further testing and examining the remains, she'd come to no further concrete conclusions about the person. The only specific artifact she had found was a small lead pellet in the skull. The tiny round hole she had seen earlier was indeed a bullet hole. But the piece of metal resembled no bullet she'd ever seen, spent or unspent. She intended to ask Hal to send it out to the crime lab in Cheyenne for identification. "I don't know what to think," she admitted. "He was in great shape, I believe, except for the bullet in his skull."

Winnie's smile faded. "Such a shame. No one will ever know who he was or what happened to him."

"He was shot." Dixie drank coffee. "To death."

"Yes, but why?"

Dixie looked over at the skull. "He was big. Almost as big as Hal. And about the same age, as near as I can tell. Wonder what he looked like?"

"Want to find out?"

Dixie looked at her.

"I'm serious," Winnie declared. She set down her mug of coffee and went over to a large cabinet. She opened the doors and took out several containers. "We don't do much reconstruction here in the field," she said. "But I keep some material on hand to show the students how it's done back at the big lab." She patted the containers. "I'm not much at human anatomy. People are just too new on the earth. I like a really old mystery. Dinosaurs are my bag. But if we work together, with what you know about muscles and attachments and epidermal patterns and what I..."

"You mean, build a face?" Dixie felt a surge of excitement. Scientific curiosity and excitement. "Try to show how he really looked in life?"

"Why not?"

"Why not, indeed." Dixie smiled. "I'll see if Hal will let us keep the skull for a while. If not..."

"If what? You look concerned."

"Nothing. If there's any objection from him, I'll take care of it. If we have to send it away, we can always cast it first, can't we?"

"I'd do that, anyway. No reason to risk destroying the integrity of the real bones when you're reconstructing." She opened a container. "In fact, if you say it's okay, I'll start a rubber mold right now. I use this liquid latex. Five, six layers. Then, I fill the mold with dental plaster. It takes to the smallest crevices perfectly. Once that sets, it'll turn out an exact replica of the original. After that, we start building. You can come out here later and help me with it. What do you say?"

Dixie thought for a moment. She was intrigued by the prospect of seeing what the man looked like, even if it was only an approximation. "Do it," she said. "We'll make arrangements to work the face later. Maybe next weekend."

"Great. By then the cast will be properly set. We can just go to town, recreating the past."

Dixie decided that would be a project worth the investment of her limited free time. Besides, it would give her a chance to get to know Winnie better.

She also decided not to tell Hal. Not until they had the face to present to him, at least.

CHAPTER EIGHT

HAL BLANE SAT BACK on the camp chair and rubbed his tired eyes. The air in the tent was hot, stifling. He'd drunk at least a gallon of coffee—excellent coffee made the right way over a camp fire in a big old pot—but it had done him no good. He was bone-weary.

He opened his eyes. Ted Travers was watching him.

"You look real beat, boss," he said. "Want me to wrap up?"

"No." Hal pulled his arms back behind his head and stretched hard. He heard his body creak and crack. Getting too old for these all-nighters? "You go home," he said to Ted. "I don't think there's much more to do."

"You want to send that stuff the doc got down to Cheyenne? I can do that on the way."

"No."

"But..."

Hal stood up. "I don't see any reason to pursue this, Ted. What're we going to do? Investigate a crime that's at least a century old? I'll get the reports typed up and sent down, but there's no point in spending money running complex forensic tests on this one."

"But, I... That is, I thought you..."

"Thought what?"

Ted recoiled slightly from Hal's pugnacious response. He'd seen his boss like this only a few times in his life and he knew that when the big guy got that stony look on his face, it was best to head for the high ground and wait out the storm.

"Nothing, boss. I guess you're right. No point in stirring up old trouble."

"Nothing to stir up," Hal declared, walking over to the small table where he'd been taking notes as Ted recounted the testimony of the diggers. "No reason even to think it was a criminal situation."

"Boss, the guy was shot in the head!"

Hal turned slowly. "Yeah? When? Why? Maybe he tried to rob somebody. Caught lead for his efforts. Maybe it was a righteous shooting. Maybe a lawman did it. Didn't bother to report it. All kinds of assassinations and legalized murders around here a hundred years ago. Remember we aren't that far away from the Johnson County War area."

Ted could say nothing.

"And how would we ever be able to find out? Answer me that."

"I guess we can't." Ted stood up. "Shoot. Seemed kinda exciting. Want me to file any of this?"

Hal considered. "I'll take care of it," he said, his tone kinder. "You've done enough. Thanks. Go get some rest."

"You need it more than me."

Hal looked at his deputy.

"I'm going," Ted said quickly. "I'm out of here."

After he left, Hal settled back down on the camp chair. What the hell was going on with him, he thought. Chewing at Ted's rear for no good reason! The man was just being thoughtful. Worrying about him...

Had Miss Esther actually put something toxic in his tea? Something to make him act so damn strange?

No, damn it! He trusted that old lady. Trusted her more than he trusted most folks he knew. She was a healer, not a harmer. A healer!

Like Dixie Sheldon.

Dixie...

He rubbed his eyes again. Maybe *that* was his problem.

He thought about her for a moment. How their dinner date had been. How kissing her had felt. How the kissing had taken fire there for a few moments. How she'd taken to Miss Esther so well. How Esther had taken to her....

How gently Dr. Dixie Sheldon had touched the bones of the long-dead man. How respectfully she had treated the remains that could feel nothing.

How cherished anything or anyone she loved would likely be....

"Hal?"

She was in the tent. By his side.

"Are you all right?"

"Yes." He opened his eyes, frowning. "Just... putting some thoughts together."

"Good. Well, Winnie and I are finished. The skeleton's ready to be shipped out. If you aren't done, I'm going to bribe someone to take me home. I'm done for. It's Sunday and I don't have to see patients unless there's an emergency."

"I'll take you. I'm ready to leave, too."

"Okay." She moved closer. "Are you sure you're all right?"

"Damn it! Does everybody around here think I need nursemaiding? Do I look like I need tending?"

"Yes." She stood back, crossed her arms and regarded him sternly. "You look like you've been to hell and back, Hal. Quite frankly, if you were my patient, I'd put you on a few days' bed rest, just to get your motor back on track again."

"Well, I don't need it. I'll catch up on my sleep and be fine."

She looked at him, hard, but said nothing. He saw a caring sternness in her blue eyes that made him feel even weaker. Her face was pale with fatigue and under those blue eyes were dark circles. But she still looked as good to him as she had when he'd picked her up for their date, all those long hours before. The sensation of weakness passed.

In fact, just standing there in that hot tent, arguing with her, knowing she was concerned about him, made him feel ...

Better. Alert. Alive! Very strong....

Damn!

"Come on," he said, going over to her and putting his hand on her arm. "Sorry to be such a cross old bear. You're right, I do need my rest. Let's get on the road. Sooner we do, sooner we both can sleep."

Dixie reached up and touched his face. He looked exhausted, and his jaw was rough with whisker stubble. Lines dug into his tanned skin by his mouth and eyes, and he appeared much older in the unforgiving morning light.

But he was undoubtedly a man still in charge and in control. Strong and tough.

"Sounds like a good idea to me." She stood on her toes and kissed him. "Did you find out who dropped the dime in the grave?"

Hal slid his arm around her waist. "No. And I'm not sure I really care right now. Or if I ever will. At first it seemed important. But not now. I guess I was responding as if it was a real crime scene."

She raised her eyebrows at that, but said nothing.

She just kissed him again.

And Hal continued to feel just fine.

Dixie dozed during the drive home. The caffeine from the camp coffee, the excitement of the burial discovery, the challenge of unraveling a hundred-year-old mystery, not even the pleasure of kissing Hal Blane could keep her alert and awake. She was able to sleep because she felt safe. Even if he was worn-out, she felt secure with Hal behind the wheel of the Jeep. Grouchy, grubby, tired Hal. He made her feel so good....

They made it to her home without incident. He pulled into her driveway and stopped. Dixie sat up and rubbed sleep from her eyes.

"Not exactly a perfect date," he said. "Next time, I'll try to do better."

"It was fine," she said, smiling at him. "I can't remember when so much has happened to me in a twenty-four-hour period before."

He smiled back. "You're a pretty tolerant lady. As well as a pretty lady." His expression sobered. "I'm covering the county this coming weekend, so we can't do anything together, but I'll..."

"Hal." She put a hand on his arm. "I start seeing your mother on Tuesday. Why don't we see how that goes before we make any plans."

"What's that mean?"

"Just... I don't know. I'm kind of uncomfortable about mixing social and professional..."

"Why?"

"I..."

"Do you think I have anything to do with my mother's condition? Is it my fault she feels bad?"

"I can't answer that, yet." Dixie regarded him steadily. "Not entirely, certainly."

"What does *that* mean? That I do have responsibility for it?"

"You are part of her family. What do you think?"

"I think this psychological stuff is horse manure. I think the sooner I get her to Salt Lake, the better."

"I agree. And I will call to make that appointment with the heart specialist, if Hattie also agrees."

"What's her agreement got to do with it? She . . ."

"It's her health, Hal. Not yours. She can make her own decisions."

"But I'm responsible . . ." He slumped down. "You're right. But I . . ."

She smiled and moved close. "Don't try to take on the world. It's too big a job. Come here, Hal. Kiss me and go away. Don't say anything. You're in a temperamental mood, and I don't want our first date to end up on a negative note." Her lips brushed his.

"Why not?" he murmured. "We seem to fight pretty well together." He kissed her mouth, moved to her throat.

"You like a good fight, don't you?" she whispered, her voice husky.

Hal sat back a little. "Well, I've never turned my back on a confrontation."

"Then why are you dismissing the dime thing? The skeleton? You saw that hole in the skull. I want to know what kind of gun . . ."

"Dixie, that is history!"

"So?"

"So, I'm not wasting my time and taxpayers' money investigating it."

"Oh."

"Don't sound so disappointed. What ever happened took place in the past, too long ago to matter to us."

"Us? Or you?"

"You know what I mean. Don't play word games with me!"

"Why not. I think it might be the only way to get your attention!"

Hal glared, then smiled. "No, you have other ways, Dr. Sheldon. Other ways that are much, much more pleasant." And he drew her close and showed her.

The kiss went on for a while.

Finally, Hal drove home, alone, and Dixie went to bed, alone. He might not want to bother doing anything about the body, she thought, but she and Winnie would go ahead with their plans, anyway. Somehow, she knew it wouldn't be a waste of time.

MONDAY, she dealt with patients, most of whom had been saving minor complaints for the weekday, rather than bothering her on Sunday. She tackled a pile of bureaucratic paperwork, and with Fran's help, completed it before six that evening.

She was busy, but she thought about Hal Blane all the time. Apparently he was busy, too, because she didn't see or hear from him at all.

His silence surprised her because she'd been sure he would want her contribution to the report. In spite of what he'd said about not wasting taxpayers' money, he'd still have to file some kind of document and arrange for the body to be reburied somewhere. She decided that he was just taking his time. There was hardly a rush; no justice was likely to be served by solving the mystery of old bone and lead. Just curiosity.

She told Fran about their find.

"That's spooky," the nurse said. "Finding a skeleton out there on the plateau in the middle of the night!"

"It wasn't really spooky. It was fascinating. I think the diggers are used to skeletons. This one just happened to be human."

"The land around here probably holds a lot more of them," Fran said. "This was a very violent place in the past."

"You mean 'When Dinosaurs Ruled'?"

"No." Fran was not laughing. "I mean the recent past. Come on, you're a Wyoming girl, born and raised, even if it was down at the university. You know the history."

"Cattlemen and sheepmen? Hired guns? Range wars? Indian wars? Gold-mining wars?" Dixie sighed. "Yes, I do. Thank goodness those days are over, and we live a little closer to peacefulness now."

"*Maybe* they're over," Fran commented. "If you want my opinion, all it would take would be a gentle nudge for some folks to step over the line again."

"Why, Fran. I didn't know you were such a cynic about human nature."

"I am, and you should be, too."

Dixie laughed. "All right. But since I kept you working late on these reports, how about if I treat you to dinner down at Sal's?"

"You've got a deal, boss!" the older woman replied cheerfully and enthusiastically.

Sal closed on Sundays, but during that time, he and Etta prepared a special stew for Monday, and the restaurant was crowded when they arrived.

They found a table toward the back of the café, but shared it with another late-coming couple. Dixie didn't know the husband and wife, so Fran introduced her.

"Reed and Lola have been in Seaside for years," Fran said. "Retired here from Denver."

"I was an accountant. Now, I'm an amateur histo-rian," Reed Turner said. His round face took on a deter-mined expression. "I want to help recreate in print exactly what happened during the turbulent past of this area."

"Really?" Dixie stifled a yawn. She wasn't bored with the company, but she was still feeling the effects of the weekend. "How can anyone know exactly?"

"Reed can," Lola declared. "He's getting all the old people to let him look at their family letters, diaries, memoirs, photographs...that sort of thing."

"Any and all family papers," Reed stated. "History is hidden right there for a man who has the brains and pa-tience to find it."

"Dixie found some history out on the tableland," Fran said. "A body."

Both of the elderly people gasped.

"I didn't find it," Dixie explained quickly. "The pale-ontological crew did. And it wasn't exactly a body. Just bones."

"Human?" Reed wanted to know.

Dixie nodded.

"My lord," Lola said. "Who was it?"

Dixie shrugged. "We have no idea. I don't expect we ever will, either." They dropped the topic then, but not before she saw a definite gleam of interest in Reed Tur-ner's eyes.

HATTIE BLANE was setting dinner on the table for her son and grandson. The sweet, yeasty smell of her day's bak-ing efforts still filled the kitchen and blended deliciously with the hearty aroma of the pot roast she was serving.

"Smells terrific, Grandma," Artie declared, pulling up to the table and reaching for fresh rolls. "Better than ever."

"Thanks." Hattie smiled. "Hal, want some butter with that roll?"

Hal didn't reply. He continued to tear at the dinner roll, dividing it into small pieces.

"Hal?"

"Dad? Earth to Dad!"

"Huh?" Hal came back from his reverie. "Sorry. I was just thinking about something."

Artie poured milk from the pitcher into his glass. "Thinking about the skeleton, Dad?"

"What skeleton?" Hattie sat down and helped herself to food. "Is someone killing cattle again? I surely hope not. That just makes me ill."

"A *human* skeleton," Artie said. "And they found it on *our* land."

"Our..." Hattie's fork clattered against the plate. "What do you mean, our land?"

"Artie, where the hell did you hear..."

"Hal Blane, do not swear at this table," his mother snapped. "Artie, what about a skeleton on our land?"

Artie Blane drew into himself. "Nothing."

Hattie looked at Hal. "All right, *you* tell me."

Hal stared down at his plate. "Nothing to tell, really. Just like Artie said. The paleontologists came across an old burial up on the edge of the tableland. That's all."

"On the tableland. On what used to be Kedrick land?"

"I think so."

"You think so? Son, you know every square inch of that property. Don't give me *think*."

"Ma, calm down."

"Grandma, it wasn't anything important...."

"Who was it?" Hattie asked softly, but bright spots glowed on her cheeks.

"We don't..."

"*Who?*" She stood up. "Hal, you must find out!"

"Ma, I..."

"Grandma, what's the matter?" Artie stood up and took his grandmother's arm. "Are you feeling sick?"

"Yes, I am." Hattie glared at her son. "Because your father is ignoring and denying..." She put her hand on her chest and sat down, hard.

"Grandma!"

Hal got up, knocking over his chair. "I'm calling the doctor," he said.

"I'm seeing her tomorrow," Hattie declared, her voice strong. "Don't you dare bother her now."

Hal strode across the kitchen to the phone and picked up the receiver. He punched in numbers.

"Harold Blane, don't you—" Hattie broke off, giving a little cry of pain.

"Dad," Artie said, clutching at his grandmother's shoulders. "Help! I think she's having some kind of heart attack."

Hal gripped the phone. "Come on, Dixie! Damn it! Answer!"

Dixie got the page while she was walking back to the office from the café. Fran had gone on home, but Dixie wanted to do a few more housekeeping chores before calling it a night. When the belt pager went off, she hurried her pace, unlocked the door quickly and got to the desk as the phone was still ringing.

"Dr. Sheldon," she said. "What's the nature of your problem?"

"Dixie! My mom's having a heart attack!"

"Hal?"

"My mother—"

"Are you at home?"

"Yes, I—"

"Exactly what happened. Describe her symptoms."

He did. Dixie listened intently. And then, in the background, she heard Hattie fussing, telling him not to bother the doctor, that she was just upset.

Very upset, judging from the voice Dixie could hear. But not suffering from anything resembling a heart attack. Just frustration and, possibly, anger.

Dixie felt a wave of relief wash over her. "I'll be right there, Hal," she said. "But I don't think you have anything to worry about. Get her to lie down. Tell her I was going to stop by on my way home, anyway."

"You were?"

"Hal, it'll make her calmer. That's what we want."

"Okay." Pause. "Uh, Dixie?"

"Yes?"

"Thanks."

"No problem. It's my job. See you in a few minutes."

When she pulled up to the Blanes' house, the front door banged open and a youth ran out. He grabbed the handle of the car door and yanked it open. "Come on, Doc," he said. "She's in the living room. Hurry!"

"Artie?" He was a reflection of his father. Rail-thin, tall and young, but still stamped with Hal Blane's image, from curly hair to big feet.

"Yes, ma'am. Come on!"

"I'm here. You can calm down, now. All right?" Dixie smiled and touched the boy on the arm.

"Okay." Artie smiled back, but it was a weak, worried smile. He swallowed hard, making his prominent Adam's apple bob. "My grandma . . ."

"Your grandma is going to be fine." Dixie went up the walk, through the front door and into the house.

It was a plain and simple dwelling. The entrance opened directly into the living room. A rectangle of plastic was set onto the carpet to ease wear immediately in front of the door. The room was done in greens, grays and oranges. Family pictures decorated the walls. Furniture was dark and seemed more than slightly worn, as if it had all been through more than one generation of owners.

Hattie lay on the sofa. She did not look fine. She looked angry. Hal sat gingerly on a chair, next to her, holding her hand and patting it soothingly.

At least, in what he apparently felt was a soothing manner. From where Dixie stood, it looked as if he were crushing Hattie's frail bones.

"Evening, Hal." Dixie said. "Looks like you have things under control."

He gave her a grateful look and released his mother's hand. "Thanks for coming so quickly," he said, standing up and moving aside. "She's in some pain, still, but she says she feels stronger."

Dixie sat down. "What happened, Hattie?" she asked. "Things get a little tense?"

"That idiot son of mine..." Hattie's complexion darkened.

"Ma!" Hal interrupted. "It was not—"

"It was, too, Dad!" Artie interjected. "You were..."

Dixie turned around. "Hal, why don't you and Artie go on out into the kitchen, or something. Let us talk."

Both males grunted, nodded assent and left the room. She heard them fussing, low-voiced, as they went down the hall. Hattie closed her eyes and sighed, obviously relieved.

Dixie laughed softly. "Okay," she said to Hattie. "Now, tell me all about it."

Hattie sat up. She touched a hand to her chest, but exhibited no sign of being in physical pain. "My idiot son," she said, "is not going to investigate the skeleton found on Kedrick land."

"I thought so. He about said as much Sunday."

Hattie's forehead wrinkled. "But why not?"

Dixie lifted her shoulders in a shrug. "He says there's no point. I suppose he's right."

"But—" Hattie pressed her hands together "—suppose it's . . ."

"Suppose it's what?"

Hattie shook her head. "I don't know. I really don't know why I'm so upset. I guess I'm thinking it might be someone my ancestors murdered or . . ."

"Why in the world would you think that?"

Hattie gazed at her. "They were bad people. I come from bad people, Doctor. We're all tainted."

"Hattie, you can't be serious."

"I am. I am. Did you know one of my ancestors was hanged in England? A highwayman. He robbed and killed. And my grandfather was a robber and a killer, too." Her voice rose into a thin, whine. She sounded fearful.

Dixie settled into her chair, thinking this was the kind of thing that would have come out eventually in therapy. Luckily, the pressure of the family argument had precipitated it for her.

"What happened to your grandfather, Hattie?"

Hattie's face seemed to shrink. "He . . . he was a bad man, Doctor."

"Couldn't have been all bad."

Hattie looked at her.

Dixie smiled. "He became part of you, Hal and Artie. You're all good people."

Hattie looked away. "We've tried to make up for it."

"I see." Dixie took a syringe out of her bag. "Look, Hattie. I know you've been upset. And you're tired. I know you'd like to relax, so I'm going to give you a shot. This won't make you sleep, but it'll help if you want to rest. In any event, it'll ease that tightness in your chest.''

"I'm not having a heart attack," Hattie stated.

"I know that." Dixie gave her the injection. "I understand, too. Stress is responsible, not anything or anyone else." She gave the woman a comforting pat on the back. "Still planning to come see me in the morning?"

"Yes." Hattie smiled. "I baked today."

"I can smell it. Delicious!"

Hattie swung her feet off the sofa. "Why don't you take yours home tonight?" she said. "It'll be fresher, and you can have some for breakfast."

"Sounds fine to me." Dixie helped Hattie to her feet. "How do you feel?"

"Better." Hattie took a deep breath. "Maybe a little woozy, but better. My chest doesn't hurt anymore."

"Good."

They walked down the hall slowly, Dixie right by Hattie's side. Hal and Artie were in the kitchen, waiting.

Dixie almost laughed when she saw them. They both had their arms crossed over their chests, both leaned up against the counter, both glared, but concern for Hattie shone in their blue eyes.

It was like looking at nearly identical twins, a generation apart in age.

"Well?" Hal growled. "What's the story?"

"Grandma, want to sit down?" Artie moved and held out a kitchen chair.

"I'm fine," Hattie said. She reached for Dixie's arm.

Hal put his hand on the chair. "Sit down, Ma. Dixie, what's wrong with her? Is she going to be all right?"

"Hattie's fine. Now, why don't the two of you sit down, and let's talk about how to keep her that way."

CHAPTER NINE

IT WAS INTERESTING from a clinical standpoint, unsettling from a personal one.

The doctor in her was pleased with the progress she saw; the woman was upset with the possible implications for herself.

She was involved with the Blane family both professionally and personally. Conflict of interest? No question about it, now.

The only question left for her to answer was: did it matter? In a place the size of Seaside, with such a small population, wasn't she likely to be in conflicts like this, no matter what? Was she to remain a social hermit, just to avoid this? And did that matter, if she was leaving in three years?

Maybe. Maybe not.

They sat at the kitchen table, the leavings of the uneaten dinner in front of them. Dixie noted that Hattie regarded the mess with distaste, but did nothing about it. The two males were oblivious to the surroundings. They were concerned only with Hattie.

That was all to the good.

Artie spoke first. "Grandma, we thought you were dying... Uh, that is, we thought..." The gleam of moisture in his eyes betrayed his emotional state. "Grandma, I don't want you to hurt that way."

Hattie smiled at her grandson. "Don't you fret," she said. "I don't hurt now. It'll take more than a little chest pain to get rid of me."

"Ma," Hal said. "Don't joke about it."

"Why not?" Dixie asked. "Humor is healing. Besides, she was not in danger. Just in discomfort. And that's what we want to learn to avoid, isn't it?" She paused, looking at the three of them. "Before it *does* become dangerous."

"Then, it could?" Hal moved his dinner plate aside and rested his elbows on the table. "Become dangerous? Is that what you're saying?"

Instead of answering, Dixie turned to Hattie. "Do you like feeling bad?" she asked.

"Of course not!" Hattie sat up straight. "It makes me useless!"

"Okay, then." Dixie took a deep breath. "Just what caused you to have problems tonight?"

The three Blanes all started talking at once. Accusations flew across the table and tempers skyrocketed before Dixie could quiet them.

When she did, she strove for understanding and compromise. The upshot of it all was that Hal grudgingly agreed to do a bit more about the skeleton, since it had been found on land that belonged to the family in the past. Hattie agreed not to nag him about it or even to speculate on it, to keep her appointments with Dixie, and also to visit Salt Lake and the heart specialist there.

"I don't want to, mind," she said. "I trust Dr. Sheldon's judgment. But if it will make your attitude improve, son, I will do it."

"Grandma," Artie said. "It's not just Dad. I want to know your heart's okay, too. I think Dad's right about this. We need to get a specialist to look at you, no matter how good Dr. Sheldon is."

Dixie noted that Hal stared at his son with amazement on his face, as if the boy had suddenly turned green or sprouted wings. She wondered when the last time Artie Blane had told anyone that his father was right about anything.

Especially in his father's presence.

She waited, wondering what was happening between the father and the son. Wondering and intrigued.

"I did some reading about heart stuff the other day," Artie continued. "You should get checked, anyway. 'Cause of your age and all." He glanced shyly at Dixie. "Am I right, Doctor?"

"You are," she replied. "I've advised it."

"All right, then," Hattie declared. "It's settled. I'll do it. Now, how about you boys eating your dinners? I can heat them up right quick." She started to stand, then gripped the edge of the table. "Oh, my," she said softly. "My, I'm so weak."

Hal and Artie both exclaimed at once and started to get up. Dixie motioned them back.

"It's just the shot I gave her," she explained. "She's really relaxed. Come on, Hattie. No more cooking tonight. Let's get you into bed. I think the boys are capable of dealing with dinner by themselves, don't you?"

"I'm not sure," Hattie replied. But she smiled as she spoke.

Dixie helped the older woman to her room. When she had her patient settled and drowsing into sleep, she shut off the light and returned to the kitchen.

It was clean. Artie was gone. Hal waited at the table, his arms crossed over his chest once more. His face was expressionless, but Dixie knew trouble was brewing.

She sat down. "Your mother's fine," she said. "Getting to sleep."

"Thanks." He uncrossed his arms and put his big hands on the table. "I do appreciate your making a house call."

"That's what we country docs do."

"But I don't appreciate your using the situation to get what you wanted."

"Excuse me?" Dixie sat forward. "I don't understand."

"Oh, come on, Dixie. You know you were aching to have me send those specimens to Cheyenne. The bone fragments and the lead shot. You and Winnie were just bursting with curiosity, and now you've got my mother on your side and . . ."

"Hold it!" Dixie stood up. "I never spoke to your mother about it. She brought it up."

"I know that. But you didn't talk her out of it, did you?"

Dixie crossed her arms defensively, defiantly. "Why should I? It seems to mean a lot to her."

"She trusts you. She likes you. You could influence her."

That did it.

"Hal Blane, I don't know who or what you think I am, but I'm here to tell you right now that I have never put anything before the welfare of one of my patients! Nothing! Especially not a little idle curiosity about an old skeleton." She put her hands on the table and leaned over until she was inches from his face.

"And especially not a moody, bad-tempered man to whom I was inexplicably attracted for a very short period of time. From now on, when we see each other, it will be for professional reasons only. I hope that satisfies you that I do not have personal interests in this matter."

She turned and walked out of the kitchen, down the hallway and out the front door. She heard him yell after her once, but she kept going.

Driving home, her temper steaming, she decided to get started with Winnie on reconstructing the skull's face as soon as possible.

That would set Sheriff Hal Blane's teeth on edge!

And that would serve the self-centered, insensitive man right! She had figured she could take a lot of what he could dish out, but that direct insult to her professional integrity was beyond the limit. He had accused her of manipulating a patient to achieve her own small goals, and Dixie Sheldon would not tolerate that kind of attitude!

So, why did she feel like crying right now? Crying for loss. Crying out of frustration. Crying for what might have been. . . .

It was a long time before she managed to fall asleep Monday night.

HATTIE CAME IN for her appointment on Tuesday morning. Little mention was made of the night before, and both of them seemed determined to avoid the topic of Hal. Dixie had Hattie talk about her childhood on the family ranch, her love of the land—an echo of what Hal felt—and her marriage to Hal's father.

"Frank was a good man," Hattie declared, closing her eyes and smiling. "Oh, he had a temper, but he was good and kind right through."

"Tell me about the temper. Did it cause you problems?"

"Oh, no, indeed." Hattie opened her eyes. "He never hit me or punished Hal in anger." She spoke so calmly and surely that Dixie knew it was the truth. "He loved us—cherished us, really. But he had a fury in him that would explode if he saw an injustice done another person, or an innocent animal."

"Did he ever hit a man?"

Hattie looked away.

"Okay. Let's talk about—"

"He killed a man," Hattie whispered.

Dixie waited, her spine cold.

"It was a long time ago, When he was young. We weren't married, yet. He was working for my father." Hattie went on to relate a chilling account of how another ranch hand had tried to rape her, and how Frank Blane had literally beaten the man to death.

"Frank was so big and strong. The other man was big, too, but Frank had that fury in him," Hattie said, her voice tight but her eyes dreamy. "Frank only hit him twice, but the man fell and broke his neck. The sheriff said it was accidental, so no charges were ever brought."

Dixie cleared her throat. "Well, killing is never a good thing, but it sounds like Frank was justified. And the death did come by accident. He couldn't have known the man would fall that way."

Hattie didn't reply.

"You married him. You must have loved him very much, in spite of what happened."

"I did. Oh, I surely did." Hattie looked down at her hands. Her fingers were twisted together, tightly. "But don't you see? It's Hal and Artie I worry about. They have the taint of a killer from both sides—mine and Frank's. And the job Hal has? Why, I think it's just a matter of time before he has to kill, too."

Dixie couldn't argue with that. The logic was convoluted, but there. Hattie would have to learn to deal with it, herself. Instead of trying to talk Hattie out of her misconception, she turned the conversation to more pleasant themes. Themes that avoided Hal.

It was not that difficult. As the older woman spoke, Dixie could see strength and integrity and even a mild sense of humor. *Those* were the factors she wanted to emphasize. Hattie eased into this positive verbal therapy without hesitation. Dixie felt a great deal of optimism about her prospects for healing.

Hattie talked for a while about her grandson. "Artie is a good boy," she said. "He doesn't get into trouble at school, and he has nice friends. But he fights with his father all the time. Rebelling, I guess. I get along with him, though. He's a thoughtful, considerate youngster. Does his chores without being asked and he's good company when he wants to be. Smart, too."

"I could tell that," Dixie commented. "And rebellion is absolutely normal in a boy his age. I'd be more worried if he wasn't acting out some resentment of his father as an authority figure."

Hattie laughed. "Then you don't need to worry. He's just fine."

Toward the end of the hour, Hattie mentioned Hal again. "I think he feels real bad about last night," she said. "He moped over breakfast this morning like a sick calf. When I asked why, he made it clear his attitude had nothing to do with me. So, it had to be you he was thinking about. Did you two have some sort of disagreement after I went to bed?"

"Hattie, don't worry yourself about Hal. He's a big boy and entitled to his moods."

"He likes you."

Dixie ignored that. "I've set up an appointment for you with Dr. Becker two weeks from this Wednesday." She handed Hattie a note. "Give this to Hal so he'll know when he needs to get you to Salt Lake."

Hattie took the paper. "You're mad at him. Why?"

"Hattie, that's not why we're here. How I feel about Hal has nothing to do with you. I'm your doctor." Dixie stood up. "The bread was delicious. I ate almost half the loaf for breakfast with some raspberry jam my grandmother sent me last month. I'm looking forward to more next week."

"I'll be here."

"Until then, try to think about the things that make you happy. And don't take on problems that belong to others. And above all, try not to anticipate trouble before it happens."

Hattie smiled. "Even if it's my own kin I'm thinking about?"

"Especially then!"

THE REST OF TUESDAY went according to expectation and schedule. Only one disquieting event broke the pattern. In the mail was a form letter from the director of rural medical care in Cheyenne. Addressed to all small clinics and hospitals in the state, it advised personnel to be aware of current funding problems. Physicians, nurses and physician assistants were encouraged to conserve financially, wherever possible. Dixie set aside the letter. Money troubles in health care. What else was new?

When Fran saw the letter, she just brushed it off as a political move. "The department starts running scared every election year," she told Dixie. "Surely you know about that, from the university."

"Indeed, I do." Dixie made a wry face. "My parents are continually in budget fights with the administration and the legislature. I guess I just didn't expect to enter the fray way out here."

"Like I told you, you need to develop some protective cynicism," Fran teased.

"I guess you're right."

She resolved to study the budget for SeaLake County and do what she could to cut spending. But it was not a high priority.

She tried not to think about what *was* her priority.

VERY LATE THAT NIGHT, when she was trying to settle into sleep, Dixie found her life changed, dramatically.

The evening was warm, so she had left the bedroom window open. As she started to drift into dreams, she heard singing.

A man's voice. A deep, rumbly, sweet sound. Soft and gentle, but strong...powerful...

Astonished, Dixie sat up in bed. Hal Blane was right outside her bedroom window, playing a guitar and singing a love song! Her body tingled. Her thoughts spun. Her heart started to do a pounding dance in rhythm with the music.

"Let me sing you of a love, before which all else fails..."

Dixie got up, shrugged into her old cotton bathrobe and went to the window. He sat, cross-legged on the ground, spotlighted by the silvery moon. He was wearing jeans and a white shirt. No uniform, no badge, no gun, no boots. She could make out that he wore moccasins, with no socks.

"Hal?"

He smiled up at her. "Evening, Dixie, honey. How are you this fine night?"

"Hal Blane, are you drunk?"

"No." He strummed the guitar. "Well, not exactly drunk. I have to admit to having a shot of whiskey before I got up the courage to come out here and do this." He plucked a high note. "I don't usually serenade ladies this way. In fact, never."

Dixie rested her elbows on the windowsill. "What do you usually do, then?"

He shrugged. "Tell 'em I like 'em a lot, I guess."

"But you're singing to me."

"Yep." He looked away. "Read the other day about the way some Indian braves courted their women. They'd sneak up outside the girl's teepee and play tunes on a flute until she came out to see what was going on."

"That's romantic. I like it. What was that song you were playing? It was pretty."

He didn't answer directly. He just resung the first verse and went on to the second.

"Journey down a thousand miles, couldn't set me free. Journey sets loose memories, bringing you to me."

He paused. Dixie remembered his love of country music. "Hal, did you write that?"

"A while ago. I've been kind of working on it. I know it's not very good, but I wanted to sing you something of my own." He looked up at her.

Her heart began to beat harder. "Why?"

He stood. "Because, Dixie, dumb as it was for me to do, I think I've fallen for you."

"You what? Hal, that's crazy."

"Hey, don't question me about this." He set the guitar against the side of the house and came close to where she stood at the window. "I know my own mind, even if my mother doesn't know hers."

Dixie stepped back. "That's an unkind thing to say."

"But it's true. If she was completely self-aware, she wouldn't need your counseling, and that's a fact." He put his hands on the windowsill and boosted himself up. "May I come in?" he asked, balancing there precariously.

"No! Yes. Hal, what's going on?" She ran to him and grabbed his arm. "For heaven's sake, don't fall!" She pulled him in.

"Ah," he said. "You do care."

"I didn't want to have to treat cuts and bruises at this time of night!"

"And if I broke my neck? I could have, if I'd slipped and landed wrong."

"Lovely thought." She put her hands on her hips. "Okay, Hal. What's going on?"

He stopped grinning. "I came here to tell you that I was so far out of line last night, I was in another country. I had no right to say the things I did about your motives. I was wrong, and I'm sorry. I apologize. I was going to come by your office today, but I couldn't work up the courage. This, I managed to do. Forgive me?"

Dixie took a second to absorb all that. "Okay." She took a deep breath. "I accept your apology. Why the midnight skulking and the guitar playing?"

"For this. For you." He didn't move, but his eyes caressed her face. "Like the Indian brave. I just had to see you. Tell you I was wrong. And that..."

"What, Hal?"

"That even if you can keep our relationship distant and professional, I can't."

"What do you mean by that?"

"I...I can't stay away from you. I haven't thought about anything but you since you waltzed out of my house. Dixie, I had to see you. I'm not crazy now, but I will be if I don't get through to you."

"You aren't seriously trying to tell me you're in love with me, are you?"

"Honey, I don't know. If I did, you'd be the first I'd tell, believe me."

Dixie stared at him.

"Um." Hal looked down at the floor and shoved his hands into his jeans pockets. "I'm not much good at this kind of talk, Dixie. Talking about my feelings doesn't come easy to me. You need to know that."

Feeling a little disoriented, she went over and sat down on the bed. "I understand. But you're doing all right, so far. Try," she said gently. "I need to hear what you've been thinking."

"All right." He cleared his throat. "Well . . . I like looking at you. You're pretty. A real pretty woman."

"Come on, Hal!"

"No, no. It's not just that. I liked the way you looked from the first minute I set eyes on you last spring. But I didn't much like you."

"I didn't think so."

"Well, you were right." He started to walk, to pace across the small room. "But then, things happened."

"What things?"

"I got to be with you. Not just watch you from a distance, judging you. That night in the jail? When you'd just come from delivering a baby and spent all that time sewing up old George. Treating him just as gently as you would a baby. My feelings started to change then. I got to watch you work. *How* you work . . ." He stopped in front of the window and stared out into the night.

"And?"

He shrugged, lifting his big shoulders, but saying nothing.

"You kissed me. Didn't that have some effect on you?"

"I've kissed a lot of women." He turned around. "No, Dixie, what's got me running in circles is who you are, not what you are. I can't seem to make it any plainer than that."

She sat, dumbfounded. "That is one heck of a romantic line, Hal Blane."

"It's no line. It's the truth. You know what really turned me into putty? What made me know I had to... do this?"

"I can't wait to hear."

"Don't make fun. I'm serious. It was the way you handled the skeleton. Like he could feel what you did to him. Like you didn't want him to hurt anymore. You were so... gentle. So... respectful. I thought about it when it happened, but thought a lot more about it the last twenty-four hours. If you deal with dead folks like that, how much more careful must you be with live ones."

"Like your mother?" she asked, beginning to get a glimmer of insight into his reasoning process. She knew, somehow, that it was vital she try to understand what he was feeling.

"Exactly." He stopped pacing and stood still. Ran a hand over his head. "Damn it, Dixie, I guess I am in love with you." He glared at her. "Don't that beat all?" He smiled wryly. "I am some kind of a fool."

That confession melted away her doubts. Tears stung her eyes. "Hal, come over here," she said, patting the bed beside her.

"No. If I get close, no telling what I'll..."

"Well, isn't that the whole idea?" She got up and went to him, putting her arms up around his neck. He was so tense, the muscles in his shoulders felt like solid steel. "Do you climb into women's bedrooms at midnight just to talk?"

He didn't touch her. "You don't love me."

"I can't honestly say. This is all new to me."

"Me, too." He put his hands on her waist. "Better tell me to leave, now, Dixie."

"Stay." She stood on tiptoe and kissed his mouth. "Maybe I don't know if I can love you," she said. "But I know I want you right now."

Hal drew back. "Don't do it unless you have some feelings for me, too."

"I wouldn't. When I heard you singing, my heart started beating faster. My body tingled. And if I didn't have feelings for you, I would never have let you in my bedroom at midnight. I'm neither that trusting nor that naive."

He touched her face, her shoulder, his fingers tracing warmth over her skin. "I'd better leave," he said huskily. "Or..."

Dixie untied the sash of her robe. "Or what?" she asked, looking up into his eyes. There was so much emotion there, it was almost frightening. This was not a man whose feelings were light and easy. Hal was no one to play with.

Did she really want to do this? In another moment, it would be too late.

She opened the robe.

And walked into his arms.

Hal trembled. He'd never felt so much desire in his life. Never felt so scared of his own emotions. Never felt so sure of what he was doing.

He ached with desire, and hurt with the pain he knew would come in the future, because he loved her. And he couldn't keep her.

Dixie knew that having sex with Hal would be making a commitment. She didn't know if she was ready. She knew she couldn't give him more than a fraction of her life. But she wanted to be with him so much, she couldn't back out now.

Hal could feel the heat and softness of her through the thin material of her nightgown. His hands moved over her, his body taking control from his mind. "Dixie!" he said, enfolding her. "Oh, Dixie. You know what you're doing to me?"

"Yes!" she replied. "Please, Hal. Make love with me." She gripped his shoulders, kissing him fiercely. Then she ran her hands over his chest and down the front of his taut jeans.

Making a sound of joy and triumph, he lifted her up and onto the bed. Within moments, they were both naked and joined. The suddenness of it shocked her, but Dixie found herself carried far beyond shock by the hot sensations that jolted her entire being.

The heat went on and on, until she was sure she would die of pleasure. Her man was a solid presence, so strong and sure, and he was giving her love as she had never felt it before.

Hal held her underneath him, his arms around hip and shoulder, his face pressed into her neck. Big and heavy as he was, he seemed no burden on her at all. Delicious heat took her higher and higher, letting her enjoy what her body could do for both of them . . .

Hal was on the edge of explosion. Dixie's small, delicate form was no fragile doll's body. She was steel and fever and liquid fire to him. She was not silent in her passion, either.

Finally, he could control himself no longer and let his body go. Too long denied and tamped down, release shook him to his marrow.

At that moment, he knew he had to have her. Not just for tonight.

Tonight was just the beginning.

CHAPTER TEN

HAL ROLLED onto his back and for a while, they lay together, limbs entwined, breathing deeply, hearts pounding. A soft, cooling breeze blew in through the open window, drying the sweat on their heated bodies. Finally, Dixie groaned and shivered.

"I didn't know you had tornadoes around here in the middle of the summer." She lifted herself up on her elbows and gazed down at her lover.

He smiled, but didn't open his eyes.

She kissed his face. "I'm going to retrieve your guitar and close the window. It's getting chilly. Even smells like it might rain."

No comment from the sheriff.

Dixie got up and rummaged around in the pile of clothing beside the bed for her bathrobe. Pulling it on, she belted it, stepped into a pair of old house shoes, went out of the bedroom and opened the front door.

The air was moving, and the humidity did promise rain. She walked around the side of the house to her bedroom window and picked up the guitar. It was an old instrument, polished and worn. She caressed it. The wood felt warm and alive.

"Play for me, pretty lady."

Dixie looked up. Hal was leaning out the window, obviously with not a stitch on. "I can't sing," she said. "I have the original tin ear, I'm afraid."

"The music you make sounds just fine to me." He held out his hand. "Come on in."

Dixie laughed and backed away. "I'll take my chances through the front door, thanks. Now. It's going to rain any second."

He grinned. "Chicken."

"Don't go away," she said.

"I wouldn't dream of it." He moved back and closed the window. The view of his naked, muscular torso was spectacular. Dixie drew in a breath, glanced around to make sure no neighbors were still up at this late hour, and then hurried around to the front of the house.

Thunder rumbled in the distance. The rain started before she reached the walk. Big fat drops pelted down, drenching her immediately. She hunched over, protecting the guitar. As Hal opened the screen door, a car drove by, headlights catching the scene in their beam. Dixie groaned once more. "So much for a discreet assignation," she said, handing him the instrument.

"Just pretend it was no one you know," Hal said, setting the guitar aside, embracing her and laughing at her distress. He had pulled on jeans, at least. "A stranger passing through town, that's all."

"Right." She brushed wet hair back from her face. "At two in the morning?"

He frowned and looked out the screen door. "That is a little odd for around here. Most folks are long into dreamland by now. Have to get up soon."

"So do we," she reminded him. She shivered as the wind blew in through the screen. Thunder rumbled once more.

Hal pulled her to him with one hand and slammed the door with the other. "Speak for yourself, lady," he said. "I have tomorrow off." He cupped her rear and bent to kiss her lips.

Dixie made a strangled protest, then melted against him. Once more, he lifted her and carried her to the bed.

This time, he focused his passion on exploration. Every inch of her. Every part of her. Dixie tried to return the favors, but he seemed determined to master her, first.

It was not much of a contest. She gave him easy victory.

And the loving he gave her was beyond anything she had imagined, much less experienced. He was a lover who read her body, mind and heart. He seemed to know where to touch her before she wanted it. To know when to be gentle and when to use his strength. To know how to take her from one pleasure to the next until she was faint with desire. To show her how much power passion could have, and how they could soar together until their cries of delight and joy faded into whispers and murmurs of adoration.

He was incredible.

MORNING CAME MUCH too quickly. The rainstorm had passed as they made love, and by five the sun was up and streaming in the window. Dixie raised her head from the pillow of Hal's broad shoulder and glared at the light.

"Daytime," she muttered. "I have to get up."

Hal said nothing. His breathing was deep and even, snoring lightly when he exhaled.

"Fine," Dixie said. "Sleep on. Let me get up and drag my carcass to work." She smiled and traced the outline of his lips with her fingertip. His muscles twitched a little, but he didn't wake.

She sat back on the bed and looked down at him.

He lay there in her bed, a gorgeous male who had taken her to places she didn't even dream existed. Unclothed, his big body was magnificent. Muscles built from years of hard work, not months of working out. No fat at the waist or abdomen. Zero. Skin tanned by the western sun, not by tanning booths. Pale below the waist, darker at neck and arms. A real tan. A workingman's tan. Unselfconscious. Unaware, and right.

His curly light brown hair was cut, not styled. Apparently, he had shaved before coming to serenade her. Now, in the morning sun, whisker stubble gleamed on his cheeks and jaw. He was a natural, to the core. *What you see is what you get....* He was a simple, straightforward man....

Or was he?

She regarded him again. Scars marred the surface of his smooth skin, one tearing a line from his left shoulder to the center of his chest and another rippling up the side of his right arm. She also recognized the old, puckering mark of a bullet wound low on his thigh. The man had been to the wars and back in his life.

Yet, this was also the man who wrote love songs and had the daring, imagination and romance to serenade her outside her bedroom window. This was a man who made love as love had never been made to her before. He . . .

He was a country sheriff, damn it. Dixie got out of bed. He was a good man, and she might be taken to heights of passion by his touch, but a man of such limited ambition and violent experience would not be the kind of partner she would eventually choose to share her life—

Realizing she was jumping the gun, Dixie brought herself back to reality. Who the heck was talking about sharing a life? They had only made love for one night! She got into the shower and ran it hot and long, then cold and fast. She needed to wake up and wake up good!

She dressed quietly, moving around the room without looking at the bed. Before she left, however, she pulled down the shade and made certain he was covered with a light blanket. Strange feelings coursed through her, but she chose to ignore them.

Winnie Nash appeared in her office after lunch. "Just thought I'd drop by," the paleontologist declared. "And see how those who treat the living live. You busy?"

Dixie waved her visitor into a chair. "Not at the moment, though that can change quickly. I don't have any patients scheduled for this afternoon. However, an emergency..."

"Can arise at any time." Winnie sat down. "I know. My father was a doctor. An old-fashioned GP, just like you. We could never rely on him to show up at family events. Maybe that's why I took on the dead."

"I won't be a GP forever."

"Right." Winnie steepled her fingers and smiled at Dixie. "Come on. You love it here. And they love you here, too. You wouldn't believe all the good things I keep hearing about you."

"It's temporary." Dixie thought of the man she had left in her bed that morning. "Just three years. Actually, less than that now."

"Okay." Winnie leaned over and picked up a large sack. "Ready to start on our mystery man?"

"Now? You brought him? I mean... You want to work on him now?"

"Hey, we don't have to, you know. If this is a bad time, I understand."

"No. It's fine. I just..." She thought of Hal, of his odd reaction to the skeleton, his reluctance to pursue any further investigation. Now that their relationship had changed, she wondered if she should do this.

"I thought it might be safer here."

"Safer?" Dixie focused her attention on Winnie. "What are you trying to tell me?"

Winnie frowned. "I don't know for sure. If I were, I'd go to the sheriff. I'd rather work on the skull away from the camp, that's all. It's just... I have this feeling..."

"Not you, too! Hal's crawling with them. He and his mother. *Feelings* seem to hang in the air here," Dixie said. "I tell you, I've never been involved with anyone so..."

"Involved?" Winnie's eyebrows went up.

"Let's see the skull," Dixie said, changing the subject. "Come on. We can set up a work area in one of the back rooms."

"That's more like it." Winnie rose, cradling the sack. "I'm dying to meet our friend, here."

"Let's get started, then." Dixie led the way down the hall to an unused room in the clinic. On the way, she told Fran where they were going to be, but not what they were going to do, thinking that the fewer people who knew about the reconstruction, the better.

While the work of reconstructing the skull began, Hal Blane sat at his desk in the attic of his house and thought about Dixie Sheldon.

He'd awakened a few hours earlier in her bed, his body still aching for her and his senses still filled with her. The bed smelled of their lovemaking.

He took a very long, very cold shower, then dressed.

The house seemed too quiet and empty without her, so he picked up his guitar and went home to another quiet, empty house. Fortunately, his mother was out, probably shopping, so he didn't have to act like a teenager and explain where he'd been the night before. He hoped, ridiculous as the hope was, that she hadn't noticed his absence. He didn't want to lie to his mother, nor did he want to tell her he had spent the night with Dixie. That might disturb the good relationship the two women had. Hal smiled wryly to himself. He was beginning to understand Dixie's problem with conflicts of interest.

Artie was out, too, but on his desk, Hal saw a note from his son. "Dad, we need to talk," it read.

Well, Hal agreed. But what they had to talk about would fill a book. He set the note aside.

Speaking of books...

As he had done for so many years, during so many personal situations and crises, Hal put his worries and thoughts aside and reached for his work.

Not police work. Research work. Research into the past.

Hours later, his mother knocked on the attic door. "Hal, are you home?" she called. "Are you in there?"

Hal was startled. He had fallen into a doze with his head on the desk. Dreams and images rushed around in his mind as he woke. Riders on horseback, thundering through a draw, up a hill...

To the cliff where the body was found. A gunshot...

Fear, pain, death...

Love...

Dixie...

Love as he had only imagined it could be...

Thunder...

"Hal!" *Knock, knock, knock.* "Are you all right?"

"Uh, yeah." He shook his head and stood up. "What is it, Ma?" He opened the door. "You okay?"

Hattie smiled up at him. "I'm just as right as rain, dear. Where were you last night? Did you hear the storm? Wasn't it unusual for this time of year?"

Hal ran his hand over his hair.

"Well, never mind that," his mother said, still smiling. "You have a visitor."

Hal's heart started to pound faster. "Who?" He ran his hand over his hair again.

"Oh, it's not her," Hattie said. "It's Reed Turner."

"Reed?" A wave of disappointment was followed by the startled realization that his mother had known who he'd wanted it to be. "What's his problem?"

"No problem, Sheriff." Reed Turner appeared at the top of the stairs. His round face was almost gleaming with eagerness. "Just wanted to chat a bit about that skeleton you found up on the tableland the other day."

"I didn't find it." Hal stiffened. "Nothing to talk about, anyway. It's just some old bones."

"Hal, you promised me you'd do something about it," Hattie whispered. "You promised! Come on. Listen to Reed," she said in a normal tone. "You might find what he has to say interesting."

"Well . . ."

"Reed, you go on in," Hattie said. "I'll bring you boys some coffee and cookies." She gave her son a hard look.

Hal gave in. "All right, Reed," he said. "I'll hear you out, as long as it doesn't take much time."

Reed smiled. "Time's what this is all about," he said.

"I'm listening."

When Reed Turner had settled himself on the old sofa in the attic office, he spoke. "I understand you and I have a few things in common, Sheriff," he said.

"That so?" Hal sat behind his desk, resting his forearms on the papers and old books scattered on the top.

"Indeed it is." Reed picked an invisible piece of lint off his shirtsleeve. "We are both amateur historians of this region."

Hal sat still.

"And we are both interested in a particular part of the past."

Hal picked up a pencil and started tapping it on the desk.

"The part where your great-grandfather..."

"Mr. Turner," Hal interrupted. "I have no interest..."

"Don't give me that, son." The old man smiled. "I've been watching you ever since we moved here. You live and breathe your family's past. I know you have managed to get yourself access to government documents and—" he regarded the messy desk, the old computer and pile of disks meaningfully "—things. I expect this study is a treasure trove of historical information."

Hal put the pencil down and sat back, one elbow resting on the arm of his chair, his chin and mouth partly covered by his hand. "Is that so? Well, what of it? I have a right to look at what I can legally get hold of, don't I? He was my ancestor."

"Yes, you do. And yes, he was." Turner sat forward, his hands clasped. "But *why* are you looking into the past? That's the interesting question, isn't it?"

"And what's your answer?"

"Gold, sir. Gold."

Hal raised his eyebrows.

Turner's smile was conspiratorial. "Don't tell me you haven't considered it, Sheriff. The gold your ancestor stole? Why, it would still be a fortune to a man like yourself."

"Mr. Turner, get out of my house." Hal didn't move.

"Oh, don't go high-and-mighty on me, Sheriff. You may wear a badge and carry a gun, but I'm too old to be either impressed or scared."

"Is that so?"

"Yes, it is." Turner licked his lips. "Now, if I've given offence, I sincerely apologize. I'm an old man, and as my wife never fails to tell me, I lack diplomatic skills. But I do not want this opportunity to pass by. As I say, I *am* old."

"You want to spend your last years in luxury on the gold my great-grandfather stole?"

"You misunderstand." Turner rose and started pacing around the small room. "I have absolutely no interest in the gold. Just the history."

"Really?"

Turner stopped and smiled. "You are a cynical young man, aren't you?"

Hal shrugged.

"Well, I suppose you're entitled. Life hasn't been all that easy for you, has it?"

Hal tensed. "What do you know about my life?"

Turner sat back down. "More than I suppose I should, actually. You see, the Kedricks have been a hobby of mine for decades. During my years down in Denver, I uncovered a number of enthralling details about your people, Sheriff Blane." He paused. "Especially your great-grandfather. A fascinating man. Are you aware that before he turned outlaw, he actually worked for the U.S. Treasury Department?"

Hal picked up the pencil again. That was something he hadn't known for sure. Only suspected from fragments of letters and documents. Perhaps Turner did have information he needed. And it might just be worth the potential cost. "What's your price, Turner?" he asked.

The old man sat back and smiled triumphantly. "I want access to your material, Sheriff. Unlimited access. Between what you know and what I know, I bet we can find out the truth."

Hal shook his head. "I'm not ready to share. Frankly, this is too personal."

Turner scowled, then smiled again. "Well, think about it, sir. Because I believe you need me."

"Maybe I do." Hal stood up. "But that's my decision. Thanks for stopping by, Mr. Turner. I'll be in touch."

"HASTINGS IS as close to an anthropologist as we've got out there at the dig," Winnie explained. She set another small wooden peg in place on the plaster copy of the skull. "He gave me a crash course in how to do this."

"Nice of him." Dixie edged around the table and set two pegs. "Didn't he want to help us outright?"

"I asked, but he said no. It was our baby, and he had other fish to fry."

"Oh." Dixie stifled a yawn. The night before was catching up to her, in spite of her fascination with the reconstruction process. "Too bad. I like Hastings."

Winnie smiled. "I guess you must like someone else a whole lot better, though. Sheriff keep you up all night?"

Dixie blushed. "Something like that."

"None of my business, of course."

"Right."

They continued to banter and chat while they worked on the skull. Winnie had explained that once they had established the race and age of the victim, it was just a matter of placing layers of soft clay to the form where muscles would have been. "Then we paint skin, add eyes and hair and, *voilà,* the past is visible."

Dixie had set out an anatomy book, and they traced tendons, major blood vessels and nerve patterns as they would have laid on and between muscles. They were so absorbed in their work that Fran had to knock twice at the door before Dixie noticed her.

"You have a visitor," the nurse said, a smile on her face. "He doesn't have an appointment, but I think you'll want to see him."

"Hal?" Dixie set down a handful of clay, her heart beating faster.

"No," said Artie Blane. He stood behind Fran. "It's not Dad. It's just me."

"Come in, Artie," Dixie said, nodding an okay to Fran. "Have you met Dr. Nash, yet?"

"No." Artie stepped into the room, his wide-eyed gaze on the half-reconstructed skull. "What's that?" He came closer, his fascination obvious.

Dixie explained. Twenty minutes later, the teenager was happily engaged in helping with the project. He had a good feel for the clay and a good grasp of anatomy. In no time they were at a point where Winnie called a halt.

"I want to let it rest a few days before I paint on skin," she said. "Let the clay do what tissue really does—settle in onto the bone."

"Is this going to look like the guy really did?" Artie asked. "Really?"

"As close as we can get without going back in time and taking a picture," Winnie declared. "Of course, I'll have to add hair and eyes and make the skin weathered and lined, like it would be for a man his age who lived outdoors a hundred years ago."

"They didn't have sunscreen," Dixie said. "He'd have gotten burned a lot all of his life even if he didn't work outdoors."

"Outdoors?" Artie repeated. "How can you know?"

"We can't for certain," Winnie said. "But his bones are dense, indicating hard physical work for many years. It's doubtful we're looking at a clerk or a schoolteacher." She regarded the half-finished head.

"This is great," Artie enthused. "To be able to bring someone back like this."

"You're good at it," Dixie said.

Artie blushed and grinned. "Thanks."

"You are good," Winnie added. "How about coming out to the dig sometime and seeing how we work on dinosaurs."

"You mean it?"

"I sure do. How about now? I'm heading back in a few minutes. One of the students can drive you home later."

Artie looked undecided. "I need to talk to Dr. Sheldon."

"I still have some personal errands to run," Winnie said. "How about if I check back here when I'm done?"

It was agreed.

Dixie took Artie to her office and shut the door. He settled into a chair, again reminding her of his father. She sat down at the desk. "Okay, Artie," she said. "Is this about your grandmother?"

"Partly." He shifted position in the chair. "And partly about my dad."

Dixie sat back.

"He's been acting real funny lately."

"Funny?"

"Yeah." Artie picked at a thread on his shirtsleeve. "Like something's wrong, and he doesn't want me knowing."

"Have you talked to him about this?"

"No." The boy's gaze wandered around the room. "Can you?"

"No." He looked directly at her. "We don't talk."

"I see." Dixie put her hands on the desk. "Artie, do you want to come here and talk to me like your grandma does?"

He picked the thread off, balled it in his fingers and tossed it. "I guess so." He frowned. "But you can't tell Dad."

"I wouldn't unless you said it was all right. But if you really have a problem, your father ought to know about it. In fact, if you do need serious treatment, I will have to tell him. It's the law."

"There's nothing wrong with me!"

"You just want to talk?"

"Uh-huh. Grandma says you make a good listener. She feels better."

"I'm glad." Dixie felt trapped. She was this boy's father's lover. If he found that out, would he trust her? Should she confess before listening to his confidences?

So much for professional objectivity and distance.

"Artie, before we decide about this, there's something you should—"

He waved his hand. "If it's about you and Dad, forget it. I already know."

"Know what?"

The boy shrugged. "You're seeing him. He didn't come home last night. No mystery where he was."

"You assume he was with me?"

"Wasn't he?"

"Yes." Dixie's discomfort with the situation was deepening, but she could see no clear way out. "Do you mind that he was?" she asked.

Artie looked away. "Guess not. Otherwise I wouldn't be here."

"Fair enough." She almost smiled, thinking how much he sounded like his father. "All right. Let's talk about your grandmother. I think she's much better, already."

Artie straightened up. "Me, too. She hasn't laughed and smiled to herself in a long time. She's doing that now."

"How does that make you feel?"

The boy smiled. It was the first real smile she'd seen on his face, and he looked much less like his dad and more like Hattie for a moment. "Great," he said. Then he so-bered. "But it's what I think she's smiling about that's got me worried. Her and Dad, both."

"Your father's smiling and laughing to himself?"

"No. He grumbles around like always. But he's in the clouds even more than before. And it ain't because of you and him."

"How do you...?"

"I know. Because he got worse on Sunday. My room's right next to his, and Sunday night, he had this night-mare."

"A bad dream? Does he have them often?" He'd slept like a baby in *her* bed.

"Nope. Oh, he snores now and then, but nothing much. This was a real corker, though! He was screaming and yelling and hollering for old Miss Esther and for you." Artie shook his head. "Scared me."

"Did you mention it to him?"

"The next morning. He like to took my head off."

"I see."

"Now, seeing that you two are getting close and all, I thought I'd talk to you about it." The boy's face grew troubled. "I don't want to lose my grandma, Dr. Shel-don. But I *really* don't want to lose my dad. Is he going crazy?"

Dixie remembered Saturday night. "No, Artie. But you're right to be concerned. There are some strange things going on. What do you know about Miss Esther?"

He shrugged, smiled. "She's a nice old lady. Talks to birds and trees and such. Kinda crazy, I guess."

"Your father took me to meet her Saturday night."

"Oh, he did?"

"Yes. And afterward he was acting...peculiar, just like you said. Then, we got the call from the dinosaur dig that—"

He was interrupted by a knock and Fran opened the door a few inches. "Another visitor, Doctor," she said. "I, um, explained you were in a confidential consultation. Um, *he* said he'd wait." The door shut.

"My dad!" Artie stood up. "Is there a back way out of here?"

"Why would you...?"

"If he thinks I've been talking to you about him, he'll nail my hide to the wall. I gotta go!"

Dixie pointed. "Well, there's the window, but I still think you ought to..."

Artie Blane was out the window before she could finish the sentence. *Like father, like son.* With difficulty she resisted the urge to laugh about it. The situation might be far from laughable, she reminded herself. If Artie was that concerned, there must be something to Hal's moodiness and nightmares.

And it was up to her to do something about that. She might be his lover, but she could also be his healer.

CHAPTER ELEVEN

ARTIE BLANE slithered out of the window and hurried around to the back of the clinic, praying that his father hadn't seen him and would not find out that he'd been talking. His old man might be interested in the pretty doctor, but he would definitely hate knowing his kid had blabbed to her.

Still, Artie was glad he had done it. For one thing, it was a load off, just telling someone else. She was a nice person. She'd listened to him.

"Artie?"

He stopped, ready to run again. But it was only the dinosaur lady, Dr. Nash. "Hi," he called. "I was coming to find you."

"I thought you'd still be with Dixie," Winnie Nash said, crossing the street. Her arms were filled with packages. "I was going to give our aged friend in there one last pat before..."

"Here." Artie took some packages from her. "The doctor's kind of busy right now. Why don't we go on?"

"Well, I..." Winnie hesitated. "Okay," she said. "Let's go."

Artie's relief at avoiding his father made him talkative. The entire ride out to the dig he chattered on, letting Winnie Nash in on matters he had kept carefully secret from other adults.

"I'd give a lot to do that. I hate it here," he confided when he found out she had traveled all over the world. "Nothing ever happens here. It's boring."

"Well, why don't you get a job, or something? Make money so you can go to school and travel."

"I'm only fifteen. Nobody will hire me."

"Maybe we will. We can always use extra hands. Especially ones as good as yours."

"You mean that?"

"I do. I was impressed with the way you worked on the skull."

"Thanks. It was kind of creepy, but I liked doing it. Sure is an ugly face, so far. Who's is it, do you think?"

Winnie glanced over at the boy. "I have no idea. But it sounds to me like you might."

Artie was silent for a while, then ventured, "You know about my mom's grandfather?"

"A little. Wasn't he some kind of . . . ?"

"Outlaw. Yeah. And I think maybe that guy was somebody he killed to keep the gold they stole."

"Really? You don't have a very high opinion of your ancestor."

"Nobody does." He lapsed into sullen silence again.

Winnie drove on to the campsite without making any effort to create conversation. Once there, Artie regained his good temper. Winnie escorted him around, briefly, then introduced him to Wayne Sussex, the graduate student responsible for directing the unskilled and volunteer workers. "He's got a good touch, Wayne," she advised. "Delicate and careful. Don't waste him on hauling wheelbarrows full of stones and junk."

"Okay, Dr. Nash." Wayne shook hands with Artie. "We'll figure out something important for this guy to do. Don't worry."

Artie felt a little less sure of himself, faced with the reality of work and responsibility, but covered up his emotions as best he could. This Wayne guy wasn't so big, but he had real wide shoulders, rough hands and a great beard. The kind of beard Artie would have liked to have, if he could've grown one. Artie decided he might like Wayne, if things went okay.

"Come on, kid." Wayne clapped him on the back. "Let's go see what we can find for you to do."

Artie trotted along beside the grad student. "I'd really like to see where you found that old skeleton first," he said. "Could I?"

"Sure," Wayne replied. He veered toward the cliff. "In fact, Hastings's down there right now, fussing around in the dirt. Maybe he could use a little help."

"Great."

They made their way to the cliff edge and down the sloped side to the ledge. Artie glanced into the valley and a mild vertigo spun his brain. He reached for the solid earth of the cliffside and put his hands on rock and dirt. Several small stones came loose and rattled on the path. "Sorry," Artie muttered. "Got dizzy."

Wayne turned and smiled at him. "Don't worry," he said. "Everybody gets the willies looking down here. Don't know why." He turned back around and started walking along the ledge.

"Maybe it's haunted," Artie muttered, following, taking careful steps. Every nerve was jumping, and he wondered how it must have been for his father to come here in the dead of night.

"Huh?"

"Nothing."

They rounded the outcrop and came to the cut where the ledge was wide and the grave had been found. Artie felt dizzy again, but this time, he had no wall to reach for. He steadied himself and stared at the scene. Two men, both older than Wayne, squatted by the long depression in the ground. One had long hair in a ponytail and the other, the older one, had a better beard than Wayne. They looked up, startled, when Wayne spoke.

"Brought a new worker down to see the grave," he said, indicating Artie. "He's—"

"Get the hell out of here, Sussex," the young one with the ponytail snarled. "We don't want amateurs tromping around, destroying evidence."

"Evidence of what?" Artie asked, emboldened by the other's rudeness. "What's going on?"

"Wayne, take the kid and leave," the bearded man said, his tone calm and reasonable. No anger in it. "This is still an exploration site. Can't have just anyone down here, Wayne. You know that."

"Sorry, sir." Wayne backed up, drawing Artie with him. "Just curious. I didn't realize it was an official site." He pulled Artie toward the cliff. "Come on, kid," he said, whispering. "Boss man says go, we go."

Reluctantly, Artie obeyed. He made the return journey with no difficulty, no recurrence of the dizziness. When they reached the top and the flat tableland, he asked, "How come they're working down there? I thought the sheriff..." He let the sentence go unfinished.

Wayne looked a little confused about it, himself. "I know. I thought so, too. But I guess the sheriff isn't interested on account of the body being so old. So Hastings and Dr. Hayden are doing a little more work." He grinned. "Anyway, I've got things that are really old. Want to see an icthyosaur?"

"Sure. What's that?"

"Come on, I'll show you. Used to be an ocean here, you know."

"Yeah. I guess I knew that. When I was little, sometimes I found rocks with shells in them."

"See? You're already a paleontologist." Wayne laughed.

Artie ran his hand over his hair. Over to the left, beyond the location of the skeleton's grave, but along the same part of the tableland edge, he saw some people digging. "What's going on over there?" he asked.

Wayne looked and nodded. "Actually, that might be a good place to put you for a start," he said. "They're roughing out a trench up there."

"Roughing out?"

"Digging to see what shows up," Wayne explained. "If and when they come across an indication there's something workable in the area, then the pros go to it and start taking earth out one millimeter at a time."

"Oh." Artie was impressed.

"But the initial trench is dug with small shovels. Want to try?"

"Sure." Besides, Artie reasoned, working there would give him a perfect excuse to look around once in a while.

And if he looked around the right way, he'd be able to see what Ponytail and Beard were up to.

Somehow, that seemed important. He might be just a kid, but he was the sheriff's kid, and darn it, he did know when somebody was up to something. Those two sure were.

HAL STRODE into Dixie's office with a smile on his face and a bunch of daisies in his hand. "Afternoon, pretty lady," he said, removing his Stetson, shutting the door and going over to kiss her. It was a friendly kiss, suitable for a meeting in her office, but with definite undertones of last night's passion. "You're busy today." He handed her the flowers. "Not roses, but the store was all out."

"I'm not really too busy," Dixie admitted, taking the bouquet of daisies. "And I don't care if they're wildflowers. It's the thought that counts. And as for what I've been doing, well, Winnie was here for a while, then . . ."

"Yeah, I saw her walking over by the hardware store." Hal put his hat on the desk and sat down in the chair his son had just vacated. "You two visiting or something?"

"Yes." She looked away from him, thinking she ought to tell him about the skull. Now that their relationship was intimate, she wanted be as honest as possible. But something held her back from speaking.

"What's the matter, Dixie?"

"Nothing. Why should anything be the matter?"

"You seem kind of . . . tense or . . ."

"Hal." She got up and went over to him. "I'm not tense. Nothing's the matter. I'm fine. Last night was wonderful, as you darn well know. What's the matter with you? Got second thoughts about what we did?" She put her hands on his shoulders and looked directly into his eyes.

"No," he said.

She believed him.

"Good." She settled down on his lap. "Now that we have that out of the way . . ." She started to give him another kiss, one that was not suitable for the office.

Hal pulled back. "I had a visitor this afternoon," he said. "What did you tell Reed Turner about the skeleton?"

Dixie thought for a second. "Not much. Just that it was found, and . . ." She looked carefully at her lover's face. "Why?"

He put his arms around her waist. "He came to see me earlier. He thinks the remains are connected to my family's dark past."

"He said he was an amateur historian. What was your impression?"

"Possibly he's just that. But I didn't like the way he kept pushing to see my family records." Hal's gaze focused on some point far off, while his hands moved on her back. "I think I might just run a check on him. He seems harmless, but a little curiosity can go a long way in changing folks' normal behavior."

"I can ask my father if he's heard about him." Dixie put her finger on his chin. "Meanwhile..."

"Yeah," he said softly, seductively.

They kissed. Lips moving tenderly, then more eagerly.

The fire began slowly. Built gradually, and—

Fran knocked on the office door.

Dixie jumped up. "What is it?" she asked, smoothing down her white coat and dress. She glanced at Hal. He was relaxed, his hands behind his head, leaning back, grinning. She gave him a mock glare, then went to the door and opened it. "An emergency?"

Fran looked embarrassed. "I don't think so. Call for the sheriff, though. Line two."

Hal got up. "I forgot to carry my pager," he said, genuinely annoyed at himself. "I wonder how dispatch knew to call here..." He went to the desk and picked up the phone and began to speak softly into the receiver.

"Gosh," Fran said under her breath, but with a smile at Dixie. "I can't imagine why they thought he'd be here."

Dixie stepped out into the hall and shut the door to give Hal some privacy. "We've had one date, Fran," she said, attempting to redirect the nurse's suspicions. "That doesn't mean—"

"Dixie," Fran said, slipping into the familiar form of addressing her boss. "Come on. Everybody in town knows he was at your place late last night."

"Oh." Dixie leaned against the wall. She remembered the car that had driven by and caught the two of them in the beam of its headlights.

"Is that a problem? Really?"

"I guess not." Dixie smiled. "And I guess it was foolish to think we could keep any secrets around here for more than a minute. Are folks scandalized?"

"Oh my, no." Fran looked away. "In fact, there's serious speculation that you two will settle down and that means you won't leave."

"Wrong. No matter what happens between us, I can't give up my plans."

"The people here like you."

"And I like them, but..."

Hal opened the office door. "Got to go, ladies. Little problem down the street needs my attention." He settled his hat on his head. "Dixie, I'll catch up with you later." His eyes spoke a promise.

Dixie felt herself blush. "Okay," she said. She watched as he strode out of the clinic, his tall frame radiating strength and confidence.

"That is a man," Fran commented. "You won't be finding his like out in California."

"I'm not looking. What's happened between us just...happened. It doesn't mean a thing for the long term. It can't."

"You sure about that?"

"Yes."

"Then, off the record and just between us girls, you are a damn fool, Dixie Sheldon."

DIXIE CONSIDERED this comment later on, toward evening, as she drove back into the high country woods, retracing their route of last Saturday night to the Fawcetts' restaurant. Her Suburban was back in fine running condition, thanks to the mechanic, Al Pringle, and she felt confident about taking the trip. She didn't even tell Fran she was headed out of town.

She wasn't going to eat at the restaurant. She was on her way to see Miss Esther.

She had a few questions for the old woman. And maybe, a few answers.

By the time she hit the county road, it was very dark. No moon lit the road, and the deer and other wildlife seemed to take that as an invitation to stroll down the centerline. Dixie drove slowly, swerving to avoid animals and thinking to herself that it would probably be easier to make this journey on horseback. At least horses didn't present a threat to bunnies and deer like the tank she was driving!

When she reached the restaurant parking lot, she saw the place was closed for the evening. There were no lights on, so she assumed the Fawcetts were out; it was too early for bedtime. She parked, left a note on her windshield and started up the trail toward the old woman's cabin.

It wasn't nearly as nice as walking with Hal. In fact, after a few minutes, it got scary. Dixie carried a powerful flashlight, but the darkness seemed to leech away the light, leaving her in a tunnel of grayness. She remembered some of the warnings about Miss Esther, and for a few moments, she entertained the notion that the old woman was using the night to discourage her.

Ridiculous! She aimed the light straight ahead and kept on walking.

Finally, she reached the clearing. The cabin was there, light glowing out of the windows, but the door was shut.

The ponies weren't in the corral. Dixie stood there, looking at the place, wishing she knew just what she should do.

Knock? Just go up and knock? What if the old woman was resting?

Or working?

A thousand fairy tales came to mind. What happened when the innocent stranger knocked on the witch's door?

Where was the damn crow when she needed him? Was he the official doorbell?

"Hello, young doctor," Miss Esther said, her voice disembodied and coming from a point right behind Dixie's right shoulder. A crow called raucously from the top of a pine tree.

Dixie yelped and jumped. She shone the light around, trying to locate the speaker.

"Come to see me, have you?" The old woman walked slowly into the clearing. Both ponies ambled behind her, like two large dogs. She carried a large basket filled with grasses, leaves, flowers and miscellaneous vegetation. "And without your fine man."

"H-hello," Dixie stammered. "I'm sorry I didn't let you know I was coming, but..."

"And how would you have done that, tell me?" Miss Esther chuckled. "Come on, child," she said. "The night's a'wasting. We have lots to do." She moved toward the cabin, the ponies right behind her.

Dixie followed. The beam from her flashlight danced along on the ground.

"Shut that thing off," Miss Esther commanded. "It ain't natural."

Dixie obeyed. Esther opened the corral gate and let her animals in for the night. Then she led Dixie into her home.

The inside of the cabin was just as Dixie remembered, except that without Hal to fill space, it seemed larger. Miss

Esther set the basket down on the table and gestured impatiently toward the dying fire. "Get it going, girl," she said. "We have things to brew."

"Um." Dixie set down her bag and light. "Where's the wood?"

"Woodpile." Esther started sorting plants on the table.

"Woodpile," Dixie repeated under her breath. "That's outside?"

Esther said nothing.

Dixie went out into the night. The wood was stacked against the right side of the cabin. She ignored the possibility of insects and gathered up an armload, thankful that she had changed into an old shirt and jeans to make this trip. She carried the logs inside and dumped them on the hearth. Esther was back in the shadows, messing with the plants and muttering to herself.

Dixie moved the hearth screen and set three logs in place on the rough andirons. Taking the ancient leather bellows from a hook beside the fireplace, she aimed air at the glowing coals until the logs started to smolder, then caught. Flames danced. Dixie sat back on her heels and watched.

"Good fire," Esther said, coming up beside her. "You do know the wood and the flame, don't you."

Dixie smiled. "I love a good fire at night. Especially in the winter when the snow's falling. Makes me feel safe."

Esther nodded. "Fire can save." She squatted in front of the hearth. "Fire can kill, too."

The two of them stared at the flames.

After a while, Esther eased herself into a standing position and went over to the table. She took a plant and handed it to Dixie. "What's this and what's it used for?" she asked.

Dixie took the offered plant. It was long-stemmed and white-flowered and it smelled like old sweat socks. "Easy," she said, pleased with herself. "Valarian. Used for calming nerves. In strong doses, it's a sedative."

"And this?"

Dixie examined a thick-leaved plant with no odor and small purple flowers. "I have no idea," she replied. "Tell me, please."

Esther smiled, the expression lifting the hundreds of tiny lines on her brown face. "Good," she said softly. "You're proud and you're honest and you're willing to admit what you don't know. Now we can get to work."

Dixie stood up, too. "Actually, I didn't come here to learn tonight," she said. "At least not about plants and things like that."

"And what did you come for?"

"Hal."

The old woman regarded Dixie for a long, searching moment. Then she smiled, put down the herbs she held and went over to sit in her rocking chair by the fire. "I see another fire's burning your ambition out of you, child. It's a good fire, too. Burning the dross and leaving the pure gold." She gestured. "Sit. We'll talk tonight. Do the learning another time."

Dixie returned to her place on the hearth. "I want to know what you know about Hal's family," she said. "And why he acted so strange after we left here Saturday night. And why..."

"Hush." Esther held up one thin hand. "Only one thing right now." She reached for her quilt and settled back in the rocker. "Forces of time and love are working on young Harold Kedrick Blane, and that's a fact. Any man would act strange under such pressure."

"Time?" The love part she could understand. But time? "What's time got to do with him?"

"Time's got us all. You know that. Cradle to grave, it rules our lives." Esther rocked. "Sometimes even beyond the grave."

Dixie waited. The old woman rocked, eyes closed.

"Seems I remember…," she said finally. "No, that ain't right. I guess I don't know so much after all…" Her voice trailed off, and she looked like she was going to sleep.

"What about the body?" Dixie asked. "What does that have to do with Hal?"

The old eyes opened. "Body? What body?"

"The one they found out on the tableland," Dixie said. "Just a skeleton, actually. Saturday. After we left you, we…" She jumped up. "Miss Esther, are you okay?"

The old woman's brown skin had turned a dirty gray and her body seemed to shrink into itself. She held up both hands, and they shook like small leaves in a hurricane. She tried to speak, but no words came out of her mouth. Just gasps for air. The thin lips began to look bluish in color.

Dixie didn't hesitate. She gathered the frail old body up, quilt and all and started to carry Esther out of the cabin. She had little hope of getting to her Suburban and her medical supplies in time, but she had to try!

She reached the edge of the clearing. The darkness of the forest waited. She slowed her pace.

"Go back."

Dixie stopped. A crow had landed on a pine tree branch almost at eye level with her. It had only cawed, loudly, but she heard the words clearly.

Esther spoke. "Go back, child." Her voice was thin and wheezy, but she no longer gasped for breath. "I was shocked," the woman said. "There's healing herbs in the cabin. Take me back, and I'll tell you what to do."

"No! I can't, Esther. I'm a medical doctor. Not a wise woman. I can't trust totally in herbs. You've probably had a mild heart attack."

Esther struggled so violently, Dixie was forced to release her. The old woman staggered, then regained her balance and stood on her own. "I had no such thing," she cried out. "Now, if you wish to be my student, you must obey me, Dixie Sheldon."

"I want to be your student, Esther, but I will not risk your life." Dixie took hold of the old woman's shoulders. "Listen to me, please. I frightened you with the news about the find. Now, let me take you into town and at least check you out on the ECG machine."

Esther reached up and put her hands on Dixie's forearms. "You didn't frighten me," she said. "I frightened myself. And your machine can't tell you anything *I* can't tell you. My heart did do a step or two of the death dance, but it's fine now. Just need to remind it who's in charge of this bag of bones, that's all." She smiled. "Have some faith in me, young'n."

Dixie hesitated. "I don't want to be responsible for your death," she said. "I want—"

"Then let's go back to my home," Esther said, taking her arm. "Help me. I am well, but I am weak."

The grip on her arm was so firm, Dixie was inclined to deny even the claim of weakness. Clearly, the crisis, whatever it had been, was past. "All right," she said. "But in return, will you promise to let me take you into town and give you a complete physical later?"

Esther nodded. "Of course. Later," she said, but she didn't look Dixie in the eye.

They walked slowly back to the cabin.

Once inside, Dixie made Esther comfortable on her bed and fixed a tea according to the old healer's specific instructions. As she prepared the brew, she learned. Only the tips of this plant, only roots of that, seeds of the other, but crushed, not ground. Water taken from a mountain stream. Boiled long enough to destroy active parasites and bacteria. Steeping done in an earthen pot.

The resulting brew smelled like steaming garbage, but Esther gulped it greedily enough and pronounced it a proper tea. Dixie was thankful her patient chose to drink it all herself. She was not inclined to try her own medicine this time!

After an hour, Esther seemed back to normal. Energetic, almost. She stayed on the bed, but sat propped up by the quilt and several ancient feather pillows. "Now," she said. "You must tell me all about the grave. Who found it, exactly where and what is being done."

"I don't think much is going to be done," Dixie told her. "After all, the body's been there for a century. Hal wasn't going to do anything, but..."

Esther's eyes closed momentarily. "But he has to, doesn't he? You see? The dead can act through the living, when they choose."

"I don't understand."

"Tell me exactly what happened after you two left me. How he behaved before and after he found out about the dead man."

"I didn't say it was a man."

"But it was. I know. Tell me."

Dixie did, including the episode when Hal had seemed to become another person. She spoke plainly and honestly. "I thought you'd drugged him," she said.

"I gave him nothing that would have made him violent or confused." Esther shook her gray head. "This is more than my poor understanding can get, child. I told you I'm not magic. Just old."

"How old?" Dixie asked.

"Older than you think." Esther smiled. "I got no records, though. When I was born, there wasn't a government law that made you keep track of young'ns."

"No state government?" Dixie didn't believe her. That would make the old woman at least a hundred years old. "Or no county..."

Esther chuckled, her good humor and strength obviously back. She swung her legs over the side of the bed. "No nothing, girl," she said. "When I breathed on this land first, your grandmomma wasn't born yet." She stood up and went over to the table. "'Course, I can't prove it, so it don't matter. Come on. Let's sort through this mess. We can talk while we do it. Talking helps me think, sometimes."

They spent the next few hours working with the herbs, grasses and flowers Esther had gathered that evening. Dixie's brain became a sponge, absorbing all the information the old woman could give her. Thoughts of Hal and mysteries and dead men vanished in the light of the knowledge she was getting.

This was what she'd come to Seaside for!

This, not Hal. This was her future....

Of course, it was! She pushed aside the tendrils of doubt, the feelings of guilt and love, the questions about emotions, and concentrated on wisdom.

CHAPTER TWELVE

SHERIFF HAL BLANE was angry. Here it was, five o'clock in the morning and still no sign of Dixie. He was mad, clean through.

And worried. Not sure which emotion was stronger, either.

He sat in his Jeep in front of her house, nursing his ego, bruises and patience. He'd been waiting only a few hours, but it felt longer. Much longer. He'd gone to sleep at home, after he'd learned from Fran that Dixie had gone out of town for the evening. But around two a.m., he'd wakened, longing for her and mildly jealous of the fact that she'd take off for parts unknown without him. Or at least without telling him where she was going to be.

Not that she'd have been able to reach him earlier that evening. The call that had taken him away from her that afternoon had led to lengthy negotiations and eventually a violent confrontation in Shift's Bar with George Preston. The cowboy had spent the day getting drunk enough to fight with anyone who challenged him, including Hal. By the time George was safely behind bars, Hal had a black eye, a bloody nose and knuckles that felt broken from decking George as a final solution to the problem.

At first, George had been willing to talk, happy, in fact, to have an audience for his drunken ravings. He hated everyone and everything and wanted everybody to know it. Hal had used up all his patience and skill at diplomatic conversation. And George had wearied of talk after a time and had gone for Hal with a knife and broken bottle.

Hal simply stepped back, then let the crazy cowboy have it with a right to the jaw.

He didn't like to use violence, but he'd had to. And to be honest, he reflected, finally knocking George to the floor of Shift's place had felt damn good. George was a troublemaker of the worst kind—cowardly and relentless. He drank to get up his courage and he did it on a regular basis. Although he'd escaped this time with nothing more than a sore jaw and head, he was a potential victim, in spite of his alcoholic bravado. Eventually, he'd get himself into a scrape that even Dr. Dixie Sheldon wouldn't be able to fix.

When Hal had last spoken to him in jail, George was full of venom and vowing vengeance on the sheriff and the world. Blaming everyone but himself and his drinking for his problems. He was trouble, waiting and looking to happen....

Hal adjusted his position on the seat. Where the hell was she? No one knew where she'd gone. No one knew when she'd be back. Fran Coble had patched up his minor injuries, and the nurse's professional attention had been all he'd needed. But not all he wanted.

He wanted Dixie. He wanted her soft, strong, sure hands on him, soothing and exciting him. He wanted to be able to talk to her about his frustration with men like George and bartenders like Benny Shift who fed them lousy whiskey until they were unable to control themselves.

He wanted...

Her.

Where the hell was she?

The rising sun's rays burned into the Jeep, promising a hot August day. Hal shut his eyes, rubbing them and feeling the grittiness of lack of sleep. He yawned.

When he looked out again, Dixie was pulling her big Suburban into the driveway.

Hal bailed out of his Jeep, jammed his hat on his head and stalked up her walkway just as she reached the front door. His temper was about to boil over when she turned and gave him a smile that melted him down to the toes.

"Morning, Hal," she said. "I spent the night out at Miss Esther's place, and..." Her cheery look of welcome faded to one of alarm as she took in the bruises and black eye. "Oh, my goodness! Are you all right? What happened to you?"

So she'd been with Esther. Hal grinned. "Nothing much. I'm okay, really. Fran fixed me up."

Dixie fussed over him, anyway, making him come inside where she could examine him carefully. She treated him like a delicate creature who would break if touched roughly.

Hal loved it!

After checking his injuries and satisfying herself that Fran had, indeed, done a proper job on them, Dixie seated him in a chair at the kitchen table and proceeded to grill him about the cause of his wounds.

"Why did you have to get beat up, too?" she asked. "You didn't duck? Was George that quick with his fists?"

"No," Hal replied indignantly. "I just tried to take care of the situation without force until it was a little late."

Dixie studied his shiner. "I guess so." She got up and put two mugs of water in the microwave. "Does this happen to you often?"

"No." He didn't feel so terrific now. She wasn't acting like a lover. She was lecturing him...like a doctor.

"Want me to take out my gun and shoot him next time? No black eye that way."

"Of course I don't want that. I'm not trying to criticize the way you do your job." The microwave dinged. Dixie added coffee to the hot water. "Here, drink this. Did you sleep last night at all?"

"Some. Fran gave me a pain pill. I dozed off for a few hours." He rubbed the back of his neck. "Had some wild dreams."

"That happens with some medications." She sat down and reached for his hand. "Oh, Hal," she said, her voice full of compassion and tenderness. "I'm so sorry you're hurt."

"I wanted to see you," he said. "When I woke up, I wanted to be with you. I came over here and..."

"I was gone. I went to see Esther, and the night just got away from me."

"With Esther?"

Dixie described some of her time with the old woman, leaving out references to Esther's dramatic reaction to news about the body. "I can't believe what an incredible person she is," she added. "How old do you think she really is?"

"No idea."

"She says she doesn't know, either. But she thinks she's over a hundred."

Hal drank coffee. "I wouldn't be surprised."

She brushed her fingers over his palm. "I wouldn't be, either. Say, it's not time for me to go to the office, yet. How about you?" She gazed at him, staring directly into his eyes.

He felt heat race all through his body. "Thought you'd never ask," he said.

They stood, embraced, warmly at first and then pas-
sionately, and headed for her bedroom. Tired as they both
were, the loving was still deep, sincere and satisfying.

Later, after Hal had left and while she was showering in
preparation for the day, Dixie reflected that they had a
special magic together in bed that she'd only dreamed of
with a lover. Too bad she had to find it with a man who
could never share the kind of life she wanted.

FOR A WHILE, life sailed uneventfully along.

Dixie and Hal continued to meet when they could, to
talk and to make love. Once in a while, they were able to
get out of town and spend time together fishing or riding,
or just having a picnic out in the countryside.

During those times, they grew more comfortable with
each other and closer in spirit, as well as in mind and body.
Dixie could see this was happening, but continued to convince herself it didn't matter. She might like Hal a lot, but
she did not love him. Their affair was only an affair and
would not interfere with her plans for the future, either
emotionally or logically. Now was now. The future was yet
to be.

In any case, it was good to have such a friend who could
be such a lover, too.

They became even closer after Hal took his mother
down to Salt Lake to see the heart specialist, only to have
Dixie's original diagnosis confirmed: nothing was organically wrong with Hattie Blane. That increased his faith and
trust in her, and helped her lose some of the remaining defensiveness she had where his opinion of her professional
work was concerned. He even agreed to sit in on the
counseling sessions, soon, once Dixie and Hattie decided
it was time.

Artie had become very involved in his work out at the dig site. With his father's permission, he'd moved out there for the remainder of the summer. Hal figured having Artie busy and out from underfoot would be good for Hattie, and it was. Or at least, it seemed to be. Hattie gained strength and confidence by the day, and everyone in town began to comment on the changes in her.

Rumors began to circulate that Hal and Dixie were considering a permanent arrangement, and *that* was why his momma was so chipper these days. No one was able to confirm or deny this. However, the topic provided fuel for gossip around town and even into the county. Everyone agreed it would be great to have Doc Dixie, as she was now called, practice in Seaside for the rest of her professional life, and if it took marriage to the sheriff to accomplish that, so be it. They'd both done good work for the people of the community, and if they were happy together, they'd likely both stay on the job.

Though Hal was aware that folks were talking, he wisely kept that information to himself, thinking Dixie probably wouldn't appreciate the gossip.

Dixie, meanwhile, was living in a happy daze of romance, research and mystery. Any spare time that she didn't spend with Hal, she spent in the woods with Esther. The old woman was an incredible source of information, and she genuinely enjoyed sharing with Dixie, welcoming her whenever she was able to make the journey. Dixie's notes and knowledge of Esther's eclectic brand of folk medicine and wisdom grew to volume size quickly.

There was a side to Esther that Dixie sensed she'd never seen, which made her more determined than ever to discover all the old one's secrets. She was as hungry for that as she was for Hal's companionship and loving.

She believed, and continued to tell herself, that Hal was for now. Esther's material was for the future.

Winnie came into town when she was able to leave the dig site, and she and Dixie finally finished the head. Once, Artie came with Winnie and helped, but he was strangely quiet and found excuses not to show up the next time. Both women figured he was more interested in working with "the guys" than hanging around, doing tiny adjustments on the face of a man who had died a hundred years before.

But they enjoyed the project immensely. Dixie had never done anything like it, and found she had talent, particularly when it came to the final touches.

"What do you think?" Winnie asked, stepping back from the table. "A moustache or not?"

"Definitely." Dixie picked up some blond-brown hair they had scrounged from the beauty parlor down on Main Street. "All real men wore them back then." She applied hair to the upper lip.

"Why blond?" Winnie regarded the results.

Dixie shrugged. "I don't know. Just seems right. The skull type is consistent with Northern European or Anglo-Saxon, according to what Hastings told you. We decided the eyes were blue, didn't we? So, the hair's right. We may have a latter-day Viking here." She picked darker blond scraps and started on the eyebrows.

"He looks fierce and tough enough," agreed Winnie. "Okay. A blondie, he is."

They added lashes around the glass eyes and a full head of hair, as well as heavy whisker stubble, and then they stood back and admired their work. The head stared back at them.

"Serious kind of fella, isn't he?" Winnie commented. "Like he's got the burden of the world on his shoulders, or something."

Dixie looked at the face. "I don't think he led a happy life, do you?"

"Like I said—" Winnie crossed her arms "—he was a serious man. Tough, mean and serious."

Dixie thought of Hal, her own serious man. Tough, as well, but certainly not mean. No. He was the tenderest man she'd ever known. Tender, clever and surprisingly easy to be with as long as nothing was bothering him.

He had sent the bullet and bone samples down to the lab in Cheyenne and hadn't yet received a report. She wondered what he'd do when he saw the head.

For some reason, she wasn't sure she wanted to know.

However, they had to do something with this thing they'd made. It shouldn't just sit back here forever, buried as the body had been.

"Now what?" Winnie asked, echoing Dixie's thoughts. "Seems a shame to leave it here."

"I know, but I can hardly put it up front in the waiting room. Someone might think it's a bizarre idea for a hat stand."

"No." Winnie laughed. "But you ought to set it out somewhere and see what happens when folks get a look." She walked around the table. "He's a handsome man. You know that? Even if he does look like he's as likely to shoot you as look at you."

"*Was*. Was likely. And see what good that attitude did him?" Dixie hadn't been able to get into the mind-set Winnie seemed to carry around all the time. For the paleontologist, the dead were as interesting and worthy of attention as the living.

"You know what I mean." Winnie grinned, showing she was only teasing. "He looks like someone I know," she added. "But I can't think who."

Dixie sat down on a stool. "I've been thinking the same thing," she said. "It'll come to me, eventually."

"Maybe your mysterious Miss Esther knows him."

Dixie turned and stared at Winnie. "That is a wonderful idea!" she exclaimed. "At least she might have some idea who he could have been. Wait a minute." She got up and went back to her office, took a Polaroid camera from the bottom drawer of her desk and returned to the workroom.

"I keep this around in case I get a family violence situation," she explained, taking a picture of the head. "If you photograph injuries, then even if the victim refuses to press charges, you've got leverage against the guy." She took the photograph out and studied it as it formed. "Not bad," she said.

"Almost as good as the real thing," Winnie declared. "Now, take another and post it in the waiting room. You might find another old-timer who recognizes the face."

Dixie did.

But it wasn't an old-timer or Esther who recognized the long-dead visage first.

It was Hattie Blane.

On Tuesday morning, Hattie came in for her regular appointment. Dixie was busy with a minor emergency—patching up a small patient who had fallen out of a tree and scratched herself up on the rough bark. So Hattie sat down and waited for her turn.

Fran was at the desk, doing some paperwork and waiting for Dixie to summon her to help, if necessary. The mother of the injured child was also there, obviously feeling guilty for having allowed her daughter to get hurt. Although Dixie had already reassured her that the child wasn't badly hurt and that tree-climbing was a normal and healthy summertime activity, the woman continued to blame herself. Hattie recognized her as Tess Pringle, Al's wife.

"I just don't know what to do," Tess said, addressing Hattie as a new audience for her guilty tirade. "She won't listen. She won't behave. She—"

"She's a child," Hattie interrupted. "Is she your oldest?"

"No." Tess twisted her thin hands together. "We have three boys, too. Sissy's the baby."

"Maybe that's why she's so rambunctious," Hattie commented. "She's trying to be like the boys."

"Why should she want to do that?" Tess asked, genuinely mystified.

But Hattie didn't answer. Her attention was drawn to the bulletin board by Fran's desk.

Fran saw the scream coming. She had been listening to the conversation between the two women, hoping that Hattie would be able to talk some sense into Tess. She glanced up just as Hattie saw the Polaroid picture pinned to the bulletin board next to the reception desk.

Hattie's skin turned gray. Her mouth opened, her eyes widened.

She screamed.

Tess jumped up, screaming also, her hands pressed to her head. Hattie screamed again, weaker this time. Tess's next yowl almost brought the roof down.

Fran knocked over her chair in her haste to get around the desk to the two hysterical women. Dixie, her hands still in surgeon's gloves, white lab coat over her dress, came racing from the small surgery room. The little girl, Sissy

Pringle, fresh bandages on her face and arms, stood in the hallway, yelling at the top of her small lungs.

The screaming and yelling went on for what seemed hours.

And then Hal blazed through the front door, his deputy, Ted, at his side. Both men shouted and demanded to know what was going on, what was wrong, who was dead and who was responsible!

Chaos reigned, until Dixie picked up a chair and slammed it down on the wood floor, making a sound like a gunshot. At that, everyone froze and was blessedly silent.

IT TOOK a little time, but Dixie managed to sort things out. She and Fran hauled Tess into an examination room while Hal tried to calm his mother in the privacy of Dixie's office. Ted took care of the little girl, distracting her with a tall tale of his own youthful tree-climbing activities.

Finally, Tess settled down, and Dixie left her with Fran. She went to her office to find Hal and Hattie. Hattie, Fran told her, was the one who started it all, though Fran had no clue why. Now that Hattie was quiet and Hal was there, Dixie intended to find out.

But the office door was open and no one was inside.

"I think they went down the hall to the back," Ted said, looking out of the surgery room. "Where you got the storeroom, I think. Say, what do you know about a face, or something, Doc? That's what Mrs. Blane was muttering about all the time."

"Oh, no!" Dixie whirled and ran down the hall. Opening the storeroom door, she found Hal and Hattie, staring at the head. Hattie's complexion was now chalk white. So was Hal's.

And when Dixie looked from him to the head and back, she knew why. Add a moustache, whisker stubble and a few years of painfully hard living to Hal Blane, and he'd be twin to the man who'd been buried up on the cliff. For him, it must be like looking into a macabre mirror. For Hattie... Who knew?

"Um," Dixie said. It was all she could manage. It sufficed to get their attention.

"What is that?" Hal asked, his tone dark, his eyes narrowed to blue glints. "Is that...?"

"It is. The skull," Dixie said, watching Hattie. Some color had returned to the older woman's face, but she trembled in her son's arms. "From..."

"From Kedrick land," Hattie finished. "Oh, my God, Hal. It's your great-grandfather. My grandfather. It's Robert Kedrick." And Hattie Blane fainted.

ARTIE BLANE CREPT slowly and carefully along the slope of the cliff. He could almost hear Hastings Clark and Dr. Hayden now.

The camp was getting set to close down for the season, so most of the people he'd worked with were busy packing up for departure. He had little to do and had been free to wander around and notice things. Something about the the way Dr. Hayden and Hastings Clark were acting had caught his attention almost immediately. He had left his post up at the top of the tableland over an hour ago. Then he'd crawled and climbed down the east side of the slope and gone into the valley where the creek ran. The trees hid him until he got under the angle of the cliff. Now, he was sneaking up the south side just under the cut where the bones had been found.

The two men he'd been observing had found something else, and Artie was determined to discover what it was.

During the days he'd been watching them, his suspicions about their motives for keeping the grave site to themselves had grown. At night, when the rest of the camp slept and a lamp still burned in Dr. Hayden's tent, Artie had snaked his lean teenage body along the ground behind the tent and listened to the two men talking in whispers.

Discussing...

Arguing...

Sometimes almost fighting. He'd seen silhouettes stand and shadowy fists clench more than once.

But nothing had ever really happened. They would quiet down and start talking again, sometimes in tones so low and intense he couldn't make out the words. They had papers and maps spread out on a camp table, as they studied and planned. It went on for hours.

Artie Blane, patient beyond his years, waited and watched and listened. And today, he was sure they had made an important discovery or come to some kind of conclusion.

He'd heard a difference in their voices today.

So, Artie climbed. Before he and his father had started squaring off about things, they used to do things together. They'd gone out into the countryside and done stuff like climbing rocks and camping and fishing, so he knew what he was doing, all right. Thanks to his dad. He slid his hand along the rock, seeking a hold.

There. He hung for a long moment, breathing.

Beneath him the creek burbled along, and the soft August wind slipped through the pines.

Above him, men talked.

Artie moved again, finding a series of hand- and footholds that brought him within yards of the ledge. Now, he could hear well.

There were three men up there. One stepped out to the edge of the ledge, kicking a few small rocks down into the valley. "Coulda fallen, ya know," he said, his voice unfamiliar to Artie. It was gravelly and rough, like a man who smoked or drank a lot. "Long way down there. Mighta fallen into the creek and been washed out to hell and China, for all we know."

Artie flattened himself against the cliff.

Hastings Clark replied. "It didn't, George," he said. "It's somewhere out on the tableland, just waiting for us to find it."

The new man hacked and spat, the gob of spittle flying over the edge and barely missing Artie where he clung to the rock. "So you say, man. But I ain't seen the gleam of no gold. So..."

Artie strained his ears. Silence. Then, "Goddam! You found it?"

"Shut up, George," Dr. Hayden said. "A little louder, and the whole camp will hear you. No. We didn't find all the gold. Hastings found this coin by the body. That's all. But we believe it's significant. Kedrick must have had it in his pocket when they buried him. It survived the disintegration of his body and clothing, of course. But it was down in the soft dirt under the hipbone. The others didn't find it, or they would have torn the area apart, looking for the strong box."

Artie felt dizzy. *Kedrick!* Kedrick? They'd found...

No, it couldn't be!

He dug his fingers and toes deeper into the crevices and pressed his cheek to the gritty rock. All his life he'd listened to his grandma talk about the bad old Kedricks, Robert Kedrick in particular. How his evil ways had finally led to the ruin of her family. *His* family.

Robert Kedrick.

That was the face he'd been helping Dr. Sheldon and Dr. Nash create.

Tears fell from his eyes and rolled down his own young face. He was unaware he wept, grieving for a man he'd never known, but whose face he had begun to see in the clay pressed over the skull.

Robert Kedrick.

His great-great-grandpa...

A thief and a murderer...

But *his* great-great-grandpa!

Who was murdered!

Murdered. Shot and tossed into a grave up there on the side of the cliff. Buried there until now.

Now those guys up there were going to steal back what Kedrick had taken. The army gold that had cost the surviving Kedricks their land, their pride, their...

The hell they were! Artie felt something both alien and friendly enter his heart. It was an anger so deep that he trembled. It was a need for revenge. It was a determination to win back what was lost!

If his great-great-grandpa had stolen gold, if *he* found it and gave it back, maybe, just maybe, they'd get the land back! For his grandma, his dad and himself.

The men were talking again.

He inched up the slope and listened.

"Season's coming to an end," Dr. Hayden was saying. "The dig will shut down on schedule tomorrow. We'll have to leave when the camp closes."

"But that doesn't mean we're gone," Hastings added. "Until we get back, secretly, you, George, are going to be here for us. Understand?"

"You're paying me to keep Blane off the—"

"We're paying you to keep anybody and everybody off this place," Dr. Hayden interrupted. "If the sheriff comes poking around, scare him away."

"He won't scare," Hastings commented. "You may have to hurt him."

"No problem." George's tone was eager. "I hate his guts."

Artie scrunched into the rock and moved upward a few more inches. If he could just see who George was, he'd be able to warn his dad. As it was, he doubted his father would even believe him. This was too much! The dead man was really Robert Kedrick, and Hastings Clark and Dr. Hayden were secretly looking for the lost gold? Right. Dad would be sure he was making it all up. Lying. Trying to get attention or something like that.

He needed proof! Identification. Something.

But the cliff turned outward, and to move higher would be not only to court a fall, but also discovery. So, he stayed put and continued to listen.

"I thought you were some kind of buddies with the sheriff," George said.

"I am. He saved my life." Hastings's tone changed. "But I like gold more than I value gratitude. So, it makes no difference to me what happens to Blane. Take him out if you have to."

Artie's blood froze. They were talking about killing his dad! Now, it didn't matter if he had proof. He had to warn his father and make sure his dad believed him!

"We'll come back," Dr. Hayden said. "But without anyone else knowing. We don't want to call special attention to ourselves by staying on to search. We must all be patient."

"It'll be worth it," Hastings added. "What gold we do find will be worth much more than it was a hundred years ago. We'll all three be rich."

"Sounds good to me," George growled. "Long as I get to deal with Blane before it's all over."

"We'll see you get your chance," Dr. Hayden said. "Maybe we can bury him right here where his great-grandfather lay. In another hundred years, someone else may dig him up and wonder who he was." The three men laughed as if this were an uproarious joke.

Artie Blane, clinging to rock and dirt yards below the trio, made a solemn pledge to himself: the future was not going to happen the way those men thought it was.

Artie was going to make sure of that! He eased himself back down toward the creek and dislodged only a few pebbles on the way.

CHAPTER THIRTEEN

HATTIE RECOVERED QUICKLY from her faint, and under Fran's care was now resting on a bed in the same room as Tess Pringle. She had indicated no desire to talk about the head, yet. She shut her eyes and let the tears flow when Hal tried to question her, so he turned on another person.

"All right," Hal said, directing his full attention to Dixie. "I want to hear every detail. And it had better be good!"

"Don't take that tone with me," Dixie snapped back. "You make it sound like I've committed a crime!"

They were in her office once more, facing off over the desk.

And over the head of Robert Kedrick. While she had tended Hattie, someone, probably Ted, had moved the skull to her desk. She doubted it was Hal—he acted as if it were poison.

"I'm sure you have," Hal roared. "I just don't know what to call it, yet." He picked up his hat, which had been placed on the desk next to the head, and threw it against the wall. "Damn!"

"Hal, calm down, for goodness—"

"Why?" he yelled, raising his hands over his head. His fury reminded her of his suddenly irrational behavior the night they first saw Esther and found the grave. "You've nearly given my mother a genuine heart attack. You... You've desecrated the dead. You... You..."

"I did what?" Dixie stood right in front of him, daring him to push her this time. "I did not desecrate your great-grandfather! I brought him back!"

"It's...wrong!"

"Why?" She stepped closer. "Hal, what are you afraid of?" She touched his face. "We're lovers. Can't you trust me?"

"Apparently not." His face was stone again, and his voice colder than winter. "Why did you do this without telling me?"

Dixie looked away. "I'm not sure. To be honest, it started out as an interesting project with Winnie. That was all it was meant to be."

"And you never mentioned it to me. You never saw...?"

"Saw what?" She looked back at him. "The resemblance? No, I didn't, really. Oh, I had a glimmer, I guess, but it didn't hit me right away. He's older, harder- and tougher-looking, different hairstyle, mustache. Besides, I had you on my mind, so it made sense that I might see your reflection in the face.

"But I did not realize this was your ancestor, Hal. Not until I saw you standing next to—" She gestured at the head. "But now I sure do. He could easily be your twin, you know."

Hal shuddered. He seemed to sag, and sat back down on the chair. "Dixie, this is going to harm my mother."

"Why?" She came over and knelt down in front of him. "Why should it harm her? Maybe it will help."

His eyes were still ice-cold. "And how do you figure that, Doctor?"

"Find out what happened!" Dixie stood. She went over to the desk and looked down at Robert. "Find out why he died."

"He robbed the army of gold." Hal's tone was as dead as his ancestor. "He was a criminal."

"Maybe. But you don't know the whole story, do you? Wasn't it rumored he escaped to South America, or something? Now, you have proof he died right here in SeaLake County. Find out more."

Hal stared at the head. "Maybe I don't want to know more."

"Chicken!"

He glared, but didn't respond.

"What about Reed Turner?" Dixie tried another tack.

"What about him?"

"Well, he's interested in the history of this area. He might be willing to work on it for you. You said he came to see you...."

Hal stood up. "Is my mother going to be all right?"

"Yes. I checked her carefully. She received a shock, but..."

He walked over and picked up his hat. Setting it on his head, he went out the office door and slammed it behind him.

Dixie stared at the door. "Well, fine," she said after a moment. "Fine. If that's what you want. Don't listen to me. Go. Run away! Fine!"

But it did not feel fine.

In fact, it felt so bad, she sat down at her desk and cried while Robert looked on, sternly.

"TAKE THE KID back to her mother," Hal told Ted as he strode into the waiting room. "You're on full duty until I get back, understand? No matter how long that takes. If you have problems, call Harlen Davis over to Cody. He's got some extra men this summer."

"Sure, boss." Ted stood up and saluted, casually. "Where are you off to?"

"Business," Hal snapped. He was out the door before Ted could ask what business.

On the other hand, the deputy mused, as he led the little girl back down the hall, maybe it was a good idea not to ask the sheriff too many questions right now. He looked as if he'd like to set someone else's head next to the one on the doc's desk.

Ted paused by the doctor's closed office door, thinking he heard the sound of crying. He hesitated. Should he check on her? Blane was in a cold rage, for sure. Had he...?

Naw. He wouldn't touch the doc. Not Hal Blane. Besides, they were supposed to be sweethearts.

He went by the closed door and into the room with the two beds. Hattie Blane was sitting up, talking to the nurse, Fran Coble. Mrs. Pringle was still lying there, looking pretty bad. "How're you ladies doing?" Ted asked, feeling awkward. "I brought Sissy back, 'cause I got to get on to the office."

Hattie regarded him, her gaze steady. "Where's my son, Ted?"

"I don't know, ma'am. He took off. Didn't say where."

Hattie stood. "Where's the doctor?"

"I'm right here," Dixie said from the doorway. Only her slightly swollen eyes betrayed her emotions. She came into the room. "How are you feeling?"

"Terrible," Tess moaned.

"Fine," Hattie said.

"Why don't you go talk to the doctor?" Fran said to Hattie. She took Sissy Pringle's hand. "We can take care of your momma, can't we, honey?"

"Sure." Sissy didn't seem eager to help out, but she gave her mom's arm a pat.

Ted left then, and Dixie escorted Hattie back down the hall to her office. "The head's on my desk," she warned. "Are you sure you want to see it?"

"I'm sure," Hattie said. Her voice was strong and steady. "And after I do, you and I are going over to my house and I'll show you pictures that will convince you that the dead man really is Robert Kedrick."

"I'm already convinced." Dixie opened the door. "He looks so much like Hal, it's downright magical."

"Or demonic." Hattie gazed at her grandfather. "I've always hated him, you know."

"Because of what he was thought to have done?"

"Because of what he did. He ruined our family." Hattie folded her arms across her chest. "It's going on to this very day. I don't expect my son has told you of his obsession, has he?" She sat down.

"Obsession?"

"That's why he's never left Seaside, I'm sure. Why he let that wife of his leave him. He won't budge. He's been studying the past all his adult life. He has a regular library up in the attic. Buries himself there for hours at a time. Works all night, sometimes. For days when he can get the time off. He's looking for proof of what happened to Robert Kedrick." She nodded toward the head.

She went on, her tone bitter. "Regardless of what happened, my grandfather deserted his family and left them penniless. My grandmother worked the land by herself until my father was old enough to take over. Then my husband did the job, but we lost the land, piece by piece. Most of it was taken for back taxes and auctioned off for debts. Hal's spent much of his time trying to prove that was illegal, but no lawyer will take the case."

"Why not?"

"Because the Kedrick history is so black. When Robert took the gold from the army, the government set out to punish us all. It's still going on to this very day. If a lawyer dares to defend us, he'll be blackballed."

"Oh, that's no reason. There are lawyers who'll defend the devil." Dixie thought a moment. "In fact, I have a lawyer friend who owes me a spectacular favor. If you'd like, I'll call him and ask him to look into this case for you."

"No. I don't want strangers involved."

Dixie considered pushing the issue, then decided the older woman had taken enough for the day. "It's your choice, Hattie," she said gently.

"Thank you," Hattie said, her tone formal. "I appreciate what you're trying to do, but it is just no use."

"Why do you say that?"

"The evil he did—" she indicated the head, "—doomed us all."

Dixie sat back down. "Hattie, the man robbed the army of some gold. It wasn't a good thing, but it wasn't exactly what I'd term evil."

"He's not your grandfather."

Dixie could think of no response to that. "Come on," she said, standing up. "I'll take you home."

"First, take that picture down in the waiting room and destroy it. Please. I can't abide the idea of other folks looking at him." Hattie looked once more at the head. "And cover that thing up."

Dixie did cover the head and took down the photograph. But she didn't destroy the picture. She put it in her desk drawer for safekeeping. Then she took Hattie home. What followed was pure revelation.

When she saw Hal's attic study, she began to understand how deeply the Kedrick obsession ran in the Blane family. Hattie had not exaggerated. Hal had books and documents and government papers piled all over the place, as well as in floor-to-ceiling bookcases. An inexpensive personal computer sat on the desk, disks scattered nearby. It was the room of a scholar. An untrained, untidy scholar, but a scholar, nonetheless. And a scholar with one intent: to find out the truth about his past.

The reason he had been so negative about talking to Reed Turner must be that he wanted to do it all himself, she decided. Just like Hattie: no outsiders allowed.

Did that include her?

Hattie went on talking.

"Hal grew up studying the past. He never did all that well in school, but when he studied what interested him, why, he became an expert almost overnight. He's like a sponge when it comes to learning things. My grandmother used to talk to him for hours when she was still alive," Hattie said, explaining some of the background. "He was just a tiny child then, but Hal cut his teeth on family legend and pain. After Grandma passed on, my mother took over passing on the stories."

She went over to a file cabinet and took out a thick folder. She opened it and held a laminated photograph out to Dixie for her inspection.

Hal and some strange woman stood stiffly in a nineteenth-century wedding pose.

No. Not Hal.

Robert. The resemblance was even strong in this younger Robert. The past, reaching out into the present... Stamping the living with the features of the dead...

"I see." Shaken, Dixie moved around the room. It was Hal's place on the planet as no other place could be. She could smell him here. See him in her mind. Feel his pain. Sense his hunger to know: good or bad, just to know the truth. A hunger she understood so well. It brought a sudden pang of longing for him that shocked her with its power. "So he inherited your grandmother's and your mother's bitterness and memories?" she asked, hoping to put some emotional distance into her thoughts.

"You could put it that way." Hattie's mouth was a thin line.

"I don't want to hurt you, Hattie, but this is more than just a medical case to me, now." Dixie went over to the desk. "I genuinely care about your son." She looked at the papers scattered there. At the labels on the disks.

"Perhaps. Perhaps you do."

Dixie looked up.

"Perhaps you'll leave him like the other one did."

"Hattie, he knew I had plans to leave in three years before I ever came here. Before he ever asked me out to dinner. Don't make this harder than it already is for any of us. We're good friends, but nothing more. I am not Hal's wife."

Hattie turned away, reddening. "I'm sorry, Doctor. I had no right...."

"It's okay. I think I understand." And maybe, even, she was telling the truth about being only friends with this woman's son. Surely, that would be reason enough to feel this kind of hurt.

Love was not necessary for pain. Simply caring for someone could cause that.

Hattie blinked back tears. "May I offer you a cup of tea? And some lunch? It's getting late, and I'm hungry in spite of all the ... excitement."

Dixie was happy to hear that—it meant Hattie hadn't been too traumatized, after all. Appetite was always a good sign. "That would be great," she said. "I'm hungry, too. And we still haven't talked today, have we?"

Hattie smiled. "No, Dixie. We haven't. And it's clear we should."

"May I keep that picture of Robert and your grandmother for a while? I promise to take good care of it."

"Throw it into the fire, if you want." Hattie handed over the folder. "The sight of that head was enough to last me the rest of my natural life!"

Dixie took the folder and didn't argue.

HAL DROVE OUT to the dig site as if the devil himself were on his tail. The sight of that face, so like his own, had stirred things in his heart and mind that he both dreaded and yearned for.

And to know that Dixie Sheldon had started this dug deep into him, giving him more agony than seeing the face.

It was a betrayal.

The story of his life!

Deep down, he knew he wasn't being reasonable, but that did nothing to stop the feelings. He was going to take Winnie Nash apart one piece at a time, then go back for Dixie! They had no right to do what they'd done! No right to exhume Robert Kedrick and remake him for all the world to see . . .

To see how much he resembled his great-grandson . . .

He slowed. The dust plume that had followed the Jeep began to envelop him, clouding the view. What the hell was he thinking!

God, had he gone insane?

He slowed some more. Up ahead, the rise that led to the tableland loomed. The scene wavered in front of Hal's eyes. He blinked, clearing his vision. What was he doing, thinking of harming either of the women? They had done nothing wrong. Just satisfied their curiosity. Naturally. Was he loco? Had the ghost of his great-grandfather driven him crazy?

Hal stopped in the middle of the dirt road. *That* was insane thinking! No one was responsible for his actions and thoughts but himself. His anger was not Dixie's fault or Winnie's. It was his, and his alone.

He put his head down and tried to cry.

He couldn't. Sweat streamed down his face, but not tears. Dust continued to swirl around the vehicle. Hal felt drawn into the vortex of a nightmare he could not escape.

Then, in keeping with his sense of horror, a dim figure seemed to be moving through the dust toward the Jeep. He closed his eyes, convinced his imagination had joined the rest of his mind in madness. When he opened them, no figure was visible. Hal leaned back and tried to calm his heart.

A fist hammered at the window by his head.

He whirled in the seat, backing away from the window and drawing his gun in one smooth movement. As his finger tightened on the trigger, he heard a familiar voice.

"Dad! It's me! Artie! Don't shoot!"

All of Hal's bones turned to water. He holstered the gun with shaking hands. "What the hell, Artie," he said, his voice rasping in his throat. "You half scared the liver out of me."

Artie opened the driver's door and climbed in. "Well, you did the same to me! What's got into you, Dad? You look like you saw a ghost."

Hal sat back, closing his eyes again. He was trembling like a leaf in a high wind. "I think I did," he said.

"Robert Kedrick," Artie said. It was not a question.

"How did you know?"

"I helped with the skull some. But there's more. Dad, we need to talk. I mean serious talk."

Hal regarded his son. There was nothing of the sullen teenager sitting beside him. The youth in the driver's seat was no child. He nodded. "Take the wheel, son," he said. "Let's get off-road."

Artie started to speak, then grinned and shifted the Jeep into gear. "Boy," he said softly. "First time. Off-road." He eased off the clutch, stuttered a bit and then swung the vehicle smoothly onto the prairie.

"First time with permission, I expect," Hal commented dryly. "You've done this before."

Artie didn't confess, but his smile widened.

They reached the grove of cottonwoods along the creek in a few minutes and Hal ordered his son to stop. They got out of the Jeep and walked over to the water without speaking.

Artie sat down on the bank. Hal had stopped shaking, but his body was still alert for danger. He chose to stand. "I saw the head today," he said. "Your grandma saw it and it spooked the hell out of her."

"I didn't see it finished," Artie said, staring down at the rushing water. "I got the creeps about halfway through. Didn't go back."

"It's something." Hal sank to the ground by his son. He stretched out his legs. "Like looking into a mirror back through time." He turned toward Artie. "Now, what have you got to tell me, son?"

DIXIE HAD TEA and a sandwich with Hattie, and the two of them waited a while for Hal to return. When it was getting close to five o'clock, Dixie had to leave.

"I have to get back to the clinic," she said, apologizing for abandoning the vigil. "I have some last-minute paperwork to do before Fran leaves. But I don't want to miss Hal. When he comes home, please let him know I have to talk to him. I'll either be at the clinic or at home.''

"I will," Hattie replied. "And I'll see he goes to you, no matter how stubborn he is about it."

"Hattie, don't push..."

"I won't. But that boy needs to think before he rushes off and does things. He's my son. I know."

Dixie couldn't argue with that.

She went back to the clinic and found matters in relatively good order, thanks to Fran.

"I sent Sissy and her mother on home," Fran said. "Once the audience was gone, Tess recovered miraculously."

Dixie smiled. "Good diagnosis, Fran. You should be the doctor here, not me."

Fran didn't smile back.

"What's the matter?"

"Read the mail." Fran handed her a stack of envelopes. "We got identical letters. The one on top."

Dixie sat down on the sofa in the waiting room and read. "They can't do that," she said when she finished the brief, official note. "They just can't."

"They did." Fran sat down on a chair, sighing. "Or at least, they're going to. The state government is cutting small rural medical services right and left, due to the loss of mineral-royalty income."

"The old economic system is failing, and no one's come up with a viable alternate solution," Dixie said sadly. She and her parents had talked about this eventuality for years, ever since she decided to go into medicine.

Fran nodded. "We all knew it was coming. Just didn't know when. We have three funded months left."

"I can't accept this." Dixie held up the paper. "I signed a contract to work here for three full years, but they can decide to close the clinic whenever they want."

"That's the government for you."

"Fran, we can't let this happen."

"You have some more mail you might want to look at before you go off on your white horse." Fran sounded tired, defeated.

Dixie glanced at the other envelopes. A large folder. From California... She opened it.

She read.

"Oh," she said, softly. "Oh, my."

"What is it?"

"Well, it seems that on the basis of the material about Wyoming healing herbs that I've sent them over the past weeks, the powers that be at California Whole Medicine have decided they can't wait three years for me. If I'm willing, they plan to repay my medical school expenses on the spot, and allow me to pay off a small percentage every year.

"They say that the new focus of twenty-first century medicine is going to be an approach that includes not only the generally accepted style of treating illness, but also the traditional natural and folk methods. Each case will be evaluated individually, instead of being treated as just one more example of a set of symptoms. It's my dream come true!" She looked at Fran. "It's an offer I can hardly refuse."

"Then take it. We're finished here, anyway."

Dixie sat very still. She listened to her mind.

Then she listened to her heart.

"I just can't do it," she said almost to herself. "At least not yet. Not until I know..."

"Know what?"

Dixie stood up. "Lots of things, Fran. Lots of things. For now, we know we still have three months before the doors have to close here. Let's make the most of the time we've got."

Fran sat still for a minute. Then she stood, too. "Okay, Doctor," she said. "You are the boss. Call the shots!"

Dixie grinned at the pun. "The first call I'm making is to the lawyer of my choice," she said. "I don't intend to wait for the bureaucrats to strike first. I'll be ready."

She picked up the phone and dialed. "M. J. Nichols, please," she said. "No, it's not an emergency. Yes, it's important. Just tell him Dixie's calling." She grinned at Fran and gave a thumbs-up sign. "Okay. I'll expect to hear from him as soon as his meeting is over. I don't care what time it is, just have him call. Thanks." She hung up.

Fran regarded her.

"An old friend," Dixie explained. "We dated in college, and it turned out we were better at friendship than romance. Once we decided that, the relationship became permanent. We've kept in close touch all these years. He's a terrific lawyer, and an even better bloodhound with a legal mystery, particularly where the government is involved. He can help. I know it."

She took the folder that Hattie had given her and motioned for Fran to come into her office. "Look at this," she said, taking out the wedding picture. She set it next to the photo of the head.

"That's truly awesome," Fran said, her tone hushed. "He's almost perfect."

"And check this out." Dixie rummaged in the folder and brought out another picture. She doubted if Hattie had been aware this one was inside when she'd surrendered the folder. It was a studio-style photograph of Hal, taken a few years ago, to judge from the face. There were fewer lines in his tanned skin, and his eyes looked less troubled.

"My God," Fran declared. "They're identical."

"That's right." Dixie took the three pictures and returned them to the folder. "And I intend to ask someone who might have seen them both during her life to tell me more about that."

"You're going to what?"

"I'm taking these to Miss Esther," Dixie said. "I have a hunch, and I'm going to give it a run. I can't do it now. I have to wait here until M.J. calls and I have to talk to Hal when he gets back from wherever he is, but first thing tomorrow, I'm driving out and showing her these pictures."

Fran's eyes sparkled with interest. "Think she knows anything about it? Really?"

"I'm not sure. But she has been here forever, and she acted strangely when I told her about the grave."

"I'll cancel your morning appointments right now," Fran said, heading for the door.

"What would I do without you?" Dixie smiled fondly at the nurse.

"No," Fran said, her tone serious. "The question is, what would all of us do without you?" Then she left the office.

Dixie considered those words while she waited for the lawyer's call.

HAL LISTENED to Artie's recitation of his grim discoveries and dangerous investigation methods with a deep chill growing inside him. At first, he was skeptical, not willing to believe in the conspiracy. He liked Hastings Clark, and although Oscar Hayden was a pompous pain, that didn't make him a bad man. When Artie talked about the man named George, however, Hal's reluctance to accept the facts faded. It had to be George Preston. The man was mean and dumb enough. His son had not only risked his life, he was now caught in the Kedrick web of death and violence and greed just as surely as if he were guilty of a crime himself.

Yet Artie was certainly an innocent. The only guilt he carried was a kinship to Robert Kedrick. Hal vowed to keep the boy safe, no matter what it took.

"So, what are we going to do, Dad?" Artie asked, when Hal sat silent for a time.

Hal cleared his throat, unable to reply immediately. They still sat on the bank overlooking the water. Hal smelled dust and water. He stared out over the creek to the prairie landscape beyond. Dry now with August heat, the grassland was still rich, the yellow stalks enough to feed large herds of wild grazers as well as domestic cattle. It was good land.

Their land, at one time.

"I don't know," he replied. "But I do know you can't be a part of it anymore. It's too—"

"Risky?" Artie stood up, his fists clenched at his sides. "Dad, I've already taken chances you wouldn't believe. Don't go trying to shove me aside now!"

"I'm not shoving. Just using some sense. You're only a kid."

"Only a kid who found out some guys are planning to kill you! You wouldn't know if I hadn't taken chances. I'm a part of this now."

"No."

"Dad, don't do this!"

Hal stared into the distance. "Artie, you're my only child. I can't let you risk your life. You still have so much future ahead of you."

"And what about you?"

Hal looked up at his son. "I don't know, Artie. Maybe I've had my future already. That's why I have to keep you safe. Get you somewhere away from here."

Tears of anger and frustration filled the boy's eyes and ran down his cheeks. Furious at himself, he scrubbed them away. "Well, you can't." He sat back down. "They know I've been working at the dig site. If I disappear, they're gonna find me. After they get you."

"Artie, that's..."

"And what about Grandma? And Dixie? And Dr. Nash? Don't they mean anything to you? Are you going to hide all of them, too?"

"I can't... Of course not."

"You don't think they're in any danger?"

"I don't..."

"Dad, Dr. Nash and Dr. Sheldon made the head. Hastings knows about it, because he gave Dr. Nash some pointers."

"That doesn't mean he'll try to..." Hal hesitated. "I guess I can't be sure what those men will do."

"You can't! And you can't hide me, either." Artie put his hand on his father's shoulder. "Dad, we have to do this together. You and me."

Hal turned. Stared at his son. "Do what?"

Artie grinned. "Take away their reason for hurting you or me or any of us. Find the gold, of course."

Hal shook his head. "Find the gold? Son, folks have been looking for Kedrick's gold for a hundred years."

Sensing a softening in his father's attitude, Artie plunged on. "Folks, maybe. But not you. You've never looked."

Hal shrugged. "I don't know where it is. Why should I?"

"Because you *do* know. Dad, you spent half your life up there in the attic, looking for it in all those old papers and books and junk. Come on, if anyone knows how he thought, you do."

"He? You mean . . . ?" Hal sat for a moment, his mind whirling. "I think like Robert would? Or could think like him, if I put myself in his place."

"Right!"

Hal regarded his son. "I'm still determined to keep you out of trouble, kid," he said. "But for right now, I guess you're in."

Artie's shout of joy echoed across the grassland.

CHAPTER FOURTEEN

DIXIE WAITED in her office until after eight o'clock that evening. While she sat there, she read and reread the two letters. One from the state of Wyoming. One from California. Letters that would change her plans. Change her life....

Well, wasn't California what she'd planned on eventually? She had already made a considerable investment in Cal Med with the research she'd done through Esther and some other folks around the area.

But she wasn't ready to leave! Not yet. She was supposed to have *three* years!

What about Hal? His problems? His mother? His...

Their... relationship?

In three years, she certainly could have sorted things out. But now, she didn't have the luxury of time.

The call from M.J. finally came through, saving her from her tangled thoughts.

"Hello, darling doctor," the lawyer said, his tone warm. "How's clinical practice in the outer limits?"

"Very funny, M.J." Dixie replied. "Listen, I need you to be serious. I... A friend of mine has a problem."

"A friend?"

"Really. It's not me, I swear. It's a friend whose entire family has been given a raw deal for almost a century by the government. Or at least some aspect of the government. I don't think the whole U.S. system is to blame, but certainly someone needs to own up to responsibility. Your kind of case, exactly.''

"All right! Give me the details." M.J.'s voice went from a teasing, bantering tone to one of professional alertness immediately. ''Tell me everything.''

After she finished talking to M.J. and getting his promise to look into the old Kedrick case as soon as he could, she went home. Hoping Hal would come to talk.... She needed to talk to him, to see if he was all right after the shock of seeing the face so like his own. Hoping he'd come to love her again as he had so many other nights....

Hoping he wouldn't, so she wouldn't have to tell him about the clinic and the job offer.

Hal never showed up, and Hattie didn't call. And Dixie spent the night alone with her thoughts.

She had some hard decisions to make, soon, and she didn't like the potential outcome of any of them.

THE NEXT MORNING, Dixie drove up to the Fawcetts' restaurant and parked. Before she got out, she hesitated, thinking. The day was unusually warm, and the clouds were thin and lacy. Sunshine cut through the pines overhead. She wasn't sure of the protocol regarding Esther's days and visits during sunlight. The only time she'd seen the old woman was after dark.

But this was too important a mission to wait on sunset. She needed some answers from Esther, and she needed them now.

"Hello, Dixie!" Sandy Fawcett waved from the porch of the restaurant. "What brings you out here in the daylight? Not visiting Miss Esther, I hope."

Dixie lifted the briefcase she carried. It contained the photographs and some hastily typed notes she had made before driving out. "In fact, that's exactly what I'm doing," she said. "I have some things I want to show her."

Sandy came off the porch. One of their large dogs, a hulking black Lab, followed her, tail wagging as Dixie greeted him. "Esther really doesn't care for daylight," Sandy said. "She's liable to be in an unpleasant mood if you go up there now."

"It's a chance I have to take."

Sandy folded her arms and regarded Dixie. "Sounds like you're serious."

"I am."

"And worried."

Dixie didn't reply.

"Is it about Hal?"

Dixie looked away. "Kind of."

"May I help?"

"You bet!" Relief filled her. "And can the dog come along? Funny, but I think I'm more scared of the woods now in sunshine than in the dark."

Sandy smiled, but her expression was not amused. "You and Miss Esther," she said. "Two of a kind." She petted the dog. "Viking here can go along, but I can't promise he'll stay with us. If he runs off, don't try calling him back."

"I won't." Dixie repressed a shiver of something very like fear, but more like dread. "I wouldn't dream of forcing anyone to do this, if they weren't willing."

Sandy smiled, this time with warmth. "I'm willing. I don't understand Esther, but I'm not afraid of her. Are you?"

Dixie hesitated. "Not of Esther. Just of what she might know."

Sandy did not pursue that.

The three then set off up the slope of ground into the woods. For a while, the Lab followed, scenting small game along the path, but not giving chase. Dixie didn't feel like talking, and Sandy seemed inclined not to chat or ask more questions.

As they neared the cabin and clearing, the atmosphere seemed to get heavier. Although it was almost September, when coolness set in up in the mountains, the temperature was still warm, and an unusually high amount of humidity hung in the air. Dixie wiped sweat from her face.

"Hot today," Sandy commented. "Muggy, too. Storm coming."

"Think so?"

"I'm sure. I haven't lived here long, but when you're out in the wilderness most of the time, you get to know things."

"Like Esther does?"

Sandy laughed softly, respectfully. "Well, goodness knows she's been here long enough."

"That's what I'm hoping," Dixie said, mostly to herself.

They reached the clearing. The door was wide open, but no one moved inside or out in the meadow. The little cabin looked forlorn and dilapidated in daylight. The magic of the dark hadn't settled on it yet, and it looked like what it really was—a home as old as its occupant.

They stood still for a moment, just looking. The dog sat down beside Sandy. Late-summer grasshoppers buzzed in the clearing, and overhead a large black bird sailed on the heated air. The place felt like an empty church.

Or a cemetery.

"Oh," Dixie said softly. "Maybe we should come back..." Her voice trailed off. *No!* She was here on an important mission. "Miss Esther?" she called. "Are you there?"

The dog barked. Once. Then whined.

Nothing stirred. Just the insects and birds.

"This is creepy. I'll wait here," Sandy said, swallowing hard and reaching down for the Labrador's collar. "Let us know what you find."

"She's all right," Dixie said, also swallowing the lump in her throat. "I'm sure. It's just that we... She's probably asleep."

"Go see."

Dixie did. She walked across the clearing and through the open door. The tiny room was stiflingly hot and smelled like smoke and wood as well as something else she couldn't identify, but no fire burned in the hearth. "Esther?" Dixie queried. "Are you here?"

A small sound drew her to the part of the room where the old woman's cot stood.

Esther was in her bed, quilt up to her chin. The quilt didn't seem to move. Her eyes were closed, and she looked two hundred years old. Dixie felt her face. It was cold as ice.

"Is she...?" Sandy asked from the doorway. The dog at her side whined again.

Dixie knelt down. "No, she's alive," she said. "But barely. I don't know what's wrong, and I'm scared to move her. She might have drugged herself for all I can tell." She examined the old woman, quickly and gently.

Then she turned to Sandy. "Run home," she said. "Call for a Life Flight helicopter up from Casper. They can land one here in the clearing. I don't dare risk moving her on my own."

"Dixie, there's a really bad thunderstorm brewing down south toward Douglas and Casper. I've been listening to weather warnings on the radio all morning. They might not be able to take off right away. Can you wait?''

"As long as I have to."

Sandy hesitated. "If she's dying, she won't like it if you interfere, you know."

"I know. But she can't die yet. She's not ready. I'm sure she isn't. Go!"

Sandy Fawcett went.

Dixie settled in at Esther's side to watch and wait. After a few minutes, to her surprise, the dog came into the cabin and sat down beside her. A soft whimper escaped his throat. Dixie reached over and patted his massive head. He licked her hand, sighed and laid down by the cot.

Esther didn't stir, barely breathed.

The day moved on past noon into afternoon and sunlight turned the inside of the cabin golden. Outside, the grasshoppers continued to buzz. A large, slow moving hornet flew in, circled around and flew out.

Dixie and the dog waited. The sunlight started to fade, and the sky grew pewter gray, then darker. Still, they waited.

LATE IN THE AFTERNOON, even though it was raining and thundering hard, Hattie heard sounds in the garage. She knew it wasn't her son. He'd have come inside to see how she was, first. The thumping and bumping startled her out of the nap she'd been taking, and then her chest began to hurt as she thought about who might be invading her home.

Carefully, she opened the closet door and took out Hal's shotgun. Even more carefully, she picked up the phone and dialed the sheriff's office. While she waited for the dispatcher to answer, she checked the shotgun to make sure it was loaded.

When she had Ted on the phone, she told him what was happening.

"Get out, Mrs. Blane," Ted said. "Throw on a raincoat and get out. I'm on my way over right now. But you go downstairs and out the front door and run. Don't even think of trying to shoot it out with anybody."

"Ted Travers, this is my home. You get here. But I'm not leaving."

"Mrs. Blane, Hal will kill me if anything happens to you."

"Just get here, then." Hattie hung up the phone. She made her way stealthily down the stairs to the first floor. Her heart was pounding, but her chest no longer hurt. She settled herself back into the corner of the kitchen, pointed the shotgun at the door to the garage, and waited.

OVERHEAD, thunder started to roll. Esther stirred. Dixie sat forward and took the old woman's hand. She gently rubbed her wrist, then felt for a pulse.

Strong and steady.

"Esther?" she asked softly. "Esther, can you hear me?"

Esther stirred again as a clap of distant thunder snapped through the air. But her eyes didn't open, and she didn't speak. The dog whined.

Dixie felt the wrinkled, brown forehead. Esther's skin seemed warmer. Though with the intense heat in the cabin and the heavy quilt over her, it was a wonder she wasn't burning up. Dixie got up and went over to the door.

No sign of the helicopter. Dixie hugged herself to avoid shivering with dread. A storm was overhead, and Esther was...

What? She turned back to the room. Esther was what? Drugged? Under some kind of herb-induced trance or coma? The smell that she'd noticed when she first entered was no longer apparent, but what had caused it might still be here. It was also vaguely familiar, now that she'd had time to think about it. What was it? Something Esther had shown her? Something they'd tested or gathered together?

She left the doorway and explored the cabin.

In a few minutes, she found it.

"HERE, son." Hal handed a small pickax to Artie. "We're liable to need this, too."

Artie took the tool and added it to the pile of equipment. "Are you gonna tell Grandma where we're going?" he asked.

"No. Just that we'll be gone a while. Let her think we're camping and fishing like we used to." Hal climbed down off the ladder and set it back against the side of the garage. "The less she knows, the better."

"She's gonna worry. How about Dixie?"

Hal winced. "Don't want her to know, either. I don't want to talk to her at all. Come on. Let's go inside and get food."

"Okay." Artie nodded and started to follow his father. They had spent the night camping out by the creek, really roughing it, like in the old days, and talking about their chances of finding the gold and how they should go about the project. As the hours of night passed, they became closer than ever before, though neither one of them would admit it openly. They were starting to form an adult-style bond with the hunt for the gold as the glue.

They had decided to go searching immediately. Not to wait until the camp was gone and the others had a chance with the camp gone. Hal and his son knew the land better. They could move and search in secret.

They'd find the gold... Get rich... Buy the land back...
Be somebody!

Lost in his dreams, Artie walked right into his father's
back. "Ma," he heard him say carefully, his voice strained
with tension. "Ma, put that shotgun away!"

"Freeze!" Ted Travers shouted the command from
somewhere behind Artie. Artie turned and saw a silhou-
ette in the garage doorway. The figure had a gun aimed
right at his head!

SHE FOUND IT in the bottom of the old pottery pot that
Esther had used to serve them tea the first night they met.
Dixie took off the cracked lid and sniffed the dregs in the
bottom.

Valerian and skullcap. Chamomile... And...

"I saw him." The voice was so thin, it sounded like a
flute song. "Saw him..."

The dog, who had been watching Dixie, but still sitting
by Esther's cot, barked.

Dixie set the pot down and hurried over. "Esther!" She
knelt down. "Esther, can you hear me?"

The eyelids fluttered, opened, shut and fluttered open.
"I saw him, child. He was dead, but I saw him."

"Who, Esther? Who did you see?"

Miss Esther sat up. She moved so suddenly, that Dixie
was taken by surprise. She fell back, startled. The dog
yipped and ran for the door. He streaked out across the
clearing and into the woods.

"I saw him!" Esther shrieked. "Again!"

Dixie waited, in shock herself.

Esther quieted. She opened her eyes. Looked at Dixie.
"I took some herbs," she said in a normal tone of voice.
"To journey into my heart."

"I saw the dregs in the pot," Dixie said, trying to keep her own voice from shaking. "Esther, you shouldn't have done that while you were alone."

But Esther just chuckled. "I have done it many times, alone." Her brown eyes clouded. "But this frightened me."

"Tell me?"

The old woman looked off into the distance. Frowned. Wrinkled up her face with the effort. "I was frightened. I was young. I can't remember. Maybe I shouldn't."

Dixie got up. "How do you feel? Physically, I mean."

"I'm rested. I'm fine."

"Let me fix you something to eat."

"I ain't hungry. Storm's coming." Esther's gaze moved to the open door. Another roll of thunder. "Smell the rain? It's hit town already, I bet."

"I know. Esther, I..."

"You came here for a reason, child. Tell me what it was."

"I don't think I should, now. You had some kind of shock while you were in a trance. I don't..."

"Why did you come here, Dixie Sheldon?" The woman's voice was strong and full of ancient power and authority.

Overhead the thunder rumbled. A *tap-tap-tap* on the roof heralded the arrival of the rain.

"I ain't lived to be this age without being strong," Esther continued. "I had a vision while I slept. I don't remember what it was, but I want to. It's important I remember. And you got something to tell me. Do it."

"It's about Hal," Dixie said. "And his great-grandfather, Robert Kedrick." She watched Esther closely, looking for signs of agitation.

"Uh-huh," Esther said, nodding. "Go on." Calm. Serene.

"I have some pictures."

Esther nodded again. "Let me see."

"I don't know..."

"Let me see!" A gnarled hand reached out and clawed at the air.

Dixie opened the folder and took out the contents. She spread the three photographs out on the quilt so that Esther had a good view of them all.

And outside, thunder slammed the air and it began to pour rain in earnest.

"YOU SCARED the life out of me, Harold Blane," Hattie said, glaring at her son. The shotgun was back in the closet and Ted Travers, shaken considerably by nearly shooting his boss *and* the boss's kid, had gone back to the office. "I thought someone was trying to break into the house."

"I said I was sorry, Ma." Hal hunkered down in his chair at the kitchen table. "I didn't want to bother you, that's all."

"Me and Dad just needed some stuff, Grandma," Artie added.

Hattie regarded the two. She was sure the boys were both lying to her.

Both of them! And that's what made her certain something was badly wrong. For Artie and his father to agree on the time of day, or even if the sun was shining, was an event of such rarity that Hattie could hardly remember the last time it had happened.

"You come clean, Arthur. You, too, Harold. I will not sit here and be lied to by my own kin. My own flesh and blood."

"Ma, we're just heading out for a little high-country time before Artie has to start school again," Hal repeated, sticking to his story.

"You know, Grandma. Fishing. Some hiking. Stuff like that."

"Stuff and nonsense!" Hattie glared.

The Blane men stared back, their gazes steady.

"All right," she said finally. "I give up. If you want to go off in the woods at a time like this, it's fine with me."

"Time like this?" Hal sat up straighter. "What do you mean, Ma? Has someone . . . ?"

"Your young lady needs you, Harold. She's waiting to talk to you about things. Do you know she's been told the clinic has to close in three months?"

"What?" Hal stood up so fast his chair went over. "The clinic closed? They can't do that!"

"I spoke to Fran this morning," Hattie said. "She told me. They got the letters yesterday afternoon."

Hal picked up his chair and sat back down. "Dixie's leaving?"

"I expect she'll have to."

"Dad," Artie said, his tone soft but urgent. "We have to get going."

Hal didn't respond. He felt as though he'd been kicked, solidly, right in the chest.

"Dad."

"Is she home?" Hal asked, getting up and going over to the phone on the wall. "Or at the clinic?" He started to dial.

"I don't know," Hattie said. She glanced out the window. "I think Fran said she was going to see Miss Esther this morning. Now, it's stormy and getting dark. I hope . . ."

"She went to see Esther?" Hal hung up the receiver. "Why?"

"Fran didn't say."

"Dad!" Artie stood up. "We have to go."

"I, um…" Hal remained where he was. "I don't… Did she go to say goodbye to Esther?" He looked and sounded as if he were talking to himself. "Is she leaving right away?" He began to pace the kitchen. "She can't do that."

"Dad!"

"Hal, she's a good person. She'll do what she has to, but unless you tell her how you feel …"

"Dad! Come on!" Artie went over to his father and shook him, grabbing his arms and staring into his face. "You know what we have to do, first!"

Hal blinked. Looked at his son. Glanced at the phone and his mother. "Yeah." He ran his hand over his face. "Ma, tell Dixie I have to talk to her before she makes any decisions. We've got to get moving now."

"In this weather?" Hattie gestured toward the window. Rain had started to fall. "You two are trying to tell me you're going out camping and fishing in this?"

"Sure, Grandma." Artie grinned. "We're roughing it."

"IT'S HIM," Esther said, taking up the old photograph of Robert and his bride. "Him that I saw." She brushed a shaking hand over her face. "Dead, he was. But alive…"

"Are you confusing him with Hal?" Dixie picked up the photo of Hal and held it for Esther to view. "They look so much alike."

"They do." Esther took both pictures in her hands. "They have the same fate, too." She looked off into the distance, and Dixie felt a cold chill run all the way through her. "They face the same death, child."

"Esther, Hal hasn't taken to riding with outlaws and robbing gold from the army," Dixie said. "And you can't know the future, wise as you are. What I want to know is the past. Did you ever see Robert Kedrick? Alive?"

Esther nodded. "I'm told I did." Her voice was high and childlike now.

"Told?"

"Yes." She put the photographs back down on the quilt. "I was just a little thing. A baby, really. When he came up here and told my Pa we could stay on his land."

"*This* was Kedrick land, too?"

"Yes, it was. It and most of the land around here. He was a man who took what he wanted, but he was generous to those who didn't have so much."

"Like your folks?"

"Yes. Not everyone was good to us because my ma was Shoshone." Esther was silent for a while. The rain beat down on the cabin roof, making a sound that evoked loneliness and loss. Dixie got up and closed the door. It became quieter.

Much quieter.

"Is that why Hal's been kind of special to you all these years?" she asked, sitting back down.

Esther didn't answer.

Dixie picked up the photograph of the head. "Esther, this is the face we reconstructed from the skull of the skeleton found over at the dinosaur dig site. It's Robert Kedrick."

Esther nodded, slowly at first, then faster. "It is, it is, it is him," she chanted softly. "He came when I was a child, to help us, and then he rode with the bad men, and they shot him, and my father..."

"Your father?" Dixie moved closer. Esther was almost whispering now. "What about your father?"

"My father gave him a decent burial."

These words were spoken in a strong voice.

"Your father? How could your father...?"

Dixie stopped speaking. Esther had risen from the bed and was walking stiffly across the small room. She reached the hearth and went to a wooden trunk set off to the left side. Opening it, she took out something wrapped in a piece of bleached deerskin. Moving more normally, she carried the packet to the table and set it down. Dixie got up and came over to stand beside her.

Esther parted the deerskin wrapping, revealing an old book. A very old book. The cover was reddish-brown leather, cracked with age. It looked like the skin on Esther's hands and face. "My father kept a journal," she said, touching the cover reverently. "In here he describes how he found Robert Kedrick's body and reburied him in the spring. How he..."

"He reburied him?" Dixie reached for the book, but the old hands stopped her. "Esther, that could be important to Hal. If he knew where the original burial site was, he might be able to find the gold, too."

Esther shut her eyes and groaned. "It may kill him, too. You have to get to him and warn him, child."

Dixie shivered. "Warn him of what?"

"The bad men. The evil men who'll shoot him down, just like they did his great-granddaddy."

Dixie felt panic now. "Esther, you have to talk as plainly to me as possible. What are you saying?"

Miss Esther took a deep breath. "I had a vision," she said. "I remembered my father coming home and telling my mother he found Mr. Kedrick, dead and frozen up in the hills above the tableland. How he'd taken the body and moved it. Put it deep in the earth where it would be safe from the coyotes."

"He reburied Robert?"

"He did. And then he and my mother went back and made the grave sacred."

"They knew he was dead. Knew where he was buried, and they didn't tell anyone? Why, Esther? Why?"

The old woman turned and regarded Dixie. "They would have been blamed, of course."

"I don't understand."

"My father and mother were hated. People were afraid of my mother's powers and called my father a squaw man. If he had admitted to finding Mr. Kedrick, everyone would have thought my father had the gold. Do you see it now?"

Dixie nodded, saddened by the knowledge. "I do," she said. "Your father did the right thing at the time. It's just too bad you never told Hal."

Esther blinked. "Until today, I didn't remember."

"But the journal..."

"It isn't written clear. Just in stories that need..."

"Interpreting?"

"Yes."

"Then, let's sit down and read it," Dixie said. She glanced out the window at the raging rainstorm. "I'm not going anywhere for a while. Not in that."

Esther nodded. "You won't. But Harold Kedrick Blane will." She pulled up a chair, sat and opened the journal.

The two women began to read.

CHAPTER FIFTEEN

HAL AND ARTIE slogged along the trail by the creek. Rain was coming down as if it were being poured from a gigantic bucket. The already soaked ground was muddy and slippery, but they had on good hiking boots and knew the terrain.

They had camped, hiked and fished along the creek and up into the cliffs for years. This time, however, their mission was far more serious. And dangerous.

On the drive out, they had decided how to approach the problem. They would reenact, as closely as they could, Robert's last hours. From records and reports submitted by the leaders of the posse chasing the outlaw band, Hal knew the nine riders had come into the valley late in the day, just before a heavy snowstorm settled in. It was the storm that had caused the pursuers to lose their quarry. In spite of making it easier to follow track, the posse had lost the riders in the heavy snowfall and had not caught up with them until over a week later, a hundred miles to the southwest.

By then, the gold had disappeared, along with Robert Kedrick.

After that, there were no written records that would help Hal and Artie trace Kedrick's actions. Although they hadn't discussed it outright, both of them were depending on something deeper than knowledge.

They were depending on the blood that ran through their veins.

As they hiked along, Hal allowed his thoughts to take whatever course they would, as he remained focused on the past.

He was concerned about Artie, but less than he had been. The boy was no longer a child; not yet a man, maybe, but capable and willing to take on a man's work. Just because the society and times into which he'd been born didn't count him as a man, that didn't make him less able.

When Robert Kedrick had been seventeen, just two years older than Artie, he had already shot a man, set up his cattle herd on appropriated land and was courting his wife.

Hal wiped rain out of his face and looked upward. The high gray cliffs above looked like giant tombstones against the darkening sky.

What had really happened here one hundred years ago? And would they find out tonight?

He shivered as the rain dripped down from his hat into his collar and ran a chill path down his skin.

They had dressed for the weather. Both were eyeball to toenails in slicker gear and warm clothing. Protective coverings over their cowboy hats. But not even the best rainwear kept out all the wetness. Hal glanced back at Artie.

The boy was clearly chilled and miserable, but game. He happened to look up just as his father looked back, and he gave an ear-to-ear grin. Hal's heart warmed with pride. This was his son!

They carried camping-and-exploration gear on and in framed backpacks. Hal needed none of his notes or books—all the information he'd accumulated over the years was safely stored in his head. As long as nothing happened to that, they were all right.

He thought of the head of Robert Kedrick, sitting on Dixie's desk.

He thought of Dixie. Of Dixie leaving to go out to California.

His foot slipped, and he grabbed at the trunk of an aspen by the side of the path.

"You okay, Dad?" Artie asked, coming up close behind. "Looked like you kind of wandered off the path for a second there."

"I'm fine. Don't worry."

Keep your mind on the business at hand, Hal reminded himself. He had to focus on the past, not the future.

They walked on. The trees were still full with summer leaves, but the rain was too heavy for them to provide any shelter. The downpour was constant, chilly and depressing.

But it had snowed on Robert. Rain wasn't so bad, all things considered.

Hal continued to place one foot in front of the other. They'd had the advantage of being on horseback, a hundred years before, but horses would have made noise that couldn't be hidden. The last thing Hal needed was for someone left at the dinosaur dig camp to notice their passage and mention it to Hayden or Clark. Besides, horses might move a man too fast past something he ought to see. The only way to be sure they'd covered everything was to do it on foot. Inch by inch.

Eventually, they reached the section of the trail that led upward toward the tableland. After that, it was even slower going.

"How far?" Artie asked, speaking loudly to be heard over the drumming of the rain and the occasional rolls of thunder. "How high up do we go?"

"I'm not sure," Hal called back over his shoulder. "I know this is the way they went. But after that, I'm not sure. We'll just have to play it by ear."

"Good deal."

They climbed, using the rock walls alongside the trail for handholds and support. The path was wide enough for two to walk side by side, but they continued in single file. Rainwater coursed down, making footing treacherous and uncertain. Twice Hal slipped, only to be caught and saved from a messy fall by his son. Once, Artie lost his balance, but Hal reached back in time to grab him and keep him upright.

Eventually, they came to the end of the trail. The path led onto a rocky, thin-soiled, relatively flat section that overlooked the tableland below. Breathing hard, both Hal and Artie moved to the edge and stared down at the camp.

"They haven't all moved out," Artie commented. A few tents still stood and lanterns glowed gold in the growing darkness. Human shapes, swathed in rain gear, moved between shelters, carrying boxes and equipment.

"No," Hal agreed. "But with the storm, they aren't likely to notice us." He turned away. "Let's get down to business."

They unslung their backpacks, unloaded gear, then got to work.

DIXIE SAT BACK, stunned by what she had gleaned from Esther's father's journal.

"Your father hid the gold," she said. "He found it when he found the body. Hid it. And he just left it there, along with Robert. He didn't take it. He didn't tell anyone. And you've known about it all these years?"

Esther stared down at the faded pages. "Yes," she said. "But I didn't allow myself to think about it." She looked up, her brown eyes full of sorrow. "Can you understand that?"

"Not really."

"Child, the gold was death. It had killed and would kill again. My family pledged never to touch it. Never to speak of it. Never to tell."

"But you must. Hal needs to know."

"Harold Blane is following his own fate. If he finds the gold himself, then what happens is on his head."

"Esther, that is cowardly!"

"No." The old woman stared her down. "It is right."

Dixie considered that. "You mean, because the gold was, in a way, Robert's, that if Hal finds it . . . ?"

"It is his." Esther stood, her gaze turning upward. "It is not and never has been mine." She paused. "The storm is moving away from here. It's heading for the place where the gold waits." She looked at Dixie. "I think we must go there, too." Her voice seemed to have an echo in the small room. "You and I."

Dixie felt a shudder moving up her back. "Esther, you've told me repeatedly that you have no special powers. That you're just old. You can't know things like that. What's going on?"

Esther shook her head. "I don't know. But I have a feeling about this night."

"Right. Well, I don't know how I can get there within the next few hours. It'll take me at least two hours to get to the main road toward the dinosaur site, even if I could get through the mud that must be on the unpaved road by now."

"There is a way over the mountain. I have walked it many times." Esther reached down and reverently replaced the deerskin over the journal. "And tonight, we won't walk, we'll ride."

"On your ponies?"

Esther smiled. "They're small, and they're old, but they can take you and me along the mountain trail. We are both light. And they are strong."

"Esther, it's been years since I've been on a horse. I don't know if I can."

"You can." She turned away and replaced the journal in the trunk. She moved over to the cabinet against the wall where she kept much of her prepared herbal material. "And you will." She took a large pouch and started to fill it with items from the cabinet.

"Let me help," Dixie said, moving to her side. "Tell me what to do."

Esther put her hand on Dixie's for a moment. "Go and put the soft halters on the ponies. They need no metal bits in their mouths. And no saddles."

Dixie suppressed a groan, thinking about riding bareback for the first time in well over a decade. But she did as she was told. She was in this so far over her head that trying to be reasonable seemed the most unreasonable thing she could do.

The ponies seemed to sense that an adventure was beginning. They came whickering over to her when she entered the corral, cooperating agreeably when she slipped on the soft hackamores. The rain had turned the ground muddy, and their small hooves made squelching noises as they shifted around, nuzzling her for a treat. They smelled warm and grassy. She scratched their foreheads and made promises, all the while regarding their bony backs with trepidation. It was going to be a long, uncomfortable trek over to the dig site.

To her relief, however, when she went back into the cabin, she saw two blanket saddles. Esther handed them to her and added a big Hudson Bay blanket. "This is for you," she said. "The rain's past, but it's going to be cold on the mountain."

Dixie stared.

Esther was dressed all in buckskins. Her long gray hair, which usually hung tangled down her back, was braided neatly on both sides of her wrinkled face. She looked like a Shoshone woman.

"We journey to the past," Esther said by way of explanation.

"I know," Dixie replied.

And she did. All those strange sensations of traveling back in time that she'd been having since she moved to Seaside suddenly made sense. She was here for a purpose. She was here to help find and redeem the past. "I know," she repeated, wonderingly. "I have no idea *how,* but I know."

THIS TIME, when sounds in the house woke her, Hattie thought that Hal and Artie had returned, having sensibly given up on their outing because of the weather. She raised her head and looked at the digital clock on her bedside table.

Eleven o'clock. Well, they could settle in on their own, as far as she was concerned. It was just too late for them to expect her to get up and take care of their mess. They were on their own. It was time to practice a little creative selfishness, just like Dixie had told her in one of their recent sessions. She closed her eyes and went back to sleep.

The noises went on, but Hattie ignored them.

It was her right.

HAL SWUNG the short-handled pickax and hacked away a large chunk of mud and rock. Artie, squatting by the depression in the ground, plunged his gloved hands into the pile and felt for something, anything solid.

"No go, Dad," he said. "Nothing here, either."

"Damn." Hal rested the ax on the toe of his boot and pushed his hat back on his head. The rain had stopped, but it was now totally dark, and the ground was gluey mud. Because they were working by the light of a hooded lantern, it was almost impossible to see clearly. Hal was going only by instinct each time he chose to dig. "He couldn't have moved too far away from the others at any time," he said, talking almost to himself. "They would have suspected something. It has to be right around here."

"But he was buried down there." Artie waved toward the ledge where the skeleton had been found. "How come you're sure the gold's up here?"

Hal shook his head. "Don't know, son. I just feel it. I still haven't figured how he got down there in the first place. Doesn't make sense. If they shot him here, they would have planted him where he fell. They didn't have time to dig for a deep grave . . ." His voice trailed off.

"What is it?"

"I didn't think of this before, but maybe that wasn't the original burial place." Hal set down the pickax. He walked over to the edge and looked down. He hunkered down on his heels and studied the terrain.

About five hundred feet below, the paleontological camp spread out on the left side of the tableland. Many of the tents had been taken down, but half a dozen housed the remaining scientists and workers. Apparently, everyone had settled in for the night, discouraged by the hard rain from doing any further packing up.

Farther to the left was the cliffside and below that, the ledge where the skeleton had lain.

Too far from where he was to make any sense at all.

Unless someone had moved the corpse, and reburied Robert Kedrick.

Whoever had done that might have reburied the gold, too.

Or taken it.

Hal considered the possibilities. He sat back on his heels and closed his eyes.

"Dad?" Artie moved close. "What're you doing?"

"Shh," Hal replied. "Thinking."

Artie got quiet.

They stayed there by the edge for a long time, each lost in his own thoughts.

Hal felt the world around him fade. He concentrated, trying to take himself back, to imagine what it had been like, what had happened. How it had happened . . .

The thunder began softly, a drumming sound thrummed up the valley like distant artillery fire, then thinned and resolved into the clatter and splash of horses' hooves racing along the shallow creek bed.

Nine horsemen tore into view, their expressions desperate and angry. One rode behind, keeping watch over his shoulder, looking for and fearing pursuit. One rode in front, his gaze steadier than that of the others and raised to the high rock rim above them, to the flat table of land he knew so well.

He was a big man with rough-hewn features and skin leathered by a lifetime in the western sun. His eyes were bluer than the clear sky and his hair was a bronzy brown. His wide-brimmed hat shaded his face.

The eight followed the leader, leaving the water, heading to the aspen trees by the creek and then back up into the huge rocks at the base of the cliff, where they disappeared. For a few minutes, the clacking sound of the horses' hooves echoed in the valley. . . .

Hal took a deep breath. He opened his eyes and glanced at his son.

Artie had a vacant, dazed expression. A streak of mud that ran down the side of his face looked like blood in the darkness. "I don't know, Dad," he said. "I think maybe they didn't come up this far."

"They did." Hal put his hand on Artie's shoulder. "Question is, did they stay up here?" He pointed out into the night toward the prairie. The storm clouds were thinning as the weather moved east, and a glow of moonlight gave the scene a silvery cast. "The posse would have been coming from out there. They'd want to be up here where they could see."

"Yeah, but when the storm came, maybe they went for the lower land. Shelter."

"He knew this land. He'd know where they could sit it out."

"We know it, too."

"But it's changed...." Hal paused. "That's it!" He stood up. "The cliffside down there eroded enough to expose the skeleton. Look at the way the water's been running down the trail up here. I'd bet my last dollar that—"

A rifle shot rang out and the bullet hit him before he could finish his sentence. Hal staggered back to the edge of the cliff. Artie screamed and grabbed for his father.

But it was too late. Without another sound, Hal Blane disappeared into the night.

DIXIE SHIFTED POSITION on her pony, trying to ease the soreness of her rear. Saddle blanket or not, she was still riding a skinny horse, essentially bareback, and it hurt. She suppressed the urge to complain out loud. Esther had been quiet during the entire hour they'd been riding, and Dixie was reluctant to intrude on the silence.

Besides, the mountain forest seemed to demand silence tonight. Even the ponies' hooves sounded muffled as they clopped along. Wrapped up as she was in the Hudson Bay blanket, Dixie felt cocooned from the outside world.

The ride had been uncomfortable, but also mystical. She traveled in a kind of waking dream, letting Esther and her pony take her where they would, trusting as she had never chosen to trust before. The world around her was dark, clean from the rain and peaceful.

Then she heard the rifle shot.

"What's that?" she asked, almost falling off her pony. "Esther, is someone shooting at us?"

Esther said nothing, but she kicked her pony in the sides and the little horse started to canter along the forest trail. Dixie's mount followed, and she had to grab hold of his mane to keep from being thrown off. In a moment, though, she had her balance and was leaning over the pony's neck, urging him on.

They raced through the trees and came out into an open space. A man knelt beside a large rock, aiming down at a target below him. Dixie screeched and threw off the blanket covering her. She kicked the pony and charged the man. Startled, he turned in her direction and yelled. For a split second, he aimed his rifle at her, but then he ducked and disappeared into the trees to her right where the slope ran uphill toward the higher mountains. The pony slid to a stop at the rock, right at the edge of the drop-off, over which the man had been aiming.

Dixie dismounted and ran to look.

Artie Blane's white face stared up at her from the ledge below. "He shot my dad!" he cried. "Dixie, he killed my dad!"

THE NOISES BECAME too insistent for Hattie to sleep. Annoyed, she threw off the light cover and put on her bathrobe. Hal and Artie were still upstairs in his study, rummaging around, making more noise than—

Hattie hesitated at the door of her room. Why were they up in Hal's study at this hour? She drew the edges of her robe together. If they'd come back all wet and dirty and tired, they would have just taken off their muddy clothes downstairs, had quick showers and gone to bed.

They would not be spending time up in the study. That was certain!

She stepped back from the door.

The telephone was out in the hall. She couldn't get to it and call for help without taking the chance of being overheard. Besides, she'd cried wolf once already today. Suppose it *was* just the boys up there? Wouldn't she be doubly a fool if she assumed it was a burglar and it really wasn't?

She had to find out what was what, and then decide how to act.

If she was facing real danger, she'd have to think and move faster and more effectively than she'd ever done before. She went back to her bed, sat down and began to plan.

"DAMN IT, Turner," Oscar Hayden whispered. "You've plowed through everything up here. How can you be so sure he's got a line on the gold?"

Reed Turner stopped looking through the file cabinet for a moment. "Because I know men," he said. "This man knows where the gold is. He's just been waiting for the right time to locate it."

"And that time's suddenly now?"

"Yes, indeed. Once your boy, Clark, found the skeleton, Blane knew he was set for life. All he had to do was wait until the remains were identified and then he could act like he was hunting for the treasure.''

"I'm afraid I still don't understand how breaking into his home and riffling through his papers is going to be of any benefit to us. Why aren't we out watching him and taking it from him when he finds it?''

"Because," Reed Turner explained, "we would only be thieves then. No better than his great-grandfather. No, my dear Hayden, what we need to do is establish prior rights that will stand up in a legal situation. Show that by scientific and historical research methods we had already located the gold.''

"So we take it, anyway.''

"Yes, but without violence. And without redress on Blane's part.''

Oscar Hayden chuckled, softly. "Mr. Turner, I do like the way you think, sir. I do, indeed.''

"Well, *I* don't," announced Hattie Blane. She reached to the side and turned on the study light. "I surely don't.''

Both men turned to the open study doorway.

Oscar Hayden gasped, and Reed Turner yelled.

WINNIE NASH WAS sound asleep when the snapping sound of a gunshot woke her. She'd slept through the worst of the thunderstorm without flinching, but that sound brought her to nerve-tingling wakefulness immediately.

That, and the fact that someone was in her tent.

Winnie eased one eye open. The tent was dark, but the tiny beam of a pencil-light cut through the gloom. Whoever it was had bent over her small camp desk and was trying to read her notes.

She opened her eye a little more.

No. Not her notes. Her private journal! Winnie reached carefully under the cot for her gun and powerful flashlight. Before she'd left Boston, her fiancé, who had never been west of New York City, had given the revolver to her, warning her against everything from rattlesnakes to bears. She'd learned to shoot the thing and kept it handy, but she'd never dreamed she'd actually need it.

She eased the weapon and flashlight up and under the blanket. With sensitive fingertips, she checked to make sure the gun was loaded and that the safety was off.

She sat up, balanced the light between her knees, aimed the gun, flicked on the light and shouted. "Hold still, sucker," she yelled. "I've got you covered!"

In the bright beam, Hastings Clark was pinned like a bug. He turned around, scattering her papers across the tent floor. Then, ignoring her repeated command to halt, he bolted into the night.

Shaken, but angry, Winnie got up. She went over to her desk and flicked on the battery light. Her journal was gone. She grabbed a sweatshirt and stuffed her feet into her boots. Still waving the gun and flashlight, she ran outside.

No sign of Hastings Clark. He'd disappeared

"Hastings," she yelled. "Where are you, you creep! Give me back my journal!"

Other paleontologists rushed out of their tents to see what was going on. Winnie yelled again for Hastings and shone the light around the camp.

Wayne Sussex came running over. "Are you all right? I thought I heard someone shooting," he said. "You weren't aiming at Hastings Clark, were you?"

"I haven't even fired my gun," Winnie declared. "But I heard a shot, too."

One of the other workers pointed toward the cliffs above the camp. "It seemed to come from up there," she said.

Winnie aimed the beam of her flashlight. The sides of the cliff had been stripped of earth and vegetation by the recent rains, and looked like the walls of a gigantic prison.

High on a narrow ledge, not twenty feet from the camp, lay a body. A man. His arm and one leg hung over the edge, his head was turned away from the drop. Winnie could see blood on his back. Dark, almost black in the glare of the flashlight. Several people screamed. She suppressed the urge to scream, herself, and directed the light beam higher.

Artie Blane knelt by the edge of the next ledge, his young face dead white in the flashlight gleam. Even from this distance, his stricken expression was clear to read.

His father lay, bleeding, maybe dead, below him.

Winnie heard another voice and took the light higher.

There, at the top of the mountain over the camp, was Dixie Sheldon. A small Indian woman stood with her. Winnie saw the heads of two horses. A rope. Two ropes.

And then Dixie was over the side and climbing down the rock.

Toward Artie. Toward Hal.

Winnie turned and snapped out specific and urgent orders to her people.

CHAPTER SIXTEEN

THE ROPES CAME from a pack on Esther's pony. The knowledge of how to use them came from a time when Dixie had done technical rock climbing for a hobby. Dixie made her way carefully down the side of the cliff, trying to keep her emotions in check as she hung far above the surface of the first ledge where Artie waited.

Waited and watched for someone to come and help his father, silently, stoically. Just like his father. Any other boy would have been screaming and crying for help.

Dixie refused to believe Hal was dead. He just couldn't be! She would know it, somehow, if he were. And Esther would have, too. Esther was the one who handed the ropes to her and said, "Get to him, child. Heal him. You know how."

So, that was exactly what she was going to do.

The rock was wet from the recent downpour, and the hand- and toeholds were slick and treacherous, but Dixie continued to move downward. Too much depended on her for any mishap to occur. Too much.

She reached Artie in a few minutes. The boy's face was streaked with tears. He helped her retrieve the ropes and retie them so that she could continue down, to Hal.

"When did he fall?" she asked. "Before or after he was shot?"

"After," Artie said, helping her snake the rope around a column of rock. "Dixie? You think he's dead?"

"No." She tested the rope. "I won't let him be." She edged over the side. "Watch that for me, and stay right where you are. I don't know who shot at your father, but whoever it was is still out there."

"I know," Artie said. "And I'm taking care of him, myself." His tone was low and menacing. The tears were gone now. His stony expression was exactly the same as the one his father wore so much of the time.

"Don't you dare!" Dixie regarded him. "Think of your father," she said. "And your grandmother. And you stay here. Don't even dream of going after the gunman."

"Yes, ma'am," he said. But there was more defiance than obedience in his face.

Dixie had no time for that, however. She adjusted the pack on her back and went over the side. The rope slid through her hands, burning her palms raw, but she ignored the pain. In a few moments, she was standing on the narrow ledge where Hal lay.

Her first close-up view of him showed her that he was indeed still alive. She wanted to shout and dance for sheer relief and joy. But she settled down immediately, getting to the task at hand.

Trying not to let her emotions take control, she knelt by his side. He was stretched out, facedown on the rock, one arm bent under him, the other hanging over the edge. One leg also dangled precariously. The other was straight and unbroken. His hat was gone, but she could see no bleeding on his face or head. His eyes were closed, his breathing was shallow.

There was blood on his back.

Dixie set up a small lantern Esther had placed in the pack. By its flickering flame, she studied his injury.

The rifle bullet had not done him too much harm. Bad enough, but not fatal. It had passed cleanly through the fleshy part of his side and lower back, missing bone and vital organs entirely. Dixie almost bent her head and wept with relief. It had been the impact that had thrown him off the upper ledge, not the fact that he had been mortally wounded.

Nevertheless, he was still in serious trouble. His right arm was probably broken, and he had been badly stunned by the fall, possibly suffering a concussion or worse. She wouldn't know until she got him to a medical center.

And to do that, she first had to get him off the ledge.

She looked up. Artie was there, staring down. "He's alive," she called out. "But I've got to get him off here. Can you go for help?"

Artie shook his head and pointed outward. He was almost grinning. Dixie turned and looked. From the east, she saw lights moving and then heard the *rattle-rattle-tat* of a helicopter. The Life Flight that she'd sent for to get Esther must somehow, miraculously, have been diverted here. As she watched, the copter turned on searchlight beams and found her and Hal on the rocky ledge. She waved, knowing she was seen and that professional help was almost there. She sent up a quick prayer of thanks.

While the paramedics and pilot in the Life Flight were obviously figuring out the best way to get to Hal, she worked on staunching the flow of blood from his wound and keeping him from going deeper into shock. Using a pressure bandage made from a variety of soft tree barks, she bound up his side. The arm she splinted. But she could accomplish nothing else for him until she had a complete medical facility at her disposal. Until then, staying with him and watching him was all she could do.

She held his hand and stroked his hair. Thought about her feelings for him. Thought about the future.

The helicopter jockeyed around, finally landing on the ledge where Artie waited. From there, they lowered one of their men and a stretcher on stout ropes.

He was a blocky, short strong man with a bald head covered by a baseball cap bearing the Life Flight logo. Over the sound of the helicopter, he yelled, "It's okay now, lady. I'll take care of him from here."

"I'm a doctor," Dixie shouted in reply. "He's my patient."

From that point on, she was in charge.

Together they secured him to the stretcher, got him up the cliff and into the chopper. After Hal was strapped onto the inside gurney, Dixie went to work. She took his blood pressure and had the paramedics record his other vital signs every five minutes. She schooled herself to keep her touch and tone professional, so as not to give away the turmoil of her emotions at seeing him so helpless.

They reached the medical center hospital at Casper in a short while. Dixie stepped aside then, and let the emergency doctors take over. Standing back, also, but keeping a close watch on the proceedings, were two men whose badges hanging from their suit coat pockets identified them as detectives. The law would have lots of questions for her soon, she realized. But now, all that concerned her was Hal's life.

With a flurry of furious activity, done efficiently and in almost complete silence, the trauma team took him into the surgical suite. No one said a word to her, but she knew they were aware that she was the primary caregiver. They'd get to her with information as soon as they knew....

Dixie took a chair in the waiting area. The detectives kept a respectful distance for the time being and she ignored them. She sat totally immobile for a few minutes, paralyzed, physically and emotionally.

When she started to sob, she scarcely noticed the two men leave the area.

She was still crying silently when M. J. Nichols appeared in the waiting room. He came over and hugged her. "I heard about it from a buddy down in the emergency room and another contact at the sheriff's department," he explained. "And I figured you'd be here. How are you doing?"

"You're a good friend," Dixie said, sniffing and wiping away tears, "I'm doing okay, now. Just making a complete idiot of myself by bawling my eyes out."

"This guy's really got to you." M.J. dug in a pocket and handed her a cloth handkerchief.

"I guess he has." Dixie took the handkerchief gratefully. All the tissues in the provided box had been long since used up and tossed into the trash can by her side. "I can't believe I'm carrying on like this."

"Dixie Sheldon," M.J. declared. "At some point in time, all of us mortals fall in love. It appears to me that you've finally taken the plunge."

Dixie stared at her old friend. "Do you really think that's what's happened to me?"

"Bet on it." M.J. gave her another hug. "He's going to make it, darlin'. Just you wait and see." M.J. smiled. The expression affected all the muscles in his round, pleasantly handsome face. He ran a hand over his thinning, dark hair. "If you're in the mood, I'd like to lay out a few items of interest that I discovered in a brief examination of the case you gave me regarding this guy."

Dixie gasped. "You already found stuff?"

"Indeed I did. And most interesting it was."

"Then tell me, please. I need to think about anything other than Hal lying in there."

"Well, first, if Hal in there is able to get up and walk out of here any day soon, I'll have his family's land case up in front of a judge quicker than you can spit."

"You're kidding me. It wasn't a legitimate governmental land takeover?"

"Not if it's based on poverty brought on by deliberate retributive measures inflicted on the widow of the alleged outlaw, Robert Kedrick."

"What are you saying, M.J.?"

"He was a government secret agent. The gang he joined as an undercover fed had been making hits for months. The gold stolen was U.S. Army gold, and someone in a position of authority knew the route it would take. And that someone didn't want the undercover scheme to become public knowledge when the gold was taken, so he hired Kedrick, an amateur.

"When Kedrick was killed and the gold vanished, that person figured if Mrs. Kedrick was made the object of public scorn and financial destitution, she'd never have the time, money, spirit or influence to look into the whole mess."

Dixie stared. "You're a wonder, M.J. But I didn't know they had secret agents back then."

"Not many departments did, but Treasury was one that did. Your Hal should be proud of his ancestor. Undercover agent for the Treasury Department, no less." M.J. preened a little. "Want to know how I found out?"

Dixie smiled for the first time in a long while. "I am all ears," she said.

"Freedom of Information Act. It's hidden in a section that not even I, with my great legal intellect, would have thought of digging into—his file was stuck out of alphabetical sequence in the Butch Cassidy-Sundance Kid records provided by Pinkerton to the government. Out of date, out of place, out of order."

"How in the world did you find it? Why could you when Hal couldn't?"

"He's too close, I think. A relative. They'd be terrified of a lawsuit. Not only that, but you have to consider that despite his obsession, he might not have really wanted to know the truth—if it had turned out the lie was the truth. Who wouldn't rather have it still questioned, at least in their own minds?

"And I have a friend whose job and great good pleasure is outfoxing bureaucrats. I just put Miranda to work on it. You remember her? The private investigator who helped with my cousin Allison's problems a few years back? She was close to uncovering everything when I started getting phone calls and faxes from Washington. They're scared of another scandal, no matter how old. I just pushed a few buttons in Washington, and, lo, the hundred-year-old records were in the fax."

"M.J., I love you."

"Yeah. But you love that sheriff guy a whole lot more, don't you?"

Dixie felt tears coming again. "Yes, I guess I do."

At that point, the doors to the surgery suite opened and a green-clad physician came out. He was a tall young man with short, sandy-colored hair and greenish eyes. "I'm Dr. Sanders," he said, addressing M.J. "Your patient is doing just fine."

"Oh, thank God!" Dixie cried.

"He's her patient," M.J. said, pointing at Dixie. "She's the doctor. I'm a lawyer."

Sanders gave him a withering look. "I see." He turned to Dixie. "The arm's not broken. Just badly sprained. It'll be a while hurting and healing, but he won't have to wear a cast. The gunshot wound was the only thing I had a question about," he said. "Someone stuffed some kind of vegetable gunk on it. Stopped the bleeding, all right, but..."

"I did," Dixie said. "It was a dried mash of inner bark of wild cherry and aspen. I—"

"Indian stuff?" Sanders looked impressed. Then he looked closer at Dixie.

"Yes, I—"

"One of them found him, then?"

"No. I treated him. I've been studying with an elderly woman who—"

"Well," Dr. Sanders said, interrupting again. "Interesting." He moved a little closer. "Where are you practicing?"

"Up in Seaside. I—"

"Why not here?" He waved his hand, then touched her shoulder. "This is the regional medical center. You're wasting your time up there in the hinterland."

Dixie stepped back and stared at him. "I don't think so," she said coldly. "May I see Mr. Blane now?"

"He's in the recovery room."

"Where's that?"

Dr. Sanders started to suggest that she continue to wait outside, then changed his mind. "Follow me," he said. "But your friend can't come."

"It's okay," M.J. said. He kissed Dixie's cheek. "Get in touch with me as soon as you can," he said.

"M.J., thanks." Dixie hugged him again. "Thanks for being there when I needed your help. I don't know what we would have done..."

"It's not over yet, darlin'," M.J. advised. "Unless something spectacular happens, he's got a long legal fight ahead of him, you know."

"I was afraid of that." Dixie paused. "But it's possible I'll be with him through it."

M.J. raised his eyebrows, but said nothing.

A few minutes later, Dixie was standing at Hal's bedside. She had borrowed a white lab coat, and no one questioned her presence.

He was pale, and he looked almost too large for the standard-size recovery bed. With his eyes closed, the stabilizing wrappings on his arm and the bandages across his torso, he looked utterly helpless.

She reached out and smoothed his hair.

"He should be waking up any time now," Dr. Sanders said. He had come in and was standing beside her. Dixie hadn't noticed him until he spoke. "The concussion's not a bad one, but it's liable to give him a headache for a few days. And he may be a little disoriented at first. The local police are going to want to talk to both of you."

"I would expect that," she said, still looking only at Hal.

"Um," Dr. Sanders said, "Is he your... I mean, are you and he..."

"We are," Dixie said.

"I see." Dr. Sanders left.

She settled in to wait for Hal. As long as it took, she would wait.

One of the recovery-room nurses eventually brought her a chair. Dixie sat down. She drank coffee, but didn't eat. The nurses came and went, checking his vital signs and making notes on his chart.

Dixie began to get sleepy.

Her eyes closed for a moment.

"Dixie!" Hal was yelling her name. "Dixie!"

Dixie stood up.

"Dixie! Don't go! Don't leave me!"

He was sitting up in bed, reaching out for something with his free left hand. His eyes were open, but he wasn't seeing anything.

Not anything in the room, at least.

"Dixie, I know where it is!" he shouted. "I can find the gold!"

She grabbed his hand, then embraced him. Nurses swarmed round, but she shooed them away. "Hal, I'm right here," she said. "Look at me."

He pushed her aside. "She's gone," he said, moaning the words. "She left me. Left us." He looked to the right. Anger replaced the grief on his face. "Is that you, Robert? Tell me the truth, damn you!"

Dixie moved back to hold him, but the head nurse stopped her. "He's having delusions. Worse than we anticipated. We're going to have to use restraints so he doesn't hurt himself." She signaled to two large orderlies.

"Robert!" Hal screamed. "You dropped it, didn't you! Buried it, too." He fell back on the bed, his breath coming in great gasps. "You old bastard," he whispered.

The orderlies took the opportunity to try applying the strap restraints. The moment they touched him, Hal exploded again. He fought them like a demon.

The two large men were thrown to the floor.

Before they could get up and go after him again, Dixie moved. Ignoring all her training in hospital protocol, she pushed past the nurses, climbed up on the bed and on her knees, took Hal's head and placed it against her breast. "Shh," she said, stroking his hair. "I'm right here, Hal. It's Dixie. I'm here with you. I'm not going away. I'm not leaving you. Not now. Not ever. I love you, Hal."

Unconscious, delirious and injured, Hal Blane sighed, relaxed, quit fighting and drifted back into healthy sleep.

After a few hours, he was moved to a regular room and Dixie took up her vigil in a more comfortable chair. She slept, herself, dozing and waking to see how he was every so often. She answered calls from concerned Seaside folk until the doctor ordered that no more personal calls be put through. The silence and lack of need to reexplain without explaining a thing was a blessed relief! The day passed and night came again. Hal slept on.

Dixie woke and watched.

And thought.

Funny, she mused, how when it all came down to one final decision, it was easy to do. She thought about that for a while, then slept some more.

The two detectives showed up and asked some questions, but, with Hal still unconscious, they didn't seem inclined to pursue matters for the time being. Dixie did nothing to discourage that attitude. Until she knew everything, she was keeping what she could strictly to herself, and M.J.

AT DAWN on the second morning, Hal woke up. "Dixie?" he asked, looking at the small, rumpled figure slumped in the chair next to his bed. "Dixie, what are you doing? You're going to get a crick in your neck, sleeping that way."

She eased into an upright position. Every muscle ached. "Hal? Are you really awake?"

"Sure." He grinned weakly. "How long have I . . . ?"

"Long enough," she replied, getting up and touching his face. "What do you remember?"

He just looked at her.

Dixie felt herself getting lost. Finally, she whispered, "I love you." Tears filled her eyes and ran down her cheeks.

"Then, it was no dream," he said softly, touching the tears. "I did hear you say you'd stay with me. Forever."

Dixie managed a smile. "We both said a lot of things."

"Don't evade the issue."

"I won't. I did say it. And I meant it."

"I know about California. And about the clinic closing. What will you do?"

"I don't know," she admitted, holding his hand tightly. "I have no idea. But I'll manage something, let me tell you."

"No," he said. "*We'll* manage something." With his good hand, he hooked the back of her neck and pulled her to him.

After that, they didn't talk for a while.

Eventually, the morning-shift nurses interrupted them, and knowing Dr. Sanders would be along soon to check on his patient, Dixie excused herself to go down to the doctor's lounge to get cleaned up.

The day before, M.J.'s married cousin, Allie Glass, had brought over some fresh clothes and toiletries for her. After she had showered and changed, Dixie was helping herself to some more coffee and a doughnut out in the main room when she overheard two older doctors discussing her.

Or, at least, discussing the treatment she'd used in the field on Hal's wound.

"Damnedest thing I've ever seen," one man was saying. "The goop was just plastered right against the open wound. No regard for sepsis at all."

The other doctor was a women, but also older, with graying hair and a severe expression on her face. "I don't know what's going on with these young people just out of medical school," she said. "They think by going primitive, all the health problems of the world will be solved."

The woman sipped her coffee. "We might as well set up a place for them to keep their leeches."

Both laughed scornfully.

Dixie scowled. But she said nothing in defense of Esther's poultice. To argue with ignorance was a waste of time. She'd need scientific proof for people like that.

And that's what she could get, working in Seaside.

If, somehow, she could manage to keep her job. Ironically, just a few months before, she would have jumped at the opportunity in California and left Seaside without a backward glance.

Now, it looked as if she was committed to life there.

Life with Hal.

Of course, she reflected, as she walked down the hall toward his room, although they had both declared love, no one had mentioned a permanent, binding relationship.

No one had mentioned marriage.

She went into his room.

"What are you doing?" she cried when she saw him. "Hal?"

He was up and getting dressed. Dr. Sanders stood by, sputtering in protest. "Tell him he can't do this," the doctor said, addressing Dixie. "He has to stay here for observation for at least another forty-eight hours."

"Hell I do," Hal declared. He held up his ripped and bloodstained shirt. "Dixie, get me a clean shirt, will you, please?"

"No! Your doctor's right. You get yourself right back in bed this minute, Hal Blane."

"Nope." He tossed the shirt aside. "Guess I just won't wear one. Still pretty warm out." He hitched up his jeans and fastened them.

He looked magnificent. "Hal, you cannot do this!" Dixie yelled.

"Mr. Blane, you mustn't..."

Hal turned and smiled at the other man. "Doctor," he said, "I really do appreciate all you've done to patch me up. But I'm fine now, and it's time I got home and went back to work." He looked at Dixie. "I'm going to have a wife to provide for, soon," he added.

Dixie couldn't speak.

"Well, if you release yourself into Dr. Sheldon's care, I suppose it's all right," Sanders said. He didn't sound pleased, but clearly he had come to terms with the fact that if Hal wanted to do something, that was what would happen.

"Okay, Doctor." Hal held out his hand to Sanders. "Again, thanks. Send the bill to SeaLake County."

"It's already done."

"Dixie, honey, do you think you can get me a new shirt someplace?" Hal asked. "I really don't want to traipse around town half-naked."

"I... Sure," she managed to say. "I'll call—"

"Morning, everybody." M.J. came into the room. He had an armload of packages. "Have I interrupted something important?"

Dixie made the introductions.

"I brought some clothes that just might fit you, Sheriff," M.J. said. "They belonged to a friend of my cousin's husband." He dumped the packages on the bed. "He's on the big side."

Dixie reached for one package, opened it and handed Hal a white shirt. Hal slipped it on. "Thanks." He smoothed the cloth. "Nice," he added. "Silk?"

"I think so," M.J. responded.

While Hal buttoned up the shirt, Dr. Sanders handed Dixie a large folder. "Here are his records, his test results and lab work," he said. "He's almost too healthy, as you probably know. It's clear he's doing fine, but if he develops any problems, get him back here as quickly as you can, Doctor.''

"I will." Dixie glanced over to where Hal was grinning broadly, and talking animatedly with M.J., who must have been sharing some good news.

"And here are his prescriptions," Dr. Sanders went on. "You can get them filled downstairs at the hospital pharmacy. They'll give you a discount." After that, he left the room.

"Dixie!" Hal didn't yell this time, but his tone was urgent and excited.

"Yes?"

"Did you hear about this?" He indicated the smiling M.J. "Did you hear?" He held his arms wide open, favoring his sprained left one.

Dixie went to him and was embraced. "I did. While you were in surgery." She put her hand on his chest and looked up at him. "It was the only good thing that happened all night."

"No, it wasn't." He continued to hold her close. "You decided you loved me."

Dixie nodded. "I did. Maybe I'm out of my mind, but I am sure about what I feel now."

"Then, what your friend has told me is only second-best," Hal said softly.

They kissed. M.J applauded.

And Dixie knew her decision was the right one. Anything other than love simply did not matter. Not now.

A LITTLE LATER, they were seated in the conference room at M.J.'s downtown law office. M.J. was going over the details of what he had learned about the Kedrick case.

"Now, as the old records stand, your great-grandfather, Robert Kedrick, was a rancher who took to larceny on the side," he said to Hal. He spread photocopies of newspapers out on the table. "Common wisdom back then assumed he either liked the wild life or needed the cash for his ranch."

Hal sat back in his chair. He had been holding Dixie's hand, but now he released it and stuffed his hands into his pockets. "That was one reason the ranch land was immediately forfeit," he said. "When the land started to go, folks figured Robert would come back and try to shoot his way clear of trouble."

"And he'd be killed."

"Yeah." Hal stared at M.J. "Only that had already happened before they started cutting away at the land."

"'They' being the government powers that be."

Dixie spoke up. "But if he was working for the Treasury Department, surely someone could have cleared his name right away."

"That's right," M.J. agreed. "So we have to figure that his official contact in Treasury had some reason for keeping quiet, don't we? Good reason to blacken Robert Kedrick's name and arrange for the eventual ruin of his ranch."

Hal's eyes narrowed. "What was the name of his contact? Have you found that out?"

"I have." M.J. handed over a document.

Hal opened it and read. "Son of a bitch," he said softly.

"Who? What?" Dixie asked.

Hal handed her the papers. "A man named Turner," he said. "Rudolph Turner."

"Reed Turner's . . . ?"

"Great-uncle." Hal looked grim.

"I talked to your dad about him, Dixie," M.J. said. "I gave him a call yesterday. And I think it's real interesting that Rudolph's great-nephew, Reed, has spent a good part of his adult life trying to figure out who the mysterious secret agent was. No one besides his great-uncle knew who the agent actually was. It could have been any of the outlaws.

"Rudolph hired Kedrick, figuring to take the gold from him after he and the gang stole it from the army. Kedrick's one big mistake was in trusting a government man. He believed the lies Turner told him.

"But once they'd all disappeared, Turner never found either the gold or the body. One member of the gang apparently confessed years later to killing Kedrick, but no one could really count on getting the truth from any of them. Because Reed Turner's ancestor was convinced that the secret agent had hidden gold somewhere before he disappeared, Reed Turner—"

"Wanted it," Hal finished. He reached for Dixie's hand again. "Honey, I need to call home and tell Ma and Artie not to trust that man, and to be on the alert for—"

A knock at the door of the conference room interrupted him. M.J.'s secretary, Barbara, opened the door and said, "Sorry to interrupt, but Sheriff Blane, there's a call for you from your office in Seaside."

"Here?" Hal stood up. "How'd they find me?"

Barbara shrugged. "Seems that your deputy's been tracking you all over town. Line two, sir." She pointed to the conference-room telephone.

Hal went over to the small table in the corner and punched a button. Dixie sat back down as she watched him pick up the receiver and speak. He was silent for a moment, expressionless as he so frequently was, and she felt relief start to ease her tense muscles.

And then Hal said, "Keep 'em locked up until I get there. Don't bother with them, yourself. I'm going to kill them both."

CHAPTER SEVENTEEN

HAL HUNG UP the phone and looked at Dixie. His expression was stony, once more, his eyes narrowed slits, his mouth tight. Two high spots of color shone on his cheekbones and there was a whiteness at the edge of his nostrils. "Let's go," he said. "I have some business to take care of at home."

"So we heard." Dixie moved close to him, praying she could reach through to his heart. "Hal, what's going on?"

"You weren't serious about the killing thing, were you?" M.J. asked.

Hal didn't answer immediately. He did, however, soften enough to put his arm around her. "That was Ted," he said. "Ma caught Reed Turner and Oscar Hayden in my study the other night. Held them prisoner with my dad's old .45 until daylight when Ted came by to see if she was all right." He shut his eyes. "If she'd fired that thing, it would likely have blown up in her face."

"Oh, my God!"

"And Artie's missing. Along with Hastings and George."

"George?" Dixie asked. "Not...?"

"George Preston. Artie overheard him talking about shooting me. Conspiring with Hayden and Hastings about the gold."

"I saw him. He was the one who shot you. Artie doesn't know that, does he?"

"I don't know. No one's seen him since the helicopter took us away the other night. Winnie says she caught Hastings in her tent, just before that, stealing her journal. She pulled a gun on him and he ran, with the journal. She'd written down details of the reconstruction you did on Robert and had also speculated about the location of the gold." Dixie felt Hal tighten his arm muscles until they shook. "No one knows where Artie is. At least no one's saying," he added darkly.

"Just what do you have in mind?" M.J. asked. "Sounds to me like you have some plans for those two your mother nabbed."

"I might. Not your business," Hal answered.

"Hal, listen to him," Dixie implored. "He's a lawyer. A *good* one!"

Hal looked down at her. "Can he get my boy back? Unhurt?"

"Listen, Hal," M.J. said. "I don't know what you have planned or think you have planned, and I guess I don't want to know, but do us all a favor and cool off first."

"I'm cool," Hal said. His arm, around Dixie, started to tremble violently.

And then Sheriff Blane fainted.

THEY DID NOT make him go back to the hospital. Not even M.J., who didn't know him well, attempted to suggest that. Instead, once Dixie had revived him and it was apparent that he was not in danger, M.J. drove them up the mountain to his cousin's house. The Glass family made them welcome and provided everything Dixie needed to see to Hal's comfort and well-being.

They gathered in the family room, with Hal reclining on the big sofa and the rest seated on chairs or the floor. Although the five children wanted to stay, their mother shooed them outside to play, giving the twins, the oldest, strict orders to keep watch over the youngest toddlers, also twins. A blond girl was the middle child, and she was followed at all times by a gray poodle called Fred.

The adults waited until the small mob disappeared, then M.J explained to Matt and Allie Glass some of the problems Hal was facing.

"That silk shirt you're wearing," Matt said to Hal. "It belonged to a friend of mine who made his living most of his adult life as a mercenary. I think I can help you. I was kind of a merc, too. He and I did some work together when I was younger. Hunt-and-rescue operations."

Dixie stared at him. "You're kidding," she said. Matt Glass was a handsome man, blond and clean-featured with a trim body, but he looked more like a professor than a warrior. His wife, Allie, was the fighter in the family, as far as Dixie knew. Allison Glass was a state senator and was considering running for the governor's slot next election year.

"He's not kidding," Allie said. "Before we married, an enemy of mine kidnapped me and almost killed me. Matt and his crew saved me." She patted her cousin's arm. "Of course, M.J. was a hero, too. If it hadn't been for him, I would have been shot in spite of what Matt did."

M.J. blushed and smiled. He'd obviously enjoyed his role as hero.

"So, what's all this got to do with my problem?" Hal asked. "I have to get up there and find my boy, and I don't really care who I take apart to do it."

"We all understand that," Matt said. "But you can't. Not if you want to give Dixie, here, and your other loved ones any future. Listen, man, I was ready to run for the high country with my niece when things got rough for us, and the law was going to take her away from me. But because of Allie and M.J. and some other good people, I kept my head and stayed and fought things out legally."

Hal frowned.

"Hell, you're the sheriff," Matt said. "You have to obey the law!"

"Hal, it would put a real spin on the Kedrick legend if you did toe the line on this," Dixie said. "But we still have to find Artie. I agree with that!"

Hal settled back on the sofa cushions. "So you were a merc?" he asked Matt.

"More of an adventurer. I didn't do any actual fighting if I could avoid it. My specialty was finding folks. Kidnap victims. Lost explorers. That kind of thing."

"Hmm," Hal said. He leaned his head against Dixie's shoulder. "What do you think, honey?" he asked.

Dixie was almost too surprised to answer, but she did. "Listen to this man, Hal. You know the terrain up there. You've certainly done standard search and rescue. You're certainly capable of dealing with violence. But I think M.J. introduced us to Matt for a reason." She looked at her friend. "Am I right, M.J.?"

M.J. just smiled.

IT ALL TOOK longer than Hal would have liked, but in a couple of hours, they had a battle plan. While M.J. and Matt made key phone calls to set things up, Dixie gave him a healing brew of her forest herbs and Allie Glass fixed him some sort of high-protein milk shake.

His head still hurt, but he felt much better.

He needed some time to be alone with Dixie and talk, but he felt better.

She'd said she loved him and hadn't denied the possibility of a future with him when he'd spoken of it in front of her friend, M.J.

Yes, he felt much, much better.

But as they flew northeast toward Seaside in Matt Glass's plane, his insides began to twist with real fear. Where was Artie? What had happened? Was his mother all right after the shock and stress of keeping two desperate men at gunpoint for hours?

What was going to be the future for his family? Was what M.J. told him about Robert Kedrick's secret role as a treasury agent actually going to make any difference?

And what about that dream he'd had in the hospital? The one where Robert had come and outright shown him what had happened to the gold...?

Artie. He had to be alive and safe! Hal clenched his fists and started to shake.

"Hal, are you all right?" He heard Dixie's voice in his ear over the roar of the propellers. Hal nodded and reached over to hold her hand.

That made him feel better.

"Dixie," he said, "I... I want... I can't promise you..."

She quieted him with a kiss as tender as the love in her eyes. "Later," she told him. "We'll have a lifetime. Later."

That was all he needed to hear.

They landed on an unused stretch of dirt road, Matt handling the small plane with an expert touch. As prearranged, Al Pringle was there to meet them with Hal's Jeep and two other vehicles, which had been driven by two of Al's sons. Hal got three police radios out of the back and gave one to M.J., one to Matt and the last one to Dixie. He didn't have much to say to anyone after that, but he thanked Al and his boys and shook hands all around. The Pringles left, and Hal spoke to his troops.

"I'll be calling all of you as soon as I have some results," he said.

"Keep cool," M.J advised. "You won't have witnesses, but if you do anything out of line, it could backfire."

"I know." Hal looked at Dixie. "Do you trust me?"

"Yes," she said.

That was enough for him. He got in the Jeep and took off for town without another word.

Dixie watched him drive away. Then she turned to her own car. "I know Esther will be waiting to hear from me," she said to M.J. and Matt. "I'll find her, and then I'll call as soon as we're on our way."

Matt held his thumb up. M.J. nodded.

And Dixie drove off.

M.J. watched her go. "I feel like I'm reliving the past," he said to Matt. "Except that my feelings aren't the same as when Allie was the one in danger. I'm much calmer."

Matt handed him a pack. "Normal to be that way. For all we know, the boy isn't in danger. We still have no evidence that he's been kidnapped."

M.J. started unpacking equipment. "I guess that's up to Hal to find out."

"Yeah," Matt said.

They didn't speak of the way Hal was planning to get the information.

HAL REACHED the jail and got out of the Jeep. He felt cold as ice inside. Leaving Dixie had stripped away his tender emotions, and now he was left only with hate.

He hated enough to kill. Easily.

He went inside, nodded to Ted and walked over to his desk. Ted, having been told over the phone hours ago how things were, said nothing. He just unlocked the big door to the cell corridor.

"Hey, there," came the call from the back cell. "Is that you, Deputy?" It was Oscar Hayden's voice. Hal repressed a shudder of fury. "We want to talk."

"You'll get your chance, Hayden," Ted Travers said. "The sheriff's here. Sheriff Blane. And he's real interested in what you have to say."

Silence from the cells. Then, urgent, desperate, frightened whispering.

Hal got a box out from the lowest desk drawer. "Set up the chair," he said to Ted. The deputy nodded.

A few minutes later, Hal was seated comfortably in the hallway, his chair back against the wall opposite the cell occupied by Reed Turner and Oscar Hayden. Hal still wore the white silk shirt donated by Matt Glass. He hadn't put on any insignia of his office. He was just a guy in jeans, boots and a borrowed shirt.

A guy who was looking for his kid.

"See, Hayden," he said, taking one of the items out of the box. "It's like this. I think you know where George and Hastings might be holed up. And I think maybe my boy is with them, so I think you and Reed here are kind of obliged to tell me."

"I don't know anything," Reed Turner said. "I just showed this man where your study was in your house."

"And likely scared my momma out of ten years of her life." Hal made an adjustment in the thing he held.

"Come on, Blane," Hayden said. "The old lady wasn't afraid of us. She pulled the biggest gun I've ever seen.... Say, that's pretty big, too. What are you planning to do with that pistol?"

"Shoot you," Hal replied.

Both prisoners started screaming for Ted Travers.

"He's left the office," Hal explained. He spun the revolver's cylinder, checking the bullets. "I don't want witnesses."

They yelled some more. Then Oscar Hayden said, "Okay, Blane. What do you want?"

Hal sighted along the long barrel. "Where's George?"

"I don't know!"

"This gun isn't traceable, Hayden." Hal cocked the hammer. "See, it belonged to my great-granddaddy, old Robert Kedrick. You know, the one you found out there."

"I didn't find him. Hastings Clark did!"

"Yeah." Hal moved the barrel up and down, sighting along it again. "But you came along right after. Clark's your student. He ran and told you about the gold coin, didn't he?"

"I don't know anything..."

The sound of the shot echoed like a cannon in the confines of the jail. A huge piece of plaster fell off the wall in the cell. The two men yelped, then fell silent.

Hal blew on the smoking end of the revolver, then aimed again. "Tell me what I want to know," he said. "Or the next shot will send you to where you can discuss the situation with Robert Kedrick, personally."

Oscar started to babble.

DIXIE WALKED ACROSS the clearing to Esther's cabin. Only one of the ponies was in the corral, and it whinnied a greeting to her. She didn't think she'd find the old woman at home, but this was a place to start. She opened the door and went inside. The cabin was, as she had expected, empty.

She went to the trunk and took out the deerskin-wrapped journal. Hands trembling, she set the book on the table and sat down to read.

An hour later, she found what she had been looking for. She rewrapped the journal, put it away and went out to get the pony. The big black crow was waiting on a fence post. As she prepared the pony for the trek, the bird watched her with its golden eyes. Dixie tried to ignore it.

The ride through the forest took less time during daylight than it had at night after the storm. The pony knew and trusted her, and they made a good pair, rider and mount. They were at the end of the trail in less than an hour.

Dixie had stashed the radio Hal had given her in a pack. She took it out and keyed in the coded signal that would indicate she had reached her destination, but had so far located none of the missing.

Then, she dismounted and walked to the edge of the cliff.

The scene below fell out like a three-dimensional map. Directly below was the shelf at the top of the trail; at the bottom of it was where Artie and Hal had dug for the gold and where Hal had been shot. Beyond that was the tiny ledge where he had fallen, and even farther below was the camp on the tableland. Off to the left was the last section of cliff, falling off to the valley and the creek. Dixie only glanced at that area. Although something compelled her to look longer, she avoided the temptation. She was here to locate George, Hastings and Artie. Not to delve into the past and its dangers and riches.

That task was reserved for Hal.

She left the edge of the heights and went over to the rocks where the gunman had been hiding. Squatting, she tried to place herself in the position where the man had been. And there at her feet was a shiny cartridge case. Dixie picked it up and put it in a baggie, using proper evidence-gathering techniques to preserve any fingerprints.

M.J had insisted on the necessity of careful evidence gathering before Hal had deputized the three of them.

She studied the ground around the rock again. No one seemed to have been here since the rainstorm, so the boot prints from the gunman were easy to follow.

She made her way through the rocks and into the woods that bordered the cliff area. Whoever it was, had obviously run along the trail that animals had made over the years. It probably led to a place where water was frequently available, she thought.

She was right. When she came out of the trees and into a meadow area, she saw a tiny stream. The afternoon sunlight gleamed on the narrow trickle of water. The high grass was turning gold, frost having struck already at this altitude. Dixie followed the gunman's trail along the stream. At the other side of the meadow, the land rose sharply upward, and she saw the shadow of a depression in the slope. Or a cave.

Low trees and thick bushes surrounded and almost obscured the area from casual view. She slowed and approached cautiously. If her guess was a good one, this was an animal den of some kind. It was.

She hadn't taken another step before a hand grabbed her roughly from behind and the cold round muzzle of a gun was pressed up under her chin.

"Afternoon, Dr. Sheldon," Hastings Clark said. "I'm really sorry you chose to come out for a house call. Kind as it was of you to do so, it may well be your last."

HAL RENDEZVOUSED with M.J. and Matt at the paleontologists' camp. Winnie Nash had been filled in on most of the details of the situation, and she had agreed to abandon the place until Hastings, George and Artie were found.

Most of the tents were gone, and the tableland looked clean and empty.

Much as it had one hundred years before, Hal reflected. "I haven't heard from Dixie, yet," he told the other two men. "But if she's located Esther, she's probably not in a position to answer her radio. She should call in—" he consulted his wristwatch "—an hour from now."

"That's what we agreed on. Five o'clock," Matt said. "She seemed to understand how important coordinating communication is for an operation like this. We should hear right on time."

M.J. changed the subject. "Professor Hayden told you that he and Clark had taken George up to a cave near the tree line on the mountain?"

Hal nodded.

"Just out of curiosity, how...?"

"Keep your curiosity in the bag," Hal advised. "They told me what I wanted to know. They aren't hurt. That's all."

"What's the best way up to the cave?" Matt asked.

Hal pointed. "The best is from the floor of the canyon where the stream bed runs. There's an old trail that crawls right up the side of the mountain to the tree line. But from here—"

"Blane!" The word fell out of the sky like a bird of prey. "Sheriff Hal Blane! Up here!"

Hal looked upward, shading his eyes against the afternoon sun. "Son of a bitch," he whispered. "He's got Dixie!"

M.J. turned around and stared upward. Dixie Sheldon stood right at the edge of the second ledge up the side of the mountain. Next to her stood a tall man with longish hair pulled back into a ponytail. He held a shotgun to her throat. "Oh, my God," M.J. breathed.

"He's negotiating," Matt said softly, holding out both hands to show he carried no weapon. "Let me try. I used to be pretty good at this. What do you want?" he shouted. "We don't intend to hurt anyone. We just want Dr. Sheldon and the Blane boy back, unharmed."

"Little late on that," Hastings called. "Tell 'em, Doc."

"Hal?" Dixie's voice seemed steady enough, given her situation. "He's hurt, but he'll be all right."

"Artie?"

"Yes, he—"

Hastings jabbed her with the end of the shotgun. "That's enough talk," he snarled, the anger and fear in his voice evident even at that distance. "Now, Blane, listen close and listen well, because I don't intend to repeat my instructions."

"Let her loose," Hal said, his voice carrying even though he spoke normally. "No instructions. No negotiations. Just let her go."

"Blane, shut up," Matt whispered. "You don't want to rattle him any more than he already is."

"I'm not intending to rattle him. I'm intending to kill him." Hal moved. His rifle was inches away from his hand....

Hastings shouted a warning....

Dixie kicked back, attempting to free herself....

And an arrow flew out of nowhere and buried itself in Hastings Clark's body. He gave a strangled yell, dropped the shotgun and tumbled from the cliff's edge, pinwheeling and hitting rock on the way down.

Hal led the other two men up the side of the mountain. As soon as Hastings's body had hit the bottom of the valley, Dixie had given a heartrending cry and disappeared from view. Hal hadn't hesitated, hadn't given a second thought to the dead paleontologist or anything else, including his sprained arm, aching head and general weakness from being shot. He'd just grabbed his rifle and started to run for the slope. He climbed upward like a man possessed, and the other two had no choice but to follow. Panting, gasping for breath, they reached the top.

No one was in sight.

M.J. swore. Matt ducked his head and drew in deep breaths. Hal bent down and studied the ground. "The cave's over that way," he said, pointing. "And that's the way she went. Come on."

He led, they followed.

Soon, they reached the meadow. The sun was too low to be seen behind the mountains now, but it was still daylight. Hal motioned for them to fan out, taking the edges of the woods while he went straight up the path of the creek. Matt nodded agreement. All three men carried rifles.

They moved in concert, as if they'd been at work together for years. Hal reached the opening of the cave without incident and flattened himself against the outside rock wall, listening.

He heard a moan. Someone was in pain. *Dixie?*

Artie? He signaled to the other two to move closer and to cover the entrance.

Hal went inside, moving silently, stalking whoever was down the tunnel in the dark. No more moans guided or goaded him. It was as silent as a tomb.

He saw a flicker of light up ahead, heard the murmur of voices, another soft gasp of pain. They, whoever they were, were just around the bend in the tunnel.

Hal bent low, checked his weapon and moved. Dropping to the ground just at the turn, he rolled forward low into the light, ready to shoot.

The first thing he saw was Dixie's face, fear and anger mingling on her fine features. The second thing was the sight of his son. Artie lay on an old, dirty blanket, his eyes closed and his clothes and face bloodied.

And then he saw George.

George Preston held a handgun, aimed at Hal's loved ones.

Hal snarled in hatred and raised his gun....

And Robert Kedrick said, "No!" Hal eased off on the trigger....

And George fell over on his ugly face.

"Hal!" Dixie cried. "Oh, Hal!" She threw herself into his arms. "I had to come back here after Hastings was shot. I knew Artie was alone with George, and that if I didn't show up, there might be a tragedy. I knew you'd find us! Artie's all right. He's just out from some medicine I gave him. Most of the blood is from George. He—"

"Hi, Dad," Artie croaked. "Just in time for the big rescue."

"Son!" Hal moved over to Artie, never letting go of Dixie. "Artie, are you...?"

"I got beat up, Dad." Artie sat up carefully, grimacing in pain as he moved. He indicated George. "But I gave as good as I got. He tried to hold the gun on us, after Dixie came back, but he just couldn't do it any longer. She gave him some kind of bug juice Esther taught her about and that took him out."

Hal released Dixie and reached for his son. "I thought I'd lost you," he said, hugging the boy to his chest, then letting him lie back down. "Artie, I'm so sorry."

"For what, Dad?" Artie grinned weakly at his father. "I had a heck of an adventure and beat the stuffings out of the guy who shot you."

"George?"

Dixie nodded. While father and son were embracing, she had moved over to examine the fallen man. As she'd suspected, he had passed out from the concoction she'd fixed for him earlier. He'd trusted her after the gentle treatment she'd given him in the jail, and that had made it easy to slip him some heavy herbal sedatives in the guise of tea.

She knew he had very nearly died, for she had seen Hal's expression when he'd entered the light and aimed his gun.

Hal had been prepared and eager to kill.

She started to ask what had stopped him, but M.J. and Matt arrived, and the time for questions was postponed.

A WHILE LATER, they stood in the meadow as the Life Flight helicopter, called by the police radio and once more sent from Casper, flew off with Artie and George. Dixie explained what had happened and how she had ended up as Hastings's captive along with Artie.

"He took Artie prisoner two days ago. He and George had supplies in the cave and decided to hold him hostage, in case things went more sour. I was trying to find Esther," she explained. "I rode over here taking the same route we took that night, and then, when I couldn't find her, I started scouting the boot prints of the man who shot you."

Hal's left arm was back in the sling. His right arm was around Dixie's shoulders. He hurt from the top of his head to the tips of his boots, but he felt fine, anyway.

"I followed the tracks," Dixie went on. "And Hastings ambushed me just outside the cave. When he took me inside, I found Artie and George. They'd run into each other a few hours after George shot you and we took you away. Artie set out to track him, just as I did, and when he found him, he went a little crazy with fury and grief over your injury. Until Hastings stopped it, they were set on beating each other to death.''

"Who shot Hastings?" M.J. asked. "We saw an arrow, but no marksman."

"Esther." Dixie's voice held a note of reverence. "And I have no idea where she is now."

"We'll find her," Matt said. "Describe her for me."

"She's a wonderful, ancient lady, who..." Dixie choked with emotion. "She saved my life by shooting Hastings. He wasn't bluffing with that shotgun."

"I was afraid of that," Matt said.

"I knew it," Hal said.

"Well, we have to find her," M.J. said. "Whatever her motive, she did kill the guy."

"We'll all look," Hal stated. "Right?" He glanced at Dixie.

"Right," she said. Then her eyes filled with tears. "I thought we were all dead."

"I know," he said. "Me, too." He kissed her. "Let's go find Esther."

They moved slowly down the side of the mountain until they reached the tableland and the camp. Hal suggested that the best way to get down to the creek was along the path that led by Robert Kedrick's grave.

There, they found Esther.

She was seated near the depression that had been Robert Kedrick's burial place. Her entire body was in shadow, and she was wrapped in the old Hudson Bay blanket she had used the night of the storm. By her side lay a bow and arrows. In her lap lay a large, dirty canvas bag. She didn't move or speak, and her dark eyes seemed glazed.

Dixie went over to her. "Esther?" she said softly, taking one withered hand in hers. "Esther, can you hear me?"

She looked back at Hal and the other two men. "She's alive. Barely."

"I'll call for the 'copter to come back," Matt said. He started to key in on the radio.

"No," said Esther. "This is my place to die." She blinked, and her eyes cleared. "Harold Kedrick Blane, come here," she commanded, her voice strong as ever.

Hal knelt down in front of the ancient woman.

She handed the canvas sack to him. "This is yours," she said. "I was only the keeper until you were ready to receive it. It's from your great-grandfather. Use it as he would have you do."

Hal took the bag. "The gold?"

"Yes. My father buried it when he buried your great-granddaddy. I knew where it was, but until the rains washed away more of the cliff, I couldn't..." Her voice faded. "Couldn't get to it. It belongs to you...." She coughed, the spasm wracking her thin body.

"Esther, let me...," Dixie began. She rummaged in the medicine pouch she still carried. "I can make you..."

"Make me a grandmother of your people, child," Esther said. "I have given the gold to your man. To you, I gave life by killing the one who would have killed you. And I gave you what I know. Now, I give you my spirit. You'll see me in the eyes of your children and their children...."

And Esther breathed a long sigh, and died.

CHAPTER EIGHTEEN

SORTING EVERYTHING OUT took some time. Time and intelligence. Love and caring. Even cunning.

Especially cunning.

Esther's death, plus the testimony of the witnesses, Matt and M.J., solved the dilemma of explaining and dealing with Hastings Clark's killing. Whatever Esther's motives had been, she was now dead, Hastings was dead and Dixie was alive. Alive, thanks to Esther. Dixie's grief over the loss of her friend was tempered by gratitude for her life and by the gifts Esther had left as a legacy.

Of those, the gold was secondary to the knowledge and love Esther had bequeathed. As soon as she could get to the project after the dust settled from the violence and terror, Dixie faxed off a report to Cal Med regarding the poultice she'd applied to Hal's wound and the tea she'd prepared to ease Artie's pain and shock, as well as the drug she'd slipped George shortly before Hal had appeared on the scene to rescue them.

Cal Med was in ecstasy and wanted more, immediately. Dixie put them off as best she could. There was too much else to do to mess with mere academic medical matters.

The gold posed more of a problem, but M.J. put his resourceful mind and legal talents to work and set up a plan that not even the most perverse IRS agent could challenge.

He made the treasure into a trust for SeaLake County, making Hal executor-manager. The money generated from investment of the funds created by the sale of the gold back to the government at present-day prices was to be used for the benefit of the citizens of Seaside and SeaLake County, not for the Blane family alone. M.J., Allie and Matt made certain that enough publicity was focused on the situation so that no politician or treasury agent could comfortably dispute the disposition of the riches.

Hal's great-grandfather's reputation was cleared, as well. M.J. made public all the information he'd garnered from Washington, and Reed Turner finally confessed that the conspiracy to brand Robert a thief and outlaw and to find the gold went back three generations in his family. The Treasury Department itself was not at fault directly, but blame still clung to the bureaucracy that had failed to investigate the accusations properly one hundred years ago.

History, Dixie's father declared, would now have to be rewritten. At least the SeaLake County section. When all the details were discovered and documented, Professor Raymond Sheldon said, SeaLake County would have itself a real western hero in Robert Kedrick.

Quite a change.

Artie Blane recovered in no time at all, demonstrating the resilience of a normal fifteen-year-old. He had inflicted considerable damage on George during their fistfight, and he was justifiably proud of the fact that he had taken steps to avenge the pain and suffering of his father.

Hattie also dealt remarkably well with the stress she'd been subjected to. In fact, Dixie believed that the experience of defending her home and holding two men at bay for hours had actually done Hattie more good than any amount of counseling. She seemed years younger, and full of confidence for the future. All mention of chest pain, fear or weakness was gone.

Reed Turner and Oscar Hayden were under indictment for their roles in the criminal activities. Even with excellent legal representation, M.J. assured Dixie that the two would do serious prison time.

The threat of losing the clinic in Seaside was now past. With the trust money from the gold, Hal not only paid off the state for the site and the existing equipment—at a bargain rate negotiated by Allie and Matt—he also began funding new and necessary supplies and apparatus.

The question remained whether there would be a medical doctor in charge, or if Fran Coble would have to maintain the place on her own, until another doctor could be found to replace Dixie, who was still faced with a choice.

Cal Med had been calling repeatedly after news of the adventure reached them. Dixie was being pressured to leave Seaside, not only by her potential employer, but also by her colleagues from medical school and internship-residency training. Everyone who contacted her thought she'd be crazy not to go on with her career. She was constantly harangued by all the people in her past whom she had trusted and cared for, her parents, most of all.

"I know you shared a remarkable adventure," her mother said. "But that's no basis for a lifetime commitment."

"He's never going to amount to any more than he already has," her father warned. "With the discovery of the gold and the truth about his ancestry, he's had his time in the sun. He may be a good man, but there won't be any more glory. Mark my words."

"You have a responsibility to society, darling," Philomena reminded her. "You have a fine mind and a willingness to work and you will just waste yourself out there in the middle of nowhere. Really, who is going to take any discovery about folk medicine seriously from a physician who lives hundreds of miles from the nearest real hospital? You have to be in the right places to get the right kind of attention, dear. You know that as well as we do.

"And he'll want children," Dixie's mother added, darkly. "I don't have to tell you what children can do to a career. If he promises to share the work, do not believe him. All men lie when they do that."

"I can't subscribe to that theory," Raymond said. "Since I certainly did my share in caring for you. But you must face reality. What, honestly, do you and this man have in common? Nothing."

What really worried Dixie, was that she was beginning to listen to their arguments. She and Hal had shared some strange and wondrous moments. They loved each other, unquestionably. In the little time they'd had for privacy, they had shared physical love tenderly and fiercely, allowing their passion to reach fiery heights neither one had known before.

They had not found time to discuss the future, however. She debated that issue alone, because he now spent hours locked up in his study, intent on his work. No one, not even Dixie could get him out until he was good and ready, and only Artie was allowed in. The furor surrounding the gold and the violence and the past was focused on Hal, so she was left out of any public attention much of the time, which gave her time to think, to doubt, to dream, to hope and to wonder.

What was next? She didn't know, and she couldn't make a decision. Not yet.

THE OFFICIAL BURIAL of Robert Kedrick took place several weeks later. Not all of the old ranch land had been returned in the deal M.J had made with the government, but enough of it to ensure Hattie's joyous satisfaction and Hal's future plans. Among those plans was a family plot with Robert Kedrick as the honored first tenant.

Esther had already been laid to rest in the soil near her cabin. Dixie intended to keep things there as close to the way Esther had left them as was possible. Her intention was to make the place a working monument to the old woman's wisdom and life. She moved the two ponies to a pasturage owned by the Dumonts, whose baby she had delivered the night she went to the jail to patch up George Preston.

Robert's funeral was the first real one he'd had, though he'd been buried twice already.

Dixie was among the many who attended. People from all walks of life, from Wyoming and beyond, came to pay their respects. Much of the population of Seaside and SeaLake County turned out. Winnie Nash and a number of her staff flew back from the East Coast for the ceremony. The Treasury Department sent a representative to put a positive spin on the role it had played in the whole sorry mess. Allie Glass had sent invitations to all the Wyoming high officials and most of them came. Guilt and curiosity, Dixie reflected, went a long way.

It was a bright October day, Indian summer weather with just a hint of winter in the breeze that blew down from the heights. Hal had chosen a site on the tableland. By coincidence, it was just about the same time of year that Robert Kedrick had been murdered.

Dixie stood at his side as the minister from the only church in Seaside read scripture and gave a brief sermon. Hal was like stone. Not a muscle moved, not a hair stirred, not a nerve twitched. He wore a business suit instead of his usual sheriff's uniform or jeans, but he still looked like a Gary Cooper clone. Solid, solitary and sullen.

Dixie suddenly felt panic. How could she think of spending the rest of her life with a man so tightly bound up into himself? A man whose emotions came out only now and then, when he was dangerously angry or when they were making passionate love?

And then, something happened that she hadn't expected.

Hal eulogized his great-grandfather.

"I didn't know Robert Kedrick," Hal said, addressing the large crowd. "Now, that might seem like a funny thing to say about a man who died a hundred years ago, but I have to confess I thought I knew him. Knew him damn good and well, too."

The October sun beat down. Hal wiped sweat from his face. The crowd was completely silent, caught up in the drama they sensed being played out before them.

Hal went on. "I knew him from the time I was old enough to understand the spoken word. I was told he was a thief and a coward, and worst of all, a man who deserted and abandoned his family to ruin. I believed every word." He paused, regarding the coffin that was poised on ropes above the grave.

"I was wrong," he said. "We were all wrong." He wiped his face again and then he took off his coat.

"Let me tell you what really happened," he said. "I know now."

A whisper of astonishment ran through the crowd. Then they all settled down to listen.

Dixie felt light-headed.

"He was an undercover agent for the Treasury Department," Hal said, his manner like that of a storyteller around a camp fire. "You all know that, but what you don't know is that he took the job because a close friend had been murdered by that same band of outlaws. Robert figured the best way to get revenge was to get them arrested, tried and executed for the crime." He paused again.

"He wanted revenge, but he was doing it all through legal channels." Hal walked over to the coffin and put his hand on the lid. "He never stepped outside the law. When it came down to it, he didn't kill, even though he was killed." His voice broke, and he stopped talking.

Dixie wanted with all her heart to go to him, but she knew he needed to stand alone. All of his life, all of his past, even before he was born, was wrapped up in this.

Hal cleared his throat and turned back to his audience. "He led the outlaw band up here," he said. "The details of the robbery are public. What isn't public is that he had made an agreement with treasury agent, Rudolph Turner, to rendezvous with the law. Turner, who had made other arrangements with one member of the outlaw band, didn't fulfill his side of the bargain." Hal stared at the coffin.

"Robert Kedrick was betrayed," he said.

The crowd murmured, then was quiet.

"He'd trusted Turner as his control in Treasury, and when he discovered the treachery, he intended to hide the gold so that no one would profit. But he was hit and seriously wounded with a rifle bullet.

"Just like I was." Hal drew in a deep breath.

"He fell from the section of the cliff, knocked over the edge by the bullet, just as I was. But he wasn't unconscious from the fall, and he wasn't rescued." He gazed at Dixie for a moment. "He did manage to hide the gold, probably shoving it deep into a crevasse in the rock. But then the others got to him and killed him, shooting him in the head to make sure of their work, burying him quickly and taking off without the loot. At that point, they were more concerned with getting away than getting rich." He wiped his face once more.

"And everyone thought Robert Kedrick was a thief," he said.

Dixie realized Hal Blane was crying. Weeping, but not even aware of it. While he told his story, his tears fell. He was mourning the past. Mourning his ancestor. Mourning the wrongs done his name. Mourning the dead.

"The body and the gold were found in the early spring," Hal said, continuing the account. "Found by Miss Esther's father. The man reburied it properly, and also hid the gold in a safer place. He was terrified that if anyone knew what he'd done, he and his family would also be killed. So he swore his small clan to secrecy.

"The gold was to be considered a trust for the future, for the Kedrick descendent who would use it for good, not greed or evil. That information was kept with his daughter for a century before she felt the time was right for me to have the treasure." He broke off and turned away, motioning to Artie.

Artie Blane moved forward. His face was pink with emotion, but he was able to pick up the thread of the story. "So old Miss Esther knew about the gold and about Robert Kedrick. The stuff was written in a kind of code in her dad's journal, but she'd sworn with the rest of her family not to tell until it would be safe for Robert's descendants to know. Until my dad came along, she didn't think anyone would be able to handle it.

"And she wasn't even sure about him, until . . . until he brought her Dr. Sheldon one night. She liked Dixie right off. And just hours after that, they found my great-great-grandfather. Miss Esther must have taken all that as a sign it was time."

It struck Dixie then, that it must have been at the exact moment Robert's bones were discovered that Hal had experienced the fainting feeling on the road driving back from their time with Esther. She watched him struggle to regain control of his emotions. Perhaps, he realized it, too.

Hal recovered. He stood next to his son, in front of Robert's coffin. "When Hastings Clark found the body," he said, "there was one gold coin next to it. Clark replaced it with a dime, figuring no one would bother much with an old skeleton. But when Dr. Dixie Sheldon and Professor Winnifred Nash reconstructed Robert's head from a cast of the skull, things began to move." He held out his hand and Hattie came forward and took it.

"My mother recognized him," Hal said. "And that opened the doors for further investigation. Gold hunting, really."

"Hastings Clark got hold of George Preston," Artie said. "He knew from town talk that George hated my dad and would be happy to help anyone hurt him. They figured if Dad got too near the gold, they'd just have George shoot him."

"Which he did." Hal looked over at Dixie, again. "But I was luckier than Robert. I was rescued."

Dixie felt tears on her own face. She wanted to move to his side, but she was rooted to the spot.

"Most of the rest of the story is known to all of you," Hal said. "But the real details of the past and the true history of Robert Kedrick are things I want to make public. You are the first to hear them, but I have a manuscript down at the university being checked by a prominent historian. All my information is documented and proven. When the manuscript is released, I have a publisher interested in taking it to a national audience." He paused, smiled for the first time. "We also have a film company interested. Remember how *Dances With Wolves* benefited South Dakota? Now there's a lot more interest in making western movies right where the story happened. They want to make it here in SeaLake County. But that's another story."

This time, the crowd murmured with excitement and delight. Dixie nearly shouted with the joy she felt for him. All of his dreams were coming true!

The service came to an end soon after that. In a dramatic gesture, all three Blanes bade farewell to their ancestor and the coffin was lowered into the soil that once again belonged to them. Dixie cried openly and noted that nearly everyone else had at least the hint of moisture in their eyes. Having shed his tears, Hal put his arms around his mother and son and said goodbye with pride and dignity.

Dixie knew then, that she loved him more than she would ever love another person on the earth.

But she had no chance to tell him. The assembly at the grave moved back to town and gathered at Sal's café, the crowd spilling out into the street. Gossip, speculation and visiting went on until late in the afternoon and after sunset.

Dixie frequently got near Hal, but never got him alone.

And he'd reverted to his stone self. She couldn't read a single emotion on his face or in his eyes. Too many people, too much talk, too much for her. The wake went on and on.

As night fell, Dixie slipped out of the café and went home. Frustrated and still confused, she knew only that she had to talk to Hal, had to tell him of her feelings. She was destined to be with him, no matter what her other plans were or became. There were ways around the problem of being a backwoods academic. She knew others who had succeeded. It wouldn't be easy, but it was possible.

She sat alone for a long time, thinking. Then she moved to her desk, uncovered the typewriter and wrote a letter to Cal Med, turning down their offer and suggesting that she would better serve the cause of research by remaining in the field.

If they didn't like that, they could just tell her they weren't interested. It didn't seem so important, anymore.

Dreams changed.

She got out her financial records and calculated how long she would have to work to finish paying back the state and be on her own. Two years and eight months. The standard procedure was for the third year to be forgiven if the physician stayed in the rural setting, but now that the state no longer had a financial obligation to the clinic in Seaside, she wasn't sure what it would mean to the bureaucrats.

And she'd already pulled in enough political favors through Allie Glass to last her a lifetime.

Four months. That was all it had taken to change her dreams, change her life.

Four months and Hal Blane. He had changed her, changed her life. The moment she had walked into that jail four months ago, her life had taken a different direction, even when she hadn't known it. She put the papers and forms back in the folders and put them away.

From outside came a strange, raw cry. Strange, and yet familiar and welcome.

Dixie sat still, frozen in place for a moment. Then she got up and ran over to the front door. Opening it, she heard the cry again. She turned on the porch light. There in the one large tree in her yard, was a crow. In the glow of the electric light, his sleek black feathers glowed. His bright little eyes shone. He cawed once more, flapped his wings and flew off, in the direction of Hal's home.

Dixie grabbed her coat and left the house.

The street was deserted as she ran along the sidewalk. Overhead, the October moon shone down, lighting her way. She knew Esther was by her side, and Robert. She felt the past and the present becoming one...

She ran up the walk to Hal's front door, flung it open and raced inside, not caring a bit who she scared, startled or offended. Hal, Hattie and Artie were in the living room. They had company. She didn't notice who the guests were.

She went over to Hal and stood in front of him, gasping for breath. "I'm staying here," she declared. "In Seaside. I want to be with you more than I want anything else in life. I love you, and that's the most important thing to me."

Hal stared up at her from his place in the easy chair.

Then, he stood and pulled her into his arms. His embrace was strong and secure. "It's all perfect now," he said, his voice breaking as it had during the eulogy. He kissed her, and Dixie responded with wild, uninhibited enthusiasm, not caring who saw or what they thought.

"Dixie?"

The sound of that familiar voice broke through. Dixie yelped and pushed away from Hal. "Dad?" She turned and saw her father and mother seated on the Blanes' sofa. "What in the world..." It suddenly hit her. "Dad, *you're* the prominent historian who's checking Hal's manuscript?"

"I am," Raymond Sheldon said, standing and smiling at his astonished daughter. "I thought you would have figured that out by now, Dixie-girl. Who else would he take such a project to in this state?"

"I should have known." She shook her head, still trying to absorb what had happened.

Her mother was smiling, too. "But I didn't."

Hal's arm rested on her shoulders, warm, reassuring. "I didn't tell you about it, darlin'," he said. "I didn't want to influence your decision about us."

She looked up at him. "I made up my mind after Esther told me I was an idiot for even thinking of leaving you."

Hal frowned.

"She sent that crow," Dixie said, grinning. "Remember him?"

"Well, then," Hal Blane declared. "I guess we have to invite the bird to the wedding."

And so, they did.

THE WEDDING took place in Seaside a few weeks later. Many of the people who had come to Robert's funeral came back for the joyous celebration of marriage.

Dixie's parents, Raymond and Philomena, had by then completely reversed their prejudgment of Hal. Raymond declared him a natural scholar and encouraged him to continue his historical writings after he finished the Kedrick project. Philomena was reassured by his plans to retire from law enforcement and dedicate his time to study, writing and his family. The income from the trust was going to go a long way in helping him achieve a number of goals, including getting some higher education, himself, and sending Artie to university in a few years.

Dixie's dreams were shaping up, as well. Cal Med expressed its dismay that she insisted on staying in Seaside, but agreed to publish her findings on a regular basis. Her discoveries as she investigated Esther's trove of herbs and her notes about their properties were worth gold as solid as the Kedrick treasure, and she was likely to be on the cutting edge of natural medicine, she was assured by the directors of the Cal Med project. "Keep the info coming," they'd said.

Before the wedding, Hal made a curious confession to her. They were spending a few hours in private at her home, just sitting in front of a fire and talking.

"If you'd gone to California, I'd have followed you," he said.

Dixie stared at him.

"No, really. I mean it. I gave it a lot of thought, darlin'. Knew I couldn't go on without you, so if it took uprooting my family and moving to be with you, I would have done it."

"But you didn't say a thing to make me think..."

"I wouldn't influence you like that." Hal smiled. "I was hoping I wouldn't have to. And thanks to the crow, I didn't."

A suspicious thought started nibbling at the back of Dixie's mind. "Crows can be tamed, can't they?" she asked.

"Sure. If you're patient enough. If you're patient enough, anything can be tamed."

"Hal! You didn't...?"

"Didn't what?" He put his arm around her. "You think I talked the crow into appearing at your door that night?"

"Stranger things than that have occurred around here."

He pulled her close, but didn't kiss her. He stared up at the ceiling. "I know. You remember how it was when I found you, Artie and George?"

"You were ready to shoot. I know that."

"I was ready to kill. But I *heard* Robert tell me not to. Like he was there. Like he was there to help me from making a mistake I'd regret. I would never live down killing a man in front of my son."

Dixie shivered, but she was not afraid. Just deeply moved. "I guess the people who have gone on before us don't like leaving well enough alone," she said, snuggling closer to her man. "Thank goodness!" she added.

"Esther did send the crow, Dixie. I have no doubt."

"Me, neither. Not now."

"First girl-child?"

"Esther Blane? Not bad. I think so. And a boy?"

"Robert, of course. If it's okay with you."

"I would have insisted," she said.

He kissed her, then, and kept on kissing her for quite some time.

My Valentine 1994

Celebrate the most romantic day of the year with
MY VALENTINE 1994
a collection of original stories, written by
four of Harlequin's most popular authors...

MARGOT DALTON
MURIEL JENSEN
MARISA CARROLL
KAREN YOUNG

*Available in February, wherever
Harlequin Books are sold.*

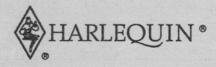

HARLEQUIN ®

Relive the romance...
Harlequin® is proud to bring you

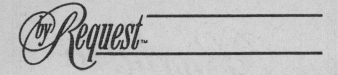
by Request™

A new collection of three complete novels every month. By the most requested authors, featuring the most requested themes.

Available in January:

WESTERN LOVING

They're ranchers, horse trainers, cowboys...
They're willing to risk their lives,
But are they willing to risk their hearts?

Three complete novels in one special collection:

RISKY PLEASURE by JoAnn Ross
VOWS OF THE HEART by Susan Fox
BY SPECIAL REQUEST by Barbara Kaye

Available wherever Harlequin books are sold.

NEW YORK TIMES **Bestselling Author**

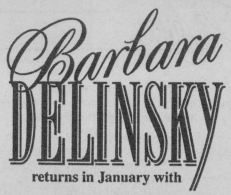

Barbara
DELINSKY

returns in January with

THE REAL THING

Stranded on an island off the coast of Maine,
Deirdre Joyce and Neil Hersey got the
solitude they so desperately craved—
but they also got each other, something they
hadn't expected. Nor had they expected
to be consumed by a desire so powerful
that the idea of living alone again was
unimaginable. A marrige of "convenience"
made sense—or did it? BOB7

 HARLEQUIN®

When the only time you have for yourself is...

™

Christmas is such a busy time—with shopping, decorating, writing
cards, trimming trees, wrapping gifts....

When you do have a few *stolen moments* to call your own, treat yourself
to a brand-new *short* novel. Relax with one of our Stocking Stuffers—
or with all six!

Each STOLEN MOMENTS title
is a complete and original contemporary romance that's the perfect
length for the busy woman of the nineties! Especially at Christmas...

And they make perfect stocking stuffers, too! (For your mother,
grandmother, daughters, friends, co-workers, neighbors, aunts,
cousins—all the other women in your life!)

Look for the STOLEN MOMENTS display in December

STOCKING STUFFERS:

HIS MISTRESS Carrie Alexander
DANIEL'S DECEPTION Marie DeWitt
SNOW ANGEL Isolde Evans
THE FAMILY MAN Danielle Kelly
THE LONE WOLF Ellen Rogers
MONTANA CHRISTMAS Lynn Russell

HSM2

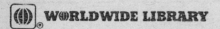 **W❁RLDWIDE LIBRARY**

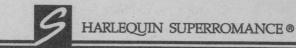

HARLEQUIN SUPERROMANCE ®

Women Who Dare will continue with more exciting stories,
beginning in May 1994 with

THE PRINCESS AND THE PAUPER by Tracy Hughes.

And if you missed any titles in 1993
here's your chance to order them:

Harlequin Superromance®—Women Who Dare

#70533	DANIEL AND THE LION by Margot Dalton	$3.39	❏
#70537	WINGS OF TIME by Carol Duncan Perry	$3.39	❏
#70549	PARADOX by Lynn Erickson	$3.39	❏
#70553	LATE BLOOMER by Peg Sutherland	$3.50	❏
#70554	THE MARRIAGE TICKET by Sharon Brondos	$3.50	❏
#70558	ANOTHER WOMAN by Margot Dalton	$3.50	❏
#70562	WINDSTORM by Connie Bennett	$3.50	❏
#70566	COURAGE, MY LOVE by Lynn Leslie	$3.50	❏
#70570	REUNITED by Evelyn A. Crowe	$3.50	❏
#70574	DOC WYOMING by Sharon Brondos	$3.50	❏
	(limited quantities available on certain titles)		

TOTAL AMOUNT	$	
POSTAGE & HANDLING	$	
($1.00 for one book, 50¢ for each additional)		
APPLICABLE TAXES*	$	_____
TOTAL PAYABLE	$	_____
(check or money order—please do not send cash)		

To order, complete this form and send it, along with a check or money order for the
total above, payable to Harlequin Books, to: *In the U.S.*: 3010 Walden Avenue,
P.O. Box 9047, Buffalo, NY 14269-9047; *In Canada*: P.O. Box 613, Fort Erie, Ontario,
L2A 5X3.

Name: _____

Address: _____ City: _____

State/Prov.: _____ Zip/Postal Code: _____

*New York residents remit applicable sales taxes.
 Canadian residents remit applicable GST and provincial taxes.

WWD-FINR

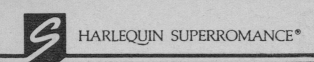

HARLEQUIN SUPERROMANCE®

WOMEN WHO DARE DRIVE RACE CARS?!

During 1993, each Harlequin Superromance WOMEN WHO DARE title will have a single italicized letter on the Women Who Dare back-page ads. Collect the letters, spell D A R E and you can receive a free copy of RACE FOR TOMORROW, written by popular author Elaine Barbieri. This is an exciting novel about a female race-car driver, WHO DARES ANYTHING . . . FOR LOVE!

Mail this certificate, designated letters spelling DARE, and check or money order for postage and handling to: In the U.S.—WOMEN WHO DARE, P.O. Box 9066, Buffalo, NY 14269-9056; In Canada—WOMEN WHO DARE, P.O. Box 621, Fort Erie, Ontario L2A 5X3.

Requests must be received by January 31, 1994.
Allow 4-6 weeks after receipt of order for delivery.   D-086-KAI-RR

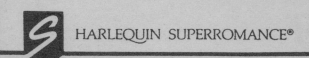
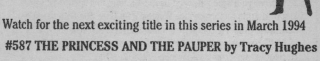